5719

D0014632

RANGER MCINTYRE: SMALL DELIGHTFUL MURDERS

RANGER McIntyre: SMALL DELIGHTFUL MURDERS

JAMES C. WORK

FIVE STAR
A part of Gale, a Cengage Company

Farmington Hills, Mich • San Francisco • New York • Waterville, Maine
Meriden, Conn • Mason, Ohio • Chicago

LIBRARY OF CONGRESS CATALOGING-IN-PUBLICATION DATA

Names: Work, James C., author.
Title: Ranger McIntyre: small delightful murders / James C. Work.
Description: First Edition. | Waterville, Maine : Five Star, a part of Gale, Cengage Learning, [2019]
Identifiers: LCCN 2018032038| ISBN 9781432850036 (hardcover) | ISBN 9781432850043 (ebook) | ISBN 9781432850050 (ebook)
Subjects: LCSH: Murder—Investigation—Fiction. | GSAFD: Suspense fiction.
Classification: LCC PS3573.O6925 R35 2019 | DDC 813/.54—dc23 LC record available at https://lccn.loc.gov/2018032038

First Edition. First Printing: April 2019
Find us on Facebook—https://www.facebook.com/FiveStarCengage
Visit our website—http://www.gale.cengage.com/fivestar/
Contact Five Star Publishing at FiveStar@cengage.com

Printed in Mexico
2 3 4 5 6 7 23 22 21 20 19

Ranger McIntyre:
Small Delightful Murders

PREFACE

Rocky Mountain National Park was established in 1915, the year Babe Ruth hit his first home run and the ocean liner *Lusitania* was sunk by a German U-boat. From 1915 the mission and purpose of the park has been the preservation and protection of singularly beautiful mountains, streams, meadows, and lakes. Despite the size of the park—nearly four hundred square miles—there are only four automobile entrances; I grew up in a cabin camp a mile down the road from the Fall River Entrance and three miles from the nearest village, Estes Park. The RMNP's flat moraines, the rushing streams and granite peaks were my playground all through grade school and high school; I knew the ways of the trout and the deer and all the seasons of the mountains. Where city kids had policemen and firemen to idolize, I had park rangers in green uniforms and flat brim hats. The places that I have created in this novel are fictional composites of all the ones I came to know as a boy. The characters are similarly fictional amalgamations of many men and women that I am proud to say I knew. From the lady who owned the drugstore to the deputy sheriff, they were clean-living people, people with moral standards, people who respected others. In dealing with children, they were kind, but strict; they expected us to act with honesty and take pride in who we were, and for the most part we did. I say "for the most part" for once in a while we broke the rules. When we did, even if we escaped punishment, there was no escaping the knowledge that people were disappointed in us.

Although the people of our community were good people, law-abiding and hardworking people, the village harbored a few stinkers of the sort that can be found anywhere. There was a woman whose clothes were too tight and whose makeup was overly garish. There was a town drunk—two town drunks, to be precise, one who seemed to be a professional and one who practiced only on weekends. There were a few "sharp" business-men who came and went after cheating too many people too many times. Once in a while a car or pickup might get stolen. We once had a murder.

I remember two signs that hung in a local store. One said "Yes, I Live Here All Year 'Round. No, I Don't Get Lonely." The other said "Lead Me Not Into Temptation: I Can Find My Own Way."

CHAPTER 1
SUMMONED TO A SHOOTING

Supervisor Nicholson was in a good mood, unusual for him. More than good: he seemed almost playful. Most other days he marched into the office, hung up his hat, assumed his official frown, and sat down in his swivel chair. From eight to five, his jaw set hard and his eyes looking icy, he read letters and reports and shuffled papers. The Department of the Interior paid him to sit in that chair. They gave him a walnut desk painted battleship gray and they gave him his assignment: take charge of four hundred square miles of trees, mountains, lakes, and streams and make it a national park. Within those 256,000 acres there were a hundred or more summer cottages, private homes, and tourist lodges. Nicholson was tasked with seeing that they didn't endanger the integrity of Rocky Mountain National Park, a job that required patience and diplomacy. The pay was good and the position was important, but most days he would rather be out there in the mountains wielding a fly rod instead of a fountain pen. He could be content with his job, but he didn't need to be happy about it. He just needed to sit there and do it.

This morning he was in this funny mood. Rocky Mountain National Park Ranger Timothy McIntyre noticed it immediately as he followed Nicholson into his office. He stood in front of the desk while the supervisor hung up his hat and sat down. What did Supervisor Nicholson have to smile about? Maybe the boss had been hitting the bottle, despite prohibition and President Coolidge's Eighteenth Amendment.

9

"Looks like a case of attempted murder, Tim," Nicholson said. "Murder."

McIntyre saw the little crinkles at the edges of the supervisor's hard gray eyes. He saw the sly way the corners of his mouth turned up.

"Oh?" the ranger said.

"Yeah," Supervisor Nicholson said. "I guess people think we're still living in the Wild West and settle arguments with a Winchester. I'm taking you off the visitor information service payroll and putting you back on law enforcement. I want you to look into it. No. Change that order: I want you to do more than look into it. I want it resolved. It's a badge and gun job, if you remember where you left your gun."

Nicholson was still smiling.

"Yessir," Ranger McIntyre replied. His reply was automatic; he was still puzzled to see Supervisor Nicholson smiling. Why would the supervisor be cheerful about putting him on enforcement? Nicholson knew that McIntyre preferred chasing lawbreakers to handing out maps and brochures and answering tourist questions. Everyone in the park service office knew it.

"Small Delights Lodge on Blue Spruce Lake," the supervisor said. "And Grand Harbor Lodge. You know where I mean. This time I want it settled for good and for all. Hand to heaven, if I hear any more squabbling from those people, I'll put the torch to both their places."

Ranger McIntyre scowled and mentally reversed himself. Maybe VIS was preferable to enforcement. He knew the Small Delights Lodge. He knew it well enough to avoid it every chance he got, even though their breakfast buffet was pretty good and there was a little trout stream where a guy might steal a few minutes to wet a fly. However, the owner was a sharp-tongued sarcastic old grouch who thought everyone was out to take advantage of him. His neighbor was a wicked virago who was out to take advantage of everybody she could. Five minutes of listening to their complaints and he would need at least two hours of quiet fly fishing to clear his mind again.

"Now I see why you're in such a good mood," McIntyre said. "John Frye rang up, did he? Somebody tried to kill him. And you want me to find out who it was, even though almost everybody around here would like to take a shot at Frye, including me. Don't you have a nicer job for me? Like doing autopsies on road kills? Maybe I could scrub outhouses instead?"

"Ranger, you don't know the half of it yet!"

Nicholson chortled and slapped his desk. The secretary poked her head around the door to see what he was laughing about.

"Dottie," Supervisor Nicholson said. "Tell Ranger McIntyre about the visitor we had from Small Delights. He wants to know what's funny."

It was Dottie's turn to grin. She had a very sweet grin. Dottie was one of those cheery people who enjoys every moment of life; to find a penny on the sidewalk or see a butterfly on a dandelion would make her whole day a pleasure. People loved her. Whenever someone said "I hope you have a good day, Dottie," she would reply "I've never had one that wasn't." She liked people. She got a special kick out of Ranger Tim McIntyre. And she loved to see him nonplussed.

"It seems the Fryes have a niece who is staying with them," she said, trying not to giggle. "Young woman named Polly Sheldon? Mister Frye didn't call us on the telephone, you see. This niece, Polly, came to the office in person yesterday afternoon to report this attempted murder. And here's the fun part. While waiting for the supervisor, she walked over to look at our wall of photos. She saw you in several of them, including your official NPS portrait photo, which everyone thinks is quite handsome. I'm afraid, Tim, that you have an admirer. I think, in fact, she's in love with you. She pointed to your picture and asked if you could handle the case personally. She'll be waiting for you at Small Delights today."

Supervisor Nicholson had a nice baritone chuckle, but Ranger McIntyre didn't appreciate the way it followed him out the door and across the sidewalk to his pickup truck. The ranger didn't need to ask why it amused the boss to think a young woman was infatuated with him. This Polly person was undoubtedly very fat with a wart on her crooked nose, was missing a front tooth, and probably had thick glasses and a wooden leg. McIntyre switched on the ignition and stepped down on the starter. His mind flashed back to the war and to a farmhouse in France where he had been forced to land his crippled Nieuport 28 biplane. He crawled into a woodshed to hide from one of the kaiser's patrols. He evaded the Germans, but only to be discovered by a huge French milkmaid with garlic on her breath and romance on her mind.

"She'll be waiting for you." Dottie's words sat like a chunk of ice on his brain.

But duty was duty. More importantly, duty was his paycheck and place to sleep. Therefore, he'd go see nasty John Frye about this latest attempted atrocity. He would talk to the fat girl with the wart on her nose and hanky-panky on her mind. First, though, he'd drive back to his cabin at the Fall River entrance station and strap on his revolver.

At eight years old, Rocky Mountain National Park was having growth pains. High on McIntyre's personal list of pains was John Frye, whose tourist lodge on Blue Spruce Lake represented a much wider problem: private commercial operations within the national park boundaries. In order to create the national park, whose mission would be "to preserve unimpaired the natural and cultural resources . . . for future generations," a bunch of bureaucrats in Washington had drawn a four hundred square mile rectangle on the map of Colorado. They declared it to be under federal management and hired a handful of men with little or no experience in either forestry or law enforcement to protect and preserve it. That was in 1915. Eight years later, the new park rangers were still trying to figure out what to do about all the private property that had been included within the rectangle. Did rangers have legal jurisdiction on private land? If they caught a game poacher, even on federal land, could they detain him or levy a fine against him, and if they did, where would they keep him, without any kind of jail, and how would they collect the fine once the poacher had left the park? If this "murder" attempt turned out to be real, which was unlikely, wouldn't it be a matter for the county sheriff to investigate?

Ranger McIntyre drove out to Blue Spruce Lake, but he dawdled on the way. He even pulled off the road at the bridge over Miner's Creek and considered whether to assemble his fly rod and make a few casts for trout, just to make sure the trout population was still healthy in Miner's Creek. But he remembered Supervisor Nicholson cautioning him that if he caught him fishing on duty again he'd be posted to Death Valley. Or somewhere with even less water. He stopped long enough to dip his canvas water bag in the creek and top up the Ford's radiator before chugging on up the road toward Small Delights Lodge. And John Frye. And some fat girl with romantic inclinations.

West of the village there were two vehicle entrances to Rocky Mountain National Park, the Fall River Entrance where McIntyre was stationed and the Thompson River Entrance where, in addition to a ranger cabin, there was a barracks for the work crew and a repair shop for vehicles. Neither of these park entrances, however, would take you to Blue Spruce Lake. In order to get to Blue Spruce you needed to leave the village and drive south along a state highway. If you stayed on it, that same highway would eventually take you to Denver after many fatiguing hours of twists and turns and steep grades. Five or six miles after leaving the village, you came to two signs a hundred yards apart. One said "Grand Harbor Lodge." The other, "Small Delights Lodge." Turn off the main road at either sign and you would drive down a dirt road into the national park where you would discover a lovely lake surrounded on three sides by pristine forest. On the fourth side, where the two access roads arrived at the lake, you'd find two sprawling log lodges for tourists.

The lodges on the lake presented a quandary for park administrators. In an ideal world of reasonable human animals, there would be no buildings in such a place. The lake would remain a beautiful mountain scene surrounded by a primeval conifer forest. Hikers would follow the natural game trails along the edge of the lake. They would sit on rocks and logs in reverential awe as if visiting a holy cathedral and when they quietly retreated they would take away any and all sign that they had ever been there.

Much of the park's federal funding, however, depended upon visitors and the visitors needed to be accommodated, and therefore virtually any lake that could be accessed by motor vehicles would soon have a dirt road cut through the forest, at the end of which the visitor would find food and lodging. Visitors couldn't be expected to enjoy nature unless they had a roof over their heads and chairs and tables and beds and running water. Blue Spruce Lake had the Small Delights Lodge operated by nasty-mouthed acerbic-tongued John Frye and his ever-suffering wife, Hattie. It was cheap, rustic, and generally had vacancies. It sat back among the pines in deep shade.

The other place, a few hundred yards away, was grandly dubbed the Grand Harbor Lodge, apparently because the rocks it was perched on overlooked a slight indentation of shoreline that could be called a harbor. It was operated by the widow

Catherine Croker, whose own outward bulges were considerable and whose manner was as autocratic as John Frye's was abrasive. Thereby lay another problem in jurisdiction. Catherine Croker held it to be her sacred privilege to cut down any and all trees that might obstruct her view of the lake. She had even ordered her manager, Thad Muggins, to chop down a hundred-year-old Douglas fir because it shaded a cabin porch on which a client wished to sunbathe. Widow Croker built cabins whenever she felt like it, diverted a creek to bring water to her place, tried to widen the dirt road before the park service caught her at it, stuck a boat dock out into the lake, burned her trash in an open pit, and generally provided John Frye with more things to complain about than John could get around to in any given eight-hour day.

Frye further believed that Witch Croker coveted his property and would probably murder him in order to acquire it. But, if Catherine wanted to kill John Frye, she'd have to stand in line: he had insulted, upset, and cheated almost every resident in the valley. Frye couldn't even buy groceries without starting an argument.

Ranger McIntyre parked his pickup truck in front of a sign saying "Guest Parking Only," which John Frye erected after discovering that someone who wasn't staying in one of his cabins had parked there in order to hike up to Skyview Lake.

He got out of the truck, dusted his tunic, wiped each boot by rubbing it against the back of his leg, adjusted the Sam Brown belt and revolver holster, squared his flat hat, took a deep breath, and advanced toward the sound of chopping coming from behind the main building. When he rounded the corner, he saw a somewhat short woman with a somewhat rounded figure standing on an upended milk crate with a small hatchet in her hand, hacking away at a thick pine tree. She was wearing bib overalls and a checked flannel shirt and wielded the hatchet like a logger using an axe.

"Aha!" the chubby woman said as McIntyre approached. She reached into the splintery hole she had chopped in the tree and wiggled something loose.

"There you are," she said when she saw McIntyre. "Just in time. Or a little late. Look at this."

She dropped a misshapen lead slug into McIntyre's hand. The base was still barely recognizable: a bullet. About a thirty caliber.

"Thirty caliber," she said. "Obviously not larger, not smaller. Uncle John was standing about where you are now. That bullet passed over his head and lodged in that ponderosa. Thought I'd save you the trouble of cutting it out of the tree."

"Over his head?" McIntyre queried.

"Come this way," she said. "I haven't disturbed anything. Follow me."

She led him about fifty yards into the shadowed forest and pointed at the ground. McIntyre bent down and picked up a brass cartridge case. The lettering around the base identified it as a .303 Savage casing.

"Somewhat unusual, wouldn't you say," she said. "Expensive rifle, not too many of them in the valley is my guess. You noticed the way it was lying. Now look back toward the lodge. From here you cannot see the tree where I extracted the bullet. I believe the assassin was standing over there, where there is a clear view of the tree. You are a hunter, probably. What do you do the instant you shoot your rifle at an animal?"

"I, uh, I guess I jack another round into the chamber. Kind of an automatic thing to do. In case you need a second shot."

"Absolutely," she said. "Now, an ejected casing from a Winchester flies upward and lands near the shooter. But with a .303 Savage the shell flies more horizontally. We may therefore presume that the marksman stood right over there by that other tree waiting for Uncle John to come out the kitchen door. He fired, he missed, he chambered another round. Meanwhile Uncle John had ducked out of sight. Our would-be killer took to his heels lest he be seen and identified. We will find footprints, but they won't be of much help."

Since this young woman seemed to be doing all the talking, the ranger said nothing. He went to where the shooter had "presumably" been and saw that she was probably right. The ground was scuffed as if somebody had sat down or knelt down. There was a crumpled cigarette butt nearby. Looking between the trees, McIntyre could see the white slash on the pine tree where she had hacked out the bullet. A good clear shot, plenty of time; there was even a handy tree branch to rest the barrel of the rifle on. And a .303 Savage was one heck of an accurate rifle. How come the slug hit the tree two feet or more above Frye's head?

"I wondered the same thing," she said, reading his thoughts as she extended her hand to shake his. "I'm Pauline Sheldon. Polly, to most people. You're Ranger Tim McIntyre. That receptionist at the S.O. seems to think a great deal of you. Well, I hope you can help clear this up. I'm the niece of Hattie Frye, by the way. And of Uncle John, of course."

He could see the resemblance. Hattie Frye was also a woman who would never be mistaken for a fashion model. No one had ever asked Hattie to try on a dress to see how it looked, and no one had ever asked her to retrieve anything from a high shelf. Like her niece, Hattie had an intensely pleasant face and the sort of demeanor that men call "even tempered" when they are talking about women. Or horses.

"Just visiting?" McIntyre inquired as they walked back to the main building.

"Probably not. Keep it under your hat—and by the way, you

do a wonderful job of keeping the brim of your ranger hat flat as a frying pan—but Aunt Hattie and Uncle John have been having financial troubles. Just before my mother died—Aunt Hattie's dear sister, you know—she asked me to take the bulk of her estate and use it to fix up Small Delights Lodge and put it back on its feet again. I was at loose ends. I had considered going into business as a woman barnstormer. They needed me here, however. Therefore, I decided to come. I'll stay until Aunt Hattie and Uncle John are back in the black. After that I'll be gone. The mountains are nice, but I prefer city life."

"Barnstormer?" McIntyre asked.

"Yes," Polly replied. "How do you keep the brim of that hat so flat, anyway? Yes, I have an airplane. One of the drawbacks to living here is that I can't have it with me. Luckily I found a farmer near the foothills who agreed to store it in his barn."

"You own an airplane?" McIntyre said.

"Curtiss Jenny JN-4," she said. "The government was selling it at a bargain price. The S.O. receptionist tells me you flew in the war?"

"A Curtiss Jenny," he said, "in training. In France, we flew Nieuports."

"Well, well," she said. "You must come flying with me. Now walk over here. I want to show you something else."

If this chubby young woman had a crush on him because of his picture in the S.O., she was doing a terrific job of hiding it.

"I've read all the works of Conan Doyle," she said as she led McIntyre toward the trash enclosure adjacent to the lodge's kitchen door. "Pure fiction, of course. Doyle's stories abound in situations that are highly improbable. Yet I find his investigative principles to be very sound. A detective could do worse than to study the methods of Sherlock Holmes, let me tell you."

The trash enclosure was constructed of upright logs, sharpened at the top like the frontier fort palisades in western movies. Polly Sheldon undid the latch and swung the heavy gate wide open. Inside, beneath a buzzing cloud of hovering deerflies and gnats, McIntyre saw a half-dozen garbage cans of various sizes.

"Look at the ground," Polly said. "Uncle John was tired of treading in mud whenever he went to dump the garbage into the cans. He salvaged that iron grill and put it down here to walk on."

It was a heavy grill, made of iron rods at least a quarter inch in diameter. It was supported on four short lengths of fence rail. One end of the grill had sunk into the damp earth, but would still keep a person's feet out of the smelly mud.

"Now look up there," Polly said, pointing.

At first McIntyre didn't see what she wanted him to. She had pointed to a pole next to the enclosure. It was an old telegraph pole, apparently, that John Frye had appropriated somewhere to use for his electric yard light. It looked like his idea had been to illuminate the garbage cans for those times when he needed to dump garbage in the dark. All at once, McIntyre spotted a wire dangling down. A length of electric wire had been connected from the light fixture to the iron grid under their feet.

"Holy cow," McIntyre said.

"Indeed," Polly said. "Uncle John is the only early riser here at the lodge. He wakes up while it's still dark, goes to the kitchen, puts a pot of coffee on the stove, builds up the fire, and takes out the trash from the previous evening. He switches on the yard light, opens the enclosure gate, and steps on the metal grill."

"It wouldn't electrocute him," McIntyre said. "Unless he was barefooted, and unless that electric wire and the grill were both insulated from the ground. The worst that could happen was that the current would blow a fuse or melt the wire in half."

"I knew you would be perceptive when I first saw your

photograph. Well done. But Uncle John, he would see the booby trap. That is the point, you see. Obviously. It's just like the bullet in the tree. Someone wants him to think they are out to kill him. Someone who, thus far, isn't very experienced in murdering people."

CHAPTER 2
ARE THERE GANGSTERS?

Catherine Croker had heard that the four Chicago men were in town. Hattie Frye told her, Hattie who seemed to know everyone in the valley and had more friends than a dog has fleas. Hattie had so many friends because she spent all day on the telephone, gossiping with village women, running up the phone bill while she let her housekeeping go to pot. Hattie, always the optimist who looked for the good in everyone, told Catherine the four men looked like they had come to try the fishing in the national park. Either that, or they were city investors looking for property to buy.

When their car pulled up in front of Grand Harbor Lodge, Catherine eased open the lace curtain to have a look before going out to meet them. She didn't think they looked like fishermen. Their car was a long, black, shiny sedan. The man in charge wore a long leather coat and had his hat at a cocksure angle; the driver wore a baggy sweater and cloth cap like a taxi driver's; the other two men wore cloth coats, which they buttoned as they stepped from the sedan. Their hats were set at the same cocky angle as that of the boss's. As they came toward the building, she saw his heavy jowls and cold, piercing eyes and she disliked him immediately. But nevertheless, customers were customers and customers were her income.

"Good afternoon," she said, stepping out onto the porch, "welcome to Grand Harbor."

"Afternoon," the man with the cold eyes said. "Not as hot

21

today. Not like yesterday."

"It was, wasn't it?" Catherine replied. "I'm always surprised how hot it can be up here in the mountains. I suppose it's because we're closer to the sun. That, and the air is extremely clear. That old sun just beats down on a person."

"Yeah, it was hot."

"Were you gentlemen interested in a room? Or a cabin? We have several available at the moment. Three boats and a canoe, if you want to fish or go rowing on the lake. A horseshoe pit, and there's a ping-pong table in the lodge. Riding stable? There's miles and miles of riding and hiking trails nearby."

He was looking around as if taking an inventory of the Grand Harbor Lodge and its surroundings.

"We're staying at that hotel in town," he said. "The one up on the hill. Right now, we're more interested in investments than in fishing or riding horses. In town, they said there were two resorts way out here at this lake. That right?"

"Yes," Catherine said. "Ours, and just around the curve of the lakeshore there's the Small Delights Lodge. You can just see the buildings through the trees there. I don't think you'd like it, though. It's run by a nasty individual who drinks and has no manners at all, and—"

The man interrupted her.

"We been there. Met him. Listen, how about we talk business?"

Without being asked, he stepped up onto the wide porch and helped himself to a lounge chair. The cloth cap man went back to sit in the car, while the other two sat on the steps of the porch and lit their cigarettes.

"Let's start at the top and work our way down," the man continued. "Like I said, we're out here from Illinois looking for investments. Let me ask you flat out, are you interested in selling your resort?"

Catherine had turned down offers before. In the beginning, after her husband died, she was merely another widow with nothing to her name except a collection of summer rental cabins. But she had ruthlessly expanded and improved on it and now she was known—and respected—as a major resort owner and "woman of means" as they say. Grand Harbor Lodge at Blue Spruce Lake was, in her view at least, one of the most desirable places to stay in the national park. She had worked hard to make it that way and she had succeeded. The only remaining challenge was to drive that odious John Frye off the lake altogether in order to take over his little resort. She saw more potential in his place than he ever could. More to the point, Small Delights had a far better access road, which she coveted, and somewhat of a better view of the lake and mountains.

"I don't think I am interested in selling," she said, trying to sound sweet about it. Trying to sound as though she appreciated the offer. "It's my home, after all, and my income. I have plans for expansion."

"Into that Small Delight place. Yeah, he told us you wanted his land."

"Yes. Well, one of these days he'll go broke. The man has no idea what it means to be an innkeeper."

"I'm not one to dicker," the man said. "Here's the deal. You name a price, my investors will negotiate. Vinny?"

The man he called Vinny got up and handed Catherine a business card with a Chicago address and phone number on it.

"Thank you," she said, "but I'm afraid I won't be interested."

"Okay," he said. "Maybe you'll think it over. Maybe you'll call up and give them a price, right?"

She only nodded at that.

"Now," he said, lighting a cigarette, "we move down the list a notch. You serve meals, right? Frye told us you got a nice private room back there, off your dining room. It used to be a bar where a man could buy a drink. Know what I mean?"

"Yes," Catherine said. "The man who built the lodge included a kind of saloon back there. I can show it to you if you'd like. We mostly use it for storage now, linens and odd chairs, that kind of thing. Ever since prohibition, you know."

"Vinny?" the boss said. "Dink?"

The other man stood up. The boss made a fist and jerked his thumb toward the building. Vinny and Dink nodded and went inside.

"Here's the deal about prohibition," he said. "Our firm can set you up a sweet little private bottle club, see? All legal and aboveboard. People come, they bring a bottle, see? Or maybe you've got lockers behind the bar where they can stash their own booze. You sell 'em the setups, have edibles for 'em, provide glassware, ice. Make it a club, charge whatever you want for membership."

This was an angle Catherine had never thought of. Miles from town, no law except for a few overworked forest rangers. Herself as hostess of a popular hangout where the wealthier people from the area would gather. People of influence and class.

"And where does your firm come into it?" she asked.

"Just for the sake of talking about it," he said, "let's say my company was able to start up a kind of what you might call a 'dealership' somewhere nearby. Some sheik is out to show a flapper a good time, see, and maybe he knows this little 'dealership' where he can buy himself a bottle. Maybe champagne, maybe a good brandy. All import, not the cheap bathtub gin your local man makes."

My God, Catherine thought. *They already know about our village moonshiner?*

"Naturally we'd like to have this place here," he continued, "make it a resort for people that want to leave the city behind, people looking to have a vacation, maybe be outa sight for a while."

"Out of the city?" she asked. "You mean Denver? There are certainly a great many moneyed people in Denver."

She could almost hear the cash register ringing up the tabs.

"Denver, sure," he said. "Chicago, too. Once in a while things are too hot in Chicago. Businessmen like to come to your mountains here and relax. Bring guests. It'd be nice if they had a dance floor, maybe. And a place to sit and enjoy a few drinks without cops busting in, if you know what I mean."

"I see," she said.

"This Small Delight dump. Is there a driveway from here to there, other than that long track of yours back to the main road and back in to Frye's place? That's what, two miles, out and back in again? All potholes and ruts?"

"I apologize for my access road," Catherine said. "The builders made it twist and curve like that in order to avoid building bridges and filling in gullies. It's on national park land and the park won't allow us to change it. I did have it widened, but the park didn't like it. But, as a matter of fact, because of the way the original properties were laid out, the boundaries do touch each other at one point near the lakeshore. A good road could be built right along there where the footpath is. It would involve moving his dilapidated storage building, cutting down a few old pine trees, and blasting some granite boulders, but it would connect the two places. John Frye, of course, will not hear of it. His own access road easement is quite short and wide."

"Yeah, okay. What about this for you to think about: suppose my firm acquires that Small Delight place, okay? We make that road along the lake. We lease cabins to our clients. They arrange a year-round caretaker, see, and he makes sure your private liquor club don't run out of good liquor. Canadian whiskey,

French brandy, champagne, the works. Our lodgers, they come over here to your place for a good time, pay dues, buy meals. That's in addition to your other customers, naturally. Could be a sweet setup for the both of us."

Catherine's mind was swirling with the possibilities. On the one hand, she wanted the man to stop talking and just let her think, but on the other hand, she had a hundred questions about how much money she would make and what class of wealthy individuals would be coming for entertainment. It thrilled her to think Grand Harbor Lodge was poised on the brink of spectacular success, unlimited income. The only obstacle was that rotten little John Frye, sitting over there with his decrepitated fish camp and his undeservedly good access road.

The double doors opened and Vinny and Dink reappeared. Vinny was carrying the rifle that had been hanging above the lodge fireplace.

"Looks good," he said to the man in charge. "There's a back entrance even. Out into the woods. This your gun?"

"Yes," Catherine said. "My husband was a hunter, you see. He even taught me to use it, but I never have."

"Sweet," Vinny said. "Kinda dangerous, though, havin' it loaded. Just hangin' there where anybody can put their hands on it. Mind if I take a shot or two? I love guns. This is a sweet one."

Without waiting for a reply, Vinny chambered a cartridge into the rifle and blasted a pine cone across the parking area. He worked the bolt action again and fired a second shot.

"Nice," he said. He handed it to the other man. "Look at this, Boss. One of them British jobs. Custom-built, right?"

"I wouldn't know," Catherine said. "I do know he bought it from an English gentleman who was staying with us."

"I'll take it and put it back," Vinny said.

26

As the shiny black sedan drove away, Catherine picked up the spent cartridge and slipped it into her pocket.

Having spent two days trying to find out who owned a .303 Savage rifle, Ranger McIntyre figured he deserved a day off. He had asked everyone who sold ammunition, from the village outdoor outfitter to Tiny's little general store out at Beaver Point. He didn't mind talking to Tiny; the huge, jovial storekeeper made excellent sandwiches and across the road from his store was a good stretch of Thompson River trout habitat. With a bit of careful timing McIntyre could arrive in time for a couple of Tiny's end-of-the-day half-price sandwiches. Afterward he could make a few casts in the river.

Tiny didn't know anyone with a .303 Savage, and neither did any of the other shopkeepers or hunters McIntyre had interviewed. He collected innumerable opinions regarding the virtues of the .30-06 over the .303, or the .30-40 over the .30-30, but none of it was information he could use.

For McIntyre, an ideal day off should begin with a breakfast at the Pioneer Inn in the village, followed by a leisurely midmorning stroll up a trail along a mountain stream to one of his favorite fishing spots. He entered the Pioneer's dining room, removed his unofficial, non-uniform Stetson, and looked around for an empty table. The one he most preferred, the one with a window view of the village and the Rocky Mountain range of mountains beyond it, was available. But the memory of that pretty photographer still hung over it. And he already had enough poignant memories of blasted love even without remembering how he and the murderess had shared breakfast there.

McIntyre chose the breakfast buffet over the menu and had just returned to his table with a platter of pancakes, sausages, Scotch eggs, and homemade biscuits when the waitress came hurrying over to him.

"It's a phone call for you," she said. "Dottie had the operator forward it from the S.O. because she said she knew you'd be here."

Blast. This was exactly why McIntyre was procrastinating with one of his official assignments, which was to talk with a telephone company engineer about finding routes for telephone lines that would connect various parts of the national park. A park was supposed to be a place of relaxation, not where a man had to race from one problem to another just because somebody could get him on a darn telephone. Supervisor Nicholson wanted telephones in all the campgrounds, at all the scenic vista points along the highway, and at the most popular trailheads. Ridiculous.

McIntyre left his breakfast cooling and stomped out to the reception desk, where the cashier handed him the telephone.

"Ranger McIntyre," he said.

"This is Catherine Croker!" came the voice through the earpiece. "You must come! Immediately."

"What's happened?" *Or*, he thought, *what's happened now?*

"They're trying to kill me!"

"You too? I'm still working on who tried to kill John Frye."

"Devil take John Frye! He can burn in hell. Someone tried to kill me with a tree!"

"You'd better tell me about it."

"You know that sharp blind curve on my approach road. Well, a few minutes ago I was going into town, driving my own road, not going too fast. I wasn't going too fast. I came to the curve and crash! A dead ponderosa came down right in front of me and I barely stopped in time not to hit it. Had I been going just a bit faster it would have crushed me. I know it. They deliberately pushed that tree over as I was approaching, I know they did."

28

"I can't be there until tomorrow," McIntyre said.

"But by that time the killer will be long gone!" she said, almost screaming into the phone.

"He's gone by now," McIntyre said. "Besides, it might have been an accident. That old dead tree was bound to come down. They all do."

"I want an investigation!" she said.

"All right, let's be calm. Is Thad Muggins still your manager?"

"Yes."

"Okay. You send Thad and one of your other men with a saw and have them cut that tree. Tell them to cut it on either side of the road, very carefully, without moving the top or the base of it. They should carefully roll the log off the road for you. Tell them not to touch the base of the tree. Just move the center section off the road."

"I understand," she said. "Evidence. You'll look for marks and that kind of thing. Now tell me, should I have the boys cover it with a tarp, in case it rains before you arrive?"

"A fine idea," McIntyre said, clenching his teeth as he watched an inn guest taking the last hot sausage from the buffet. "But tell them to be careful about leaving footprints. I'm trusting you to keep that evidence safe."

McIntyre had no intention of examining the log that had blocked Catherine Croker's road. Maybe Polly Sheldon could use her magnifying glass on the bark and find the assailant's initials, but McIntyre wasn't going to play Sherlock Holmes of the Forest. He hoped that Catherine wouldn't tumble to the realization that he had given her all those instructions merely in order to keep her out of his hair for a while. It was still his day off. He was going to finish his breakfast and go fishing.

His afternoon on the trout stream was everything a fisherman could want. He thought about all those poor people who were sitting in offices down in the city where the summer heat came up off the dirty sidewalks, climbed the walls of the office buildings, and flowed over the sills of the open windows where desk workers perspired and waited for five o'clock.

Vi Coteau was probably one of those. He could picture her at her desk in the FBI office, wearing a silky short-sleeve dress all light and summer-like and staying comfortable in the soft breeze of a portable electric fan. McIntyre wondered if Vi Coteau would like fly fishing. Even if she didn't, she would love a mountain day like this. What was not to like about it? The sky was absolutely cloudless, a columbine-blue dome over mountain and valley. The creek was as clear as gin and beautifully cold against his feet. The brook trout rising to strike at his Royal Coachman swam to the surface like little ballet dancers moving in graceful curves. McIntyre caught more than half a dozen and released them again.

Maybe the lunkers are hiding behind that shadowy rock over there, he thought. *It's a long cast. There's a willow bush just waiting to snag my line. Still, if there's any keeper-size trout in this hole, that's where they'll be.*

He flicked the Coachman across the creek. As the quiet swirl of current caught it and carried it around the boulder he had a glimpse, the merest shadow of movement, of a large trout coming out of hiding. There was a crash of water and McIntyre jerked the tip of his fly rod up and the fish was hooked.

Had it been a brookie, it would probably have gone to the bottom of the stream where it would try to resist the pull of the line until it was tired out and could be dragged to the bank. A German Brown, on the other hand, would likely make an aggressive dash upriver, heading for the fast current while staying down under the surface out of sight. But this fish, this fish broke surface almost immediately. It came arching up out of the creek, curved glistening in the air, dove again, and then rose again into the air shaking the hook. McIntyre saw the flash of color along its side as it rose a third time, gained slack in the line, threw the Royal Coachman, and vanished. A rainbow trout.

I love rainbows, McIntyre thought. *Love the way they fight.* While he reeled in his empty dry fly he let his mind drift backward in time to another beautiful day. It was the day when the one certain love of his life had caught and landed her first rainbow trout. Her outburst of joy, the way her entire being seemed very, very happy to be alive in that one moment. It was a large rainbow and she had exhausted it too far to let it go. That evening in his cabin by candlelight he cooked it along with the brookies they had taken and they supped on trout with canned sweet corn and homemade bread. She pronounced it the best-tasting trout anyone had ever eaten. And before they went to bed she made a solemn vow that she would not stop fishing until she had caught another just like it, and another after that.

"From now on," she said, laughing, "you may address me as the Woman of the Rainbows."

Rainbows.

Examining his Royal Coachman to see if the hook needed sharpening, while thinking of rainbow trout, McIntyre remembered something. There was a Rainbow Road near Blue Spruce Lake. A retired British military man and his wife lived on that road, a mile or so over the hill past Small Delights and Grand Harbor. The previous summer McIntyre had paid the couple a visit, just to say hello and let them know who he was, and, on the wall, he had seen the man's rifle. Anyone who had been in the war would recognize it instantly as a .303 Enfield. Could you shoot a .303 Savage cartridge in a .303 British Enfield rifle? It might be worth looking into. He'd pay the major a visit. Despite Supervisor Nicholson's stern warning about being transferred to Death Valley, McIntyre would take along his fly rod. On up the road from the Brit's cabin, there were some fine fishing holes along Fanton's Creek.

CHAPTER 3
ARSON AND A DEADFALL

Ranger McIntyre slept soundly and woke up eager for action. He made himself a sensible breakfast of oatmeal and toast and coffee, brushed his uniform, rubbed the dust from his boots, and packed up his lunch and fly rod. After gassing up the National Park Service pickup truck, he set out for Rainbow Road. He had the .303 Savage cartridge case in his pocket: he intended to find out for himself whether it would fit into the chamber of the retired Englishman's .303 Enfield rifle.

He was less than fifty yards past the Grand Harbor Lodge access road and was approaching the road to Small Delights when he saw a column of grayish-black smoke twisting up into the still morning air.

A fire!

It was a serious one, from the look of that smoke. It looked like it was close to Small Delights Lodge, which made it particularly serious because Hattie Frye at Small Delights had a horror of fire. Everyone in the area knew about her pyro phobia: at the slightest danger of forest fire the neighbors would say "Oh no! Where's Hattie?"

McIntyre swung the pickup off the main road and drove the lodge road as fast as the bumps and ruts would allow. *You'd think John Frye would maintain his road once in a while,* McIntyre thought, *instead of telling guests that the road was the national park's responsibility.*

He came around the corner to discover a large truck burning

33

in the middle of the road, blazing up like a regular bonfire. Mc-Intyre brought the pickup to a sliding stop, jumped out and stripped off his hat and tunic, unstrapped his fire shovel from the fender, and went to work.

The ranger had scooped up and thrown a dozen shovels of dirt onto the burning truck when he realized that he was not alone. Someone else was on the other side of the blaze, also throwing dirt. The heat was intense. The tires popped and burst into greasy flame, along with the wooden bed and sideboards. Thankfully there was no wind; the heat and stinking smoke was going straight up instead of being blown into his face. His anonymous helper moved around closer to him, scraping up dirt and throwing it like an experienced forest firefighter. He saw who it was. Pauline "Polly" Sheldon from Small Delights Lodge.

"We'd better fall back!" she shouted over the roar of the flames. "Gasoline! The tank could blow!"

I was just about to think of that, McIntyre thought. He threw another shovel of dirt and made a retreat, followed by Polly Sheldon. They sat side by side on the bumper of his pickup, panting from exertion as they watched the truck burn. If the gas tank blew up they would have their work cut out for them chasing spot fires in the thick forest.

"Is that Aaron Rule's truck? The garbage man?" McIntyre said.

"Yes," she said. "I saw the smoke from the lodge. Aunt Hattie is going crazy. She came along with me far enough to see that the road was blocked. When I ran back for a shovel I saw her pushing the old rowboat into the lake and climbing into it to escape. Terribly afraid of fire."

"You were handling that shovel like a pro," McIntyre said.

"Surprised?"

"Well, it's just that . . ."

"Just that people don't expect a girl to know how to use a fire shovel? Or is it just that I'm a fat girl?"

"Hey," McIntyre said. "Where is Aaron, I wonder? I just remembered. He ought to be around here somewhere."

"Dunno," Polly replied.

"Ought to look for him. Did you see him in the truck?"

"No. First thing I did when I got here was to look. The cab door was wide open but there wasn't anyone inside."

The roar of the fire became intense as the solder melted on the fuel line and allowed gasoline to pour out. The tank was on the back of the cab just behind the driver's seat where it had been shielded from the flaming truck bed by several cans of wet garbage. Now the solder melted around the fuel cap; it fell into the tank and the tank became a blowtorch sending orange flame twenty feet into the air. But it didn't explode.

"That's a break for us," McIntyre said. "Let's just pray there's nothing flammable in those trash cans."

Polly stood up and walked back toward the burning truck, scanning the ground as she went. Despite the heat, McIntyre went near enough to the truck to throw more dirt. He managed to extinguish the front tires and smothered a small blaze where oil from the engine had dripped on the ground. The wooden bed of the truck burned through and gave way, letting the load of garbage cans crash to the ground. The fuel tank was still sending a jet of flame skyward but seemed to be cooling down a little. It was only by the grace of God that the forest hadn't caught fire.

"Here's tracks!" Polly called.

Off one side of the road, where their shovels hadn't disturbed the earth, she had found fresh boot tracks leading into the trees.

"Looks like they're headed for the creek," McIntyre said.

Beside the creek they found Aaron Rule, the trash collector. He was nearly unconscious and in terrible pain from a horribly scorched arm which he had been soaking in the cold water. Mc-Intyre ran for the first aid kit from his pickup while Polly urged Aaron to his feet and supported him as they made their way back to the road.

Ranger McIntyre drove as fast as he dared. The unfortunate Aaron sat back against the seat in agony, his arm cushioned in two pillows from the lodge. McIntyre kept reassuring him that they wouldn't be long before they were at the doctor's office, but the miles into town seemed to drag along at snail speed.

"Do you know what happened?" McIntyre said.

"Don't know," Aaron said between agonized moans. "Fuel line, I guess."

"Fuel line?"

"Aw, hell, Tim. I shoulda knowed. I smelt it right away."

"What, gasoline?"

"Yeah. After I picked up Grand Harbor's garbage. The old girl, Croker, she even give me coffee and biscuits this morning. Still complaining about me putting damn dents in her garbage cans, though."

He pressed his head against the back of the cab and moaned again.

"I got back in my truck so's to drive over to Small Delights and that's when I smelt it. Gas line runs from the tank under the seat, acrost the floorboards, out the firewall to the engine, see? I'm purty sure gas was leakin' at the carburetor and runnin' back along the line inta the cab. Engine heat must've set her off."

The effort of talking had taken Aaron's mind off of his pain, but it was too much for him. He slumped against McIntyre's shoulder, unconscious. And the miles kept crawling.

After leaving Aaron with the doctor, McIntyre went to the

RMNP supervisor's office and stuck his head through the door just long enough to tell Dottie what had happened.

"If anybody needs me, I'll be at Blue Spruce Lake. I want to be sure the fire's out and I need to look around and find out how it happened."

Back at the scene of the fire, he found John Frye in a state of high dudgeon.

"And where the hell have you been?" Frye demanded. "We coulda used your help towing Rule's damn truck off the road. How are customers supposed to use the road with this damn burned-up garbage truck in the way? Look at this mess!"

"I had to rush Aaron to the doc. He's seriously burned. Got back as quick as I could."

"Well, without your help we got the fire put out. Damn that Aaron, anyway. He oughta learn to keep up a truck so's it don't catch fire. And just you listen to me, Mister Ranger Man. This here is your property, government property right up to that there post with the tin sign on it. So, this damn smokin' wreckage is on your land and so it's up to you to take it the hell outa here. And do it quick. I don't want guests seein' a burned-out truck on my road. And it's gonna spook ol' Hattie every damn time we drive past it, she's that afraid of fire. You haul it outa here."

"I'll check with the S.O. about it," McIntyre said.

"Check my hat, dammit. Move that thing off my road."

Polly saved McIntyre from further conversation with John Frye by coming up and asking the ranger if he would step over to the wrecked truck for a moment. The metal was still hot.

"I used a stick to open the engine cover with," she explained. "Even with my gloves on it was pretty darn warm. Now, you look down there where the gas line goes through the firewall and tell me what you see."

"Nothing," he said.

Polly reached around him and jiggled the brass connection on the gas line.

"It's cooled off now. That connector ought to be tight. In fact, I'm thinking the heat from the fire should have made it pretty near impossible to unscrew. But look how loose it is. And there's scratches in the brass. See where I wiped the soot away? You're going to say those wrench marks could have been made any time, but I disagree. I think the fuel line was deliberately loosened. Somebody wanted this garbage truck to catch fire while it was parked at Small Delights, that's what I think. Aaron stopped and collected the garbage at Grand Harbor Lodge before driving here. I bet if we sniffed around, we'd find a puddle of gas where he parked to load our garbage. Right behind the kitchen. It's a miracle it didn't ignite there. I'm thinking it dripped on the exhaust pipe as he drove away until it caught fire, right here on the road. What do you think?"

I think I'll just give you the badge and gun and I'll go fishing, McIntyre thought.

"Sounds plausible," he said.

"Hey! Ranger!" John Frye called. Apparently, he wasn't finished with his ranting and raving.

"Hey! What am I supposed to do about my garbage? You better talk to that other trash guy, what's his name, tell him to chase his butt over here. There's all this garbage on the road. Next week my cans will be full again. What am I supposed to do, dump 'em in the woods? The park service trash truck picks up cans at the campgrounds, have them come collect mine while they're at it."

"John," McIntyre said. "Your garbage isn't my job. However, I'm willing to ask around and see if I can find somebody. Grand Harbor will be in the same predicament. Meanwhile, why don't you dig a garbage pit? Keep it at least fifty yards back from the edge of the lake. Build a frame and door for it, like a cellar door, to keep varmints out of it."

"Dig!" Frye said. "You ever try to dig around here? It's all rocks and roots. Tell you what: you send your trail crew boys out here and I'll let them dig me a garbage pit. That way it'll be regulation and meet with your fussy standards. Damn government."

Frye stomped off, probably heading for the old storage shed where he hid his secret stash of booze. Once he was out of earshot, Polly Sheldon came up to McIntyre.

"I looked into that falling tree, too," she said, "the one on the road to Grand Harbor. I made photographs. When I have the time to go to town, I'll drop them off to be developed and order you extra copies. Have you seen the place where the log nearly hit Catherine's car? I had a good look around. It's a classic. A Burmese booby trap. They call it The Sleeping Python. They dug a narrow trench across the road and laid a long fence rail in it, one end sticking back into the trees along the road. A strong cord tied to the end was looped over a tree branch to keep the tree trunk from falling. The tree trunk was rigged to fall, you see. All that held it upright was that cord. Car wheel runs over the fence rail, pushes it down, slip knot releases, and bam!"

"Swell," McIntyre said. "I guess your Uncle John probably didn't rig it to hit Catherine?"

Polly laughed.

"Uncle John? I seriously doubt it. If you haven't noticed, Uncle John is a city kind of man. No, it was done by a woodsman. Somebody with experience at trapping animals. Funny, though."

"Funny?"

"That tree trunk wasn't much thicker than a telegraph pole. And the trigger rail, it was set too far back. It's funny that a man would know how to set up a trap like that and not make it lethal."

"So far," McIntyre said, "none of these so-called attempts on people's lives have been lethal. It looks like they were just meant to scare people. But now they've gone and hurt Aaron, burned his arm and ruined his garbage business. I'm going to find out who did it."

McIntyre got into his truck and drove to the Small Delights main building. He had told Polly he was going to make sure Hattie was all right and reassure her that the fire was out, but his grumbly stomach was hoping that Hattie would be serving lunch to the guests and would ask if he was hungry. Unfortunately, lunch hour was over and Hattie was lying down with a sick headache from the fire scare.

Now he was hungry and he reeked of smoke and sweat. His uniform shirt was stained and wrinkled and his pants had streaks of charred wood and soot. He was in no condition to go calling on a retired British military man. He needed to drive back to the Fall River entrance station and take a shower and cook supper. He'd stop off at the S.O. and tell Dottie that he'd given John Frye permission to dig a garbage pit and to report that there was a burned-out truck and several hundred pounds of wet garbage sitting beside a national park road.

Digging. Rocks and roots, John Frye said. Something about digging began to peck away inside his skull. He had better take a look at that Burmese booby trap before he went home to clean up.

He turned onto the Grand Harbor access road and stopped where the deadfall had been. The log was lying just off the side of the road but the trigger, the long fence rail, was still in the shallow ditch someone had dug across the road. McIntyre got out of his pickup and knelt down to examine it. The marks in the dirt showed that whoever had dug it across the road hadn't used a pick even though the ground was hard and rocky. They hadn't used a full-size garden shovel, either.

McIntyre took his own fire shovel from the pickup and fitted it into the trench. The guy who laid the trap probably used a fire shovel or an entrenching tool. Every park service vehicle carried one. For that matter, any driver might be carrying a small shovel in his car. Then McIntyre noticed a paint streak on a rock sticking into the side of the shallow ditch. He used his shovel to pry the rock out: the streak was a trace of olive drab paint. Civilian shovels were usually painted black, if they were painted at all. Most people would let them rust. Park service fire shovels were painted olive drab.

The culprit would want a short shovel. A man seen on the road carrying a long-handled shovel might attract notice; an entrenching tool could be hidden under a long jacket. McIntyre would have liked to look in the trunk of that Chicago sedan, just to see if they carried an army surplus folding shovel. It wouldn't prove anything, however: almost anybody could "borrow" a fire shovel from any park service pickup.

McIntyre sighed. One more thing to do. Would it be worth his time to check ranger vehicles and see if any shovels were missing? Or had been used lately?

"There was a phone call for you," Dottie said. "From the FBI. Since Supervisor Nicholson is gone for the day, you can use the phone in his office. I'll ring up the operator and tell her you're ready to take the call."

"Okay, thanks."

"What does the FBI want with you? Have you been making moonshine out there at Fall River?"

"Maybe I'm working as a spy to expose nosy secretaries in government offices," he said. "Put them on the line. And don't listen in."

Dottie stuck her tongue out at him and tapped the phone cradle to signal the operator. McIntyre went into the supervisor's office and closed the door. The supervisor's upholstered swivel chair fitted him comfortably; for a brief moment, he thought it would be pretty nice to have a clean office with wide windows and a swivel chair, and a receptionist to do the paperwork, and lots of time to go fishing. And he could boss people around. Supervisor Nicholson had hired two new rangers that spring. It might be fun to just sit here thinking up jobs for them to do.

When the phone rang, he picked up the earpiece and the candlestick mouthpiece and leaned back in the chair with them like an important executive.

"Ranger Tim McIntyre," he said.

"Just the man I've been looking for."

It was Vi Coteau, assistant to the FBI agent in Denver and supervisor of the Denver office. During several all-too-brief meetings with her, including going to the movies, McIntyre had found out that Vi Coteau was not only beautiful and a very classy dresser but was more intelligent than her boss. She could also shoot better than her boss, and with any weapon the FBI had in its arsenal. McIntyre fantasized about having a pinup calendar picture of Vi in one of her flapper-type filmy dresses, high heels, and designer cloche, smiling and holding either a Thompson submachine gun or a Browning Automatic Rifle, a BAR. He had never been a man for calendar girl pictures on his wall, but Vi with a machine gun? Wow.

Vi lowered her silky voice to give it a serious tone.

"Ranger McIntyre, the FBI has discovered your fingerprints on several dozen trout belonging to the U.S. Government and we want you to come to Denver and explain how they got there and take me to lunch."

"Woolworths again?"

"Can you afford the Brown Palace? Or the Daniels & Fisher Tearoom?"

"Not unless I can trade poached trout."

"Then Woolworths it is."

"Egg salad sandwiches?"

"You remembered!"

He remembered. The first time they met, Vi took him to lunch at Woolworths. She told him she had three weaknesses. One was egg salad sandwiches, one was nonpareil candies, and she wouldn't tell him the third one.

"Are you just checking up on me, or did you actually want something?"

"Just checking up," she replied. "They gave me a new office telephone that I'm trying out. The mouthpiece and earpiece are all in one piece. Very handy. I can even hold it with my shoulder and type as I talk. How are you? Any more murders in the park?"

"No, but I've got a couple of attempts. A man took a shot at a guy and missed by at least two feet. They also tried to electrify his garbage cans but didn't get the wire grounded right. They tried to drop a log on his chief competitor but missed, and they probably torched a garbage truck, too. How about you? Anything better than that?"

Her laugh was all soft and all female, seductive enough to send a warm tingle all the way down into his knee-high boots.

"Oh, we solved a case of espionage. And one of counterfeiting. We thought we had a kidnapping, but it was just a senator's daughter running away from home. No shootings, though."

"Speaking of shootings, I had a thought," McIntyre said. "You guys have a ballistics lab, right?"

"Yes, we do. And for the record, I'm not a guy."

"Hmmm? Well, well."

"You sound as if it comes as a surprise."

"Oh, no," McIntyre said. "I noticed right away that you're not a guy. Anyhow, that shooter's slug was in a tree and it's pretty smashed. I think it came from a .303 Savage. Is there any way you could measure it and let me know if it's a .303? The base of the bullet is still nearly round, just a little distorted. But I don't have anything to compare it with. That, and maybe the base expanded a little when it was fired."

"Mail it down to me," Vi said. "I'll take a look at it."

"Great. I'll owe you that lunch," he said.

"Speaking of buying me lunch," she said, "if I were to take off for a day or two and wanted to see Rocky Mountain National Park, do you suppose I could find a ranger willing to show me around?"

"I imagine you could," McIntyre said. "We have two new ones. You could have your pick. Russ Frame came to us from Yosemite, he's a very neatly dressed military type guy. Very fit and very tidy. Or there's Charlie Nevis. His voice is kinda wheezy and his uniform is usually baggy. Well, let's face it: he's a slob. But he's a pretty good woodsman and is really good with mechanical stuff."

"Wow," she said. "How to decide? I'll pick a day to visit, and you can have your available rangers lined up outside the barracks for me to choose from. How about that?"

"Like an inspection parade. Sure, we can do that for you. Now tell me what you really phoned about," he said.

"Okay. About two weeks ago the Denver police broke up another speakeasy. My boss, Agent Canilly, was in on the raid because the bootleg alcohol supposedly crossed state lines. Came from Canada. The funny thing was, the guy who ran the joint didn't seem too concerned that he'd been put out of business. Two days ago, one of the bartenders decided he'd had enough of being in jail and volunteered to cop a plea. He said he had heard that it wouldn't matter about the Denver gin joint because 'the Boss' had plans to relocate to a resort town. In the mountains."

"Then you want to know if we have a hidden speakeasy in

the national park, one that we don't know about? Let me think a minute. How many unknown illegal operations do we have? I don't know."

"Don't be such a silly ranger. Agent Canilly wants you to report suspicious strangers, that's all. I described your reputation for hanging out in lodge kitchens and dining rooms and he thought those would be ideal places to hear about any lodges or fancy homes that might be up for sale. Or men who've been asking about buying a resort."

"Hey!" McIntyre said. "I don't spend all my time eating free meals."

"Oh?" she said.

"Once in a while I go fishing. Or in rainy weather I stay at the entrance station and do a jigsaw puzzle. I can't resist a good puzzle. I guess you could say it's a weakness I have, like you and your egg salad sandwiches."

"Don't forget nonpareils. I can't resist them, either."

"Yes," he said, smiling at the memory of their lunch date in Woolworths. "And that third thing you can't resist? What was that again?"

"Goodbye, Ranger Tim McIntyre. Remember to mail me that .303 slug."

"All through?" Dottie asked sweetly, as McIntyre came out of Supervisor Nicholson's office. "What do the feds want you for? Poaching? Extortion of free lunches? Or did the FBI tumble to the fact that you're using a government truck for your own private vehicle?"

"Say! You can stop teasing about that. I told you I'm looking for a car to buy. Besides, Nick said I could use the truck as long as I paid for the gas. Speaking of looking for things, however, I'm going to call a meeting of rangers and assistant rangers and any work crews who can make it. Day after tomorrow at the ranger barracks, 9 a.m. sharp. Can you spread the word?"

"I'll help, sure. What's it about?"

"FBI says we should be on the lookout for a bootleg opera-tion, maybe a dance hall or other kind of hangout. Plus, I need to locate anyone who owns a .303 Savage. Preferably a man with enough free time to go around rigging up booby traps. Maybe someone who doesn't have a regular job."

"Like a park ranger?" Dottie said, smiling as innocently as only she could.

"Smart aleck," he replied. "If anyone wants me, tell them I've gone back to the station to shower and clean up. I really need it."

"Agreed," she said. "You're making my office smell like an old tire incinerator."

CHAPTER 4
WHO BROUGHT THE BEAR?

Driving through the village on his way to the office, Park Supervisor Nicholson saw McIntyre's government pickup truck parked outside the Pioneer Inn. *That's kind of odd,* he thought: *on Tuesday mornings McIntyre usually tries for a free breakfast at the Staghorn Lodge. Maybe the Pioneer has a new chef. Or a new waitress.*

Dottie was her efficient little self that morning. On his desk, Nicholson found two letters ready for his signature, two memos he needed to deal with, and a note telling him he had a phone call to return. The phone call was from John Frye, who had rung up the park office three times before eight o'clock. Nicholson sighed, hung up his hat, sat down in his chair, and, in keeping with his personal policy, addressed himself to the most distasteful job first. It was like what Mark Twain or someone said about eating a live frog each morning: if you do that, it will be the worst thing you'll have to do that day.

After his conversation with Frye, Nicholson came out of his office.

"Dottie," he said, "would you call the Pioneer Inn and have McIntyre report to the office. You might phone Catherine Croker at Grand Harbor, too. Ask if they've had any trouble with marauding bears at her place. She'll no doubt give you an earful about garbage piling up, but listen politely. We need to be nice to our residents."

"A bear? Frye says there's a bear problem at Small Delights?" McIntyre asked. "We don't have a bear population anywhere near Blue Spruce Lake. Remember how the animal wardens wanted to bring some into the area and re-establish them?"

"Nevertheless," Supervisor Nicholson said patiently. "John Frye's been burning up the phone lines this morning. According to him, a ferocious giant silvertip grizzly was hiding outside the back door, waiting to grab his guests, one of whom was mauled and chewed up and only managed to escape when John picked up a stick and attacked him."

"John attacked the guest?"

"The bear, wise guy."

"The translation of which is that a lodge guest surprised a little brown bear and John came out and took a shovel to the poor creature."

"Maybe. But you still need to look into it."

"Wait a minute. You put me on enforcement, not wild game management. I don't think I can arrest a bear for eating garbage. Might not even be one of our bears. Could be a forest service bear. I know: let's send the new summer ranger, Russ Frame. Mister Neat and Tidy. He can collect all the details and file a report. He could inventory the garbage to see what's missing."

"And also take down the bear's name and license number, I suppose," the supervisor said. "No dice, Ranger. I put you in charge of all trouble at Blue Spruce Lake and you're the guy who's going out there and take care of it. Have you got a rifle?"

"Not with me. But I found my revolver. See?"

"Swell. Tell Dottie to give you a rifle from the gun closet as you leave."

"Ranger Russ Frame has a rifle. I saw the rifle case next to his bunk. Let's send him."

"Gun, McIntyre. Take a gun, go. Keep John Frye away from

me. I don't care if you have to stand sentry duty over his garbage all night, just deal with his bear problem."

"I could take a few potshots at his telephone line," McIntyre suggested. "That way he couldn't call you, at least not for a while."

"Just take care of the bear, Tim," the supervisor said. "Go. Take a gun. Remember to take bullets. Deal with it."

All the way out to Blue Spruce Lake Ranger McIntyre was dreading another encounter with Polly Sheldon, the pushy self-appointed frontier detective. But when he got to Small Delights Lodge, he discovered to his own large delight that Polly was nowhere to be seen.

"Dunno where she got to," John Frye said with a snarl. "Never around when I need her. She's either in there feeding her fat face or poking around in the woods. She oughta be with Hattie. Hattie imagined she smelled smoke again last night, so none of us got any sleep. First, she thought she heard a car motor, that's what woke her up. She thought she smelled smoke, too. Never saw a woman as afraid of fire as she is. It's a damn phobia, that's what it is. I just about got back to sleep when she yells at me 'there it is again' and she said she heard that car motor and I told her to shut the hell up and go to sleep."

"Probably a tourist who got lost and drove down your road. You might as well tell me about this bear problem of yours," McIntyre said.

"It ain't my bear problem. It's yours. That's a government bear. It's your responsibility. C'mon, I'll show you where it happened."

John Frye repeated the story he had told Supervisor Nicholson over the phone, namely that a huge grizzly bear had been lying in ambush when an early-rising guest went out the back door of the lodge to enjoy a cigarette. The bear started biting and mauling the man. The man yelled bloody murder, Frye heard the racket, grabbed the first stick he saw, and attacked the animal, beating it off.

"Where is this guest? I'd like to talk to him."

"Gone."

"What?"

"Demanded his refund. For all three nights him and his wife was here. Says he ain't gonna stay in a place where a man can't go outside for a quiet smoke without a bear attacking him. Said they was gonna go into town and stay at a civilized place like the Livingstone. I figure we lost a week's worth of business and I'm gonna send Nicholson a bill for it. It's his bear."

"I guess that's between you and the supervisor," McIntyre said. "You say this bear attack happened right here?"

"Right here where we're standing. But I gotta leave you to it. Gotta go see if Hattie's calmed down enough to feed what's left of our customers."

McIntyre immediately observed two things, starting with the footprints. The earth around the garbage enclosure showed well-defined tracks, thanks to a soft evening rain. Judging by the size of the bear prints John Frye's "huge marauding grizzly" was probably not much larger than a big dog. He took out his notebook and sketched two of the prints. They were the tracks of a bear, of that there was no doubt, but it was no grizzly.

The other thing he noticed was that there were no claw scratches on either the gate to the garbage enclosure nor on the back door of the lodge. It was too early in the summer for a bear to be hungry enough to come near humans. Maybe a bear would investigate the lodge just before hibernation, if natural food was in short supply. Maybe. If a bear did come hungry, it would have at least tried the door to the kitchen. Good smells come out of a kitchen. It would also have tried to climb into the garbage enclosure. Either way there'd be claw marks somewhere.

McIntyre tried to line up the pieces of the picture like it was a jigsaw puzzle. A young bear wandered in during the night. From the tracks, it looked as though the bear didn't know where it was. It sniffed around and either sat down or lay down, probably to wait for daylight. There was a wild rose bush growing against the corner of the lodge: several tufts of coarse hair were caught on it, so dark brown as to look almost black. Mister Bear wasn't particularly hungry or afraid, but maybe he was lost or confused and tired. He lay down beside the rose bush. Around sunrise a guest came out of the door and either tripped over the bear or surprised it. The bear probably lashed out with a paw. The guest screamed and John Frye came barreling out of the kitchen with a shovel handle or a broom and started beating on the poor creature.

The tracks clearly showed that the bear had gone off into the forest. Judging by the distance between footprints and the way the claws had scruffed up the ground, the animal was moving away from these screaming humans and their clubs as quickly as possible.

McIntyre lost the tracks in the forest. He went back to the lodge to see if he could determine which direction the animal had come from in the first place. It wouldn't mean anything, but at least it would look like the park service was investigating. He was bent over, trying to find more tracks, following the service road behind the garbage enclosure, when he came to a fresh set of tracks of quite another kind. They were the fresh tracks of a vehicle, and not an ordinary one.

Polly Sheldon came bustling out of the woods. She spotted the ranger and made a beeline for him at flank speed, coming on like a tugboat. She was carrying a shotgun.

"There you are," she said. "What species of bears do you have in your national park, anyway? This was definitely not a grizzly."

"I already knew that," McIntyre said. "Those tracks aren't grizzly tracks. Just a small, garden variety brown bear. Was that gate to the garbage cans secured last night? I found it open."

"I don't know," Polly said. "Now, listen to me. I made a wide circuit back in the trees, starting at the lakeshore near Grand Harbor and looping around to the south. I saw no evidence of bears whatsoever. No rotten logs broken open, no hair caught on trees where they might have scratched their backs, no ground squirrel holes dug into. No scat, no paw prints, nothing. In short, that bear does not live around here."

"I could have told you that, too," Ranger McIntyre said. "And stop waving that shotgun. In fact, break it open. Thank you. First off, we don't have many grizzlies left in the park and they all stay near timberline this time of year. We have a brown bear population, but our crews have been trapping and relocating them to the north side of the park where there's more natural food and fewer humans. We haven't seen one in this valley for three summers. And if one was living around here, which I doubt, he wouldn't be eating John's garbage. Plenty of natural food out there."

"All right," Polly said. She pulled the two shotgun shells out of the gun's breech and put them in her shirt pocket. "What is your explanation? What are we going to do about it? Families will not want to rent rooms or cottages if they think there are bears hanging around."

"Well," McIntyre said, "I suppose we could set fire to the forest, drive the bear out into the lake, go out in your rowboat and shoot him. Either that or wait to see if he comes back to the garbage. But that's strange, too. He didn't climb the enclosure, which means the gate was opened. One garbage can was tipped over, but the lid is sitting on top of the other cans like someone had opened the can, put the lid down, then tipped the can over. Anyway, if this bear has gotten a taste for human garbage, we'll need to trap him and relocate him. You might hire a hunter with dogs to track him, but I don't think it would do any good."

"Hmmmpphh," she said. "What have you found there? Just more tracks?"

"Interesting tracks," McIntyre said. "Wheels. Two wheels, wide wheels, wheels without any tread at all, just smooth. What do you suppose made them?"

Polly moved closer to see for herself.

"Stop there!" McIntyre said. "Don't mess it up. Do you have a mirror in that handbag of yours?"

"I have a compact with a mirror in it, yes."

She took out a tortoise shell compact the size of a saucer and opened it to show the mirror.

"Hold it near the ground and reflect the sunlight across this area here."

In the reflected light, the tracks were as obvious as if they had been inches deep. Two parallel indentations where two wide, plain wheels had rolled along. McIntyre followed them toward the garbage enclosure, where they stopped. The light from Polly's mirror also revealed a deep groove at a right angle to the tracks. Beyond the groove they saw the bear's paw prints. McIntyre sketched the scene in his notebook.

"What is it?" Polly asked.

"A jigsaw puzzle," the ranger replied. "There was a light rain yesterday evening. Some time after it stopped raining, a truck with no tread on its tires backed in here off the service road. There's enough slope that it could have rolled in with the engine turned off. I saw tracks like that in France, lots of them. The Army used White trucks, heavy brutes with wooden wheels and solid rubber tires with no tread. Anyway, the truck, whatever kind it was, backed up to this point next to the garbage enclosure. But I'm still puzzled about it."

"Why? What's wrong?"

"That gouge in the dirt. They let down the tailgate and that's where it dug into the dirt. It's too close to the wheel tracks. And it shouldn't be there at all. The tailgate on a White truck wouldn't reach all the way to the ground."

"I'm beginning to see where you're going with this," Polly said. "Well, what if it wasn't a tailgate but a ramp of some kind, and what if they stopped the truck and pulled forward a few feet before letting it down?"

"Yeah," McIntyre said, musing. "That could explain it."

"You're saying that someone quietly backed in here last night, released a bear, and drove away again. Right?"

"Right. Except a truck would have made enough noise to wake everybody up. And whoever did it, where did they get the bear from?"

"And whoever did this," Polly asked, "what's the point?"

"To scare people into leaving, maybe? Like John's frightened guest. Tourists always want to climb the mountains and hike the trails and swim in the lakes, but they want assurances that there aren't any snakes, bears, or mountain lions. Whoever did it might have been thinking that a bear as small as that one, a young bear, would be attracted to the garbage and would decide to hang around for a few weeks. I think the bear had recently fed, though, and wasn't hungry. When he found himself in a strange place in the dark he just lay down."

They heard the kitchen door slam and turned to see Hattie Frye bustling toward them.

"What are we going to do?" Hattie asked. "What are we going to do?"

"To start with, John needs to secure this garbage. Haul it to the dump, after which he should wash out the cans with soap. Make sure a bear can't open the cans or find a way into the enclosure. Keep your ground floor windows and doors closed at night. Tell guests not to leave anything that smells like food in their cars. John does have a burn pit up in the trees, right? Up there next to the hot water boiler?"

"Yes," Hattie admitted, "but I'm afraid when he lights it! I can't sleep for fear it's going to set the place on fire."

"You might have to put up with it, at least until our bear goes away. Tell John he needs to burn paper stuff like bread wrappers, lard boxes, even tin cans if they had food in them."

"It will be all right, Aunt Hattie," Polly said, putting her arm around the older woman's shoulders. "I'll sleep in the lounge with my shotgun. We'll deal with the bear. The rangers will trap it or I'll shoot it. Ranger McIntyre will find out who brought that bear here in the first place, won't you, Ranger?"

"Who brought it here?" Hattie went from anxious to full-out terrified. "Oh! It must have been that Thad Muggins, that awful man! He's just the sort! Or it was those gangsters trying to buy Small Delights from us. I think it's time we simply sold and moved to Denver. Just sell it to them. Living out here in the woods is making me into a nervous wreck."

McIntyre hadn't thought of Muggins, the general foreman at Grand Harbor Lodge. He was a woodsman, and a good one. From what Catherine Croker and Hattie had told him about the men in the long black sedan, they seemed like his best suspects, except that McIntyre couldn't picture them capturing a bear and stealing a truck to transport it in without being seen.

Transporting the bear. A small piece of the jigsaw puzzle snapped into place.

"Can I use your phone?" he asked.

Polly waved in the direction of the lodge. McIntyre found the phone on the reception desk and asked the operator to connect him with the Fall River station.

"Fall River Entrance, Jamie Ogg speaking."

"Jamie? Tim. Everything okay over there?"

"Sure, boss. Just your average number of cars coming

through. One guy wanted to know where the redwoods are. His wife seemed kinda upset when I told him that the redwoods are in California."

"Jamie, you know that bear trap you built last summer? The one we can tow behind a truck? You used the wheels and axle off of that wrecked White truck, didn't you?"

"Right."

"Is it still sitting behind the cabin there?"

"Funny you'd ask," Jamie replied. "The trail crew borrowed it a week ago to trap a nuisance bear at the Boulder Creek campground."

"What's funny about that?"

"The funny thing is that they caught the bear the other night and drove back to the barracks with it. Parked the truck and trailer way over by the slash pile there, where the bear wouldn't smell the kitchen all night long. Next day they were too busy to take it anywhere and they fed the animal and left it there. I fed it again and gave it some water that night. But next morning it was gone."

"Gone?"

"Yup. The new guy, Russ Frame, he looked all around for tracks but didn't find none. The tailgate was still fastened shut but the cage was empty."

"No tracks, you say. You mean there were no bear tracks?"

"Nope," Jamie said. "No bear tracks. But Russ and I found something weird about the tire tracks."

"What?"

"Judging from the tire tracks, somebody, maybe some animal lover, maybe some guy from the barracks, somebody drove the truck away with the trailer still hitched onto it. We think they released the bear and brought the truck back. They parked it in just about the same place. That's what it looked like to us, anyhow."

"Good man, Jamie."

"I found out another thing you oughta know, too," Jamie said.

"Which is?"

"Well, while me and Ranger Frame was looking for bear tracks we got to talkin' about marauding bears and swapping bear stories and such like that and I kinda kidded him by sayin' I should strap on my Colt revolver before we go crashin' into the willows after a bear and he said maybe he oughta bring his rifle, just kidding of course. I asked him what kind he had."

"What did he say?"

"Said he has a .303 Savage lever action."

CHAPTER 5
SOME PUZZLING PIECES

Ranger McIntyre drove down the alley to the rear of the outfitter's store. He backed his pickup against the freight dock as if he was there to load something. However, he didn't go into the outfitters; instead, he looked furtively up and down the alley before slipping into the side door of the village telephone exchange next to the outfitters. Upstairs he found a young woman handling the switchboard. She looked very pretty. Even with heavy black headphones clamped over her perm, and even with the black speaking tube hanging over her frilly white blouse, she looked both trim and attractive.

"Jane?" McIntyre said.

She turned around and pulled one of the earpieces away.

"Ranger McIntyre! Good morning! How nice to see you."

"You, too," he said. "You're back for another summer at the ol' switchboard, I see."

"I need to pay for college," she said. "Oops! Excuse me while I connect this call."

In between phone calls, of which there were not many, Jane and Ranger McIntyre chatted about this and that, about college and rangering, families and friends. Jane had always been interested in McIntyre's various investigations. Like him, she loved a puzzle. He told her about the trouble out at Blue Spruce Lake.

"You see," he said, "it's starting to look like a coordinated conspiracy. Somebody knew when John Frye would likely be standing under his yard light. Somebody knew that he dumps the kitchen garbage each morning. Somebody knew how to loosen the gas line on the garbage truck and make it stall on Frye's approach road. They even knew what time of night to drive a trailer behind Small Delights and not wake him up."

"Golly," Jane said. "It's thrilling! It's like in those espionage novels, spies with binoculars and long dark overcoats! Wow! They use the phone to tell their accomplices, that's what you think?"

"You got it. You're on duty early in the morning and late in the evening, right?"

"Right. The summer girl shift, they call it."

"Here's what I was wondering. Legally, we can't listen to phone conversations or violate anyone's privacy, nothing like that. But I was thinking maybe if you happened to notice unusual traffic between two phone numbers, maybe you could drop me a hint. Casually, you know."

"A hint. You mean like I can't mention any names, but there are two teenagers who phone one another exactly at 4 p.m. every day and talk for nearly an hour. Like that? They're both on the same party line, the 0-4-0 line, and they tie it up. No one else on that line can use it for an hour, which makes old Mrs. Lennox hopping mad?"

McIntyre laughed.

"Let me see if I can work this out," he said. "Hmmm. I know Mrs. Lennox lives on Pleasant Vale Road, which must mean that the 0-4-0 party line runs along that road. There's only one teenage girl living along that road. Her mother works at the toggery, which doesn't close for the day until after five o'clock. There's a couple of teen boys living on that road. One of them washes dishes at the lunch counter and gets off work around three or three-thirty. He would be home by four o'clock."

Jane clapped her hands.

"You got it!" she said.

"Elementary," McIntyre said.

"What?"

"Never mind."

"Okay. I'll let you know anything suspicious. As long as I can do it legally."

"Good girl," he said.

The next morning, he was wide awake while it was still dark outside. Ranger Tim McIntyre turned this way and twisted that way, but the bed was uncomfortable no matter which way he lay. He couldn't keep his mind from fussing with a dozen dumb thoughts. With a groan of resignation, he swung his feet to the floor, lit the gas lantern, and pulled his pants on. He took the lantern out to the horse shed where he pitched fresh hay for Brownie and put oats in her trough. Instead of going inside when he had finished, he stood there in his undershirt looking at the mountains outlined against the eastern sky. As the sky gradually became lighter, one by one each tall spruce tree separated from the black silhouette and seemed to be stretching its top branches toward the approaching sun.

The last of the morning stars faded and blinked off and the sky turned pale blue. Not a cloud anywhere to be seen, and not a breath of a breeze. Out in the forest a coyote yipped, but otherwise McIntyre's world was silent, deep, pine-scented, and at peace.

"You know what, Brownie?" he said to the mare. "You haven't had any exercise lately. And you being government property, it's my official duty to keep you in shape. Why don't we take a little ride up to Fall River Lodge and have breakfast? On the way back, we can investigate the Mystery of the Missing Trash Cans. I'll take my fly rod along and it will look like we're fishing instead of investigating."

Admittedly, Brownie the Mare knew next to nothing about the finer points of human grammar but it seemed that "we" wasn't quite right. The human would be doing the riding while the mare picked her way through dew-damp branches along a dark trail where rocks and roots waited to trip her up. But she did like the sound of the words "Fall River Lodge" because the hostler there liked horses and always had a horse treat in his overalls, usually a carrot or half an apple.

Minnie March was outside, peeling potatoes for breakfast and filling her ample lungs with clean mountain air. Minnie could tell the cook or the cook's helper to prepare the potatoes, but it was a job she liked to do herself. It offered a few minutes of luxurious peacefulness, a quiet time as the sun was coming up, sitting outside in the chilled mountain air, taking pleasure in every little detail that the rising light brought into view. She took satisfaction in the keen sharpness of a knife and the slippery feel of a freshly peeled potato.

She recognized Ranger McIntyre at a distance. Brownie was almost prancing-happy, lifting each foot with clipped precision and looking kind of cocky about being a handsome horse on a nice morning. Ranger McIntyre looked a little sure of himself, too, sitting straight in the saddle with his flat-brim ranger hat set exactly level, one hand holding the reins loosely and the other hand resting on his leg. He was coming for breakfast and he was in a fine mood. More than that: Minnie spotted the jacket rolled up and tied atop the slicker behind the saddle. From experience she knew it was McIntyre's fishing jacket, wrapped around his fly rod case. No doubt after breakfast, he planned to leave his tunic and hat on the saddle while he slipped into his jacket and then into the willows along Fall River.

Minnie turned the job of peeling potatoes over to the cook's assistant. She and McIntyre made their way through the kitchen to the small table outside the door of her office, just inside the doorway leading to the dining room. From there she could monitor the comings and goings of the kitchen staff while staying out of sight of the lodge guests.

The cook brought coffee and orange juice. He recommended the Belgian waffles and fried eggs and McIntyre eagerly agreed, although riding through the early morning air had left him hungry enough to try anything on the menu. Except broccoli.

"Took the first choice, eh?" Minnie said, teasing him. "How do you like it, being a pushover?"

"Listen, Minnie. It's not as easy as it looks, being a pushover. What's going on at the lodge these days?"

"What I want to know," Minnie replied, "is, who are these city dodgers in the black sedan? That's what I want to know. They've been up here three different times, wondering if I want to sell the lodge. Ever since Mike died, you know, I've had people say they wished they could buy it. But they're mostly people who've never seen a Rocky Mountain winter. They don't realize that running a lodge is plain hard work. Plus, you have to make all your year's money in just three months. And I tell them so. But one of these jaspers, the boss one, he just brushes that off and makes me a higher offer."

"They give you any trouble?"

"No, no trouble. The one who acts like he's the boss asked all about the hydroelectric plant Mike built when he electrified the lodge. The other three only stand around trying to look sinister. But no trouble."

"This is off the subject," McIntyre said, "but I've heard folks refer to your late husband as 'Max.' "

"Sure," Minnie said with a laugh. "That's what his parents called him, but he never liked it much. Other people, mostly kids from his school days, they called him 'Slim' and he didn't like that name, either."

"Tell you what," McIntyre said, moving his silverware and coffee cup to make a place for the cook to set down a plate of waffles, eggs, and sausage. "I'll snoop around town and see if I can find out more about the city slickers in the sedan. I'll let you know."

"While you're at it," Minnie said, sipping her coffee, "find out what's up with your other ranger, that Nevis guy."

"Charlie Nevis?"

"That's the one. Baggy pants, poor haircut, sloppy appearance. Wheezy voice."

"Why? What's he been doing?"

"I'd call it lurking," Minnie said. "The housekeeping girls noticed it first, him just hanging around the cottages. Tom, the hostler, he said Nevis wanted to know all about how many horses we had and whether they'd wander away if they ever got out of the night corral. I saw him myself, checking out the hydroelectric building. I asked him could I help him, but he sorta shrugged and said he was only making sure he was familiar with the layout of the lodge in case of a fire or other emergency. Sounded like horse pucky to me."

"His patrol route and mine don't cross each other very often, but I'll make a point of having a talk with him. Could you pass me that maple syrup?"

The mention of patrols reminded Ranger McIntyre that he should be out there on the job. He really should. Looking for people who parked illegally to take photos of elk. People who used burnt sticks to write their names and hometowns on the rocks. Tourists who were illegally collecting rocks, firewood, artifacts, anything that wasn't nailed down. But the series of near-miss "accidents" at Blue Spruce Lake was more than just a burr under his saddle or a pebble in his boot. The Blue Spruce incidents smacked of threat and bullying and if the human bully ever had an archenemy, it was Timothy Grayson McIntyre of the RMNP. He needed time to think about it, time to mentally assemble the pieces.

He did most of his best thinking with a fly rod in his hand.

He thanked Minnie March for breakfast, retrieved Brownie from Tom's pampering, and rode in the direction of the river. Below Fall River Lodge, the river meandered a mile or more through a flat meadow. There were hardly any trees, but a jungle of willow bushes grew all along the bank. Brownie obediently followed the game trail along the river, her strong chest pushing the limber willow branches aside. She stepped carefully: beaver were known to dig deep canals in the willow thickets, deep enough to break a horse's leg.

They came to the clearing that McIntyre had been thinking of. It was an open spot among the willows where the lazy river took a long U-turn. Against the opposite bank were deep, dark holes where brookies and rainbows lurked. He dismounted and changed his tunic for the fishing jacket. He assembled his fly rod and took a careful look around to make certain no one could see him, particularly the supervisor. Nicholson was also known to carry a fly rod on patrol and was one of the few woodsmen clever enough to sneak up on McIntyre. But there was no one in sight across the whole wide meadow. Other than a couple of scraggly spruce trees, the tallest thing in the meadow was Brownie.

"Brownie!" he said. "Hide. Hide!"

It had been part of her training. The mare went to her knees and rolled over on her side in the cool grass.

"Good horse. Stay."

From the narrow strip of gravel, McIntyre could cast his fly across the current to the other side of the stream, where a deeply cut bank made a dark shady hiding place for the trout. He opened his fly wallet and chose a smallish fly, a Number Sixteen Gray Hackle, which he tied to the thread-thin tippet.

The first few casts were fun. The water flowed like molten glass, transparent enough that he could easily track his tiny dry fly as it floated on the current; whenever a little brook trout rose up from the depths to attack, McIntyre would flick the fly away at the last second. He didn't want to hook any trout too small to keep. He smiled and watched the little fish swim back down toward the bottom.

As it almost always did, his mind eased itself into the rhythm of the river and surrendered to the quiet harmony of the wide meadow. He began to envision all the parts of the Blue Spruce Lake situation as being parts of a whole picture, the way he had seen the entire battlefield layout during the war, looking down from his Nieuport biplane high above the reach of guns and explosions and the shouts of soldiers. The rifle bullet in the tree. The electric wire fastened to the iron grid. The .303 cartridge case left in the woods and the timing of the burning garbage truck. A prowling bear. And moving around the edges of the picture, that dark sedan with four city slickers in it. Looking to buy "properties" one of them said. There was a ranger who didn't seem to care about looking like a ranger, one who asked too many questions about properties and who hung around places where he shouldn't be.

Crimes had been committed, no doubt of that. Suspected arson, endangerment of human life—that booby-trapped log across the road, don't forget that—maybe even extortion going on that he didn't know about. And it wouldn't take too much of a leap to imagine that those men in the sedan were connected with illegal liquor. That, or gambling. Everybody in the village who had run into them said the same. They looked like the type who would be up to something sleazy.

Watching his fly float on the stream, McIntyre saw an underwater shadow detach itself from the bluff bank. It didn't come dashing up to grab the fly the way the little brookies did;

this one moved almost lazily upward toward the Gray Hackle. Aha! The one he'd been waiting for, the lunker of the hole. Probably a German Brown. Patience. Stay absolutely still. Let the dry fly float the current. The fish is coming. He's slow and careful, which is how he got that size, but he's coming for it.

Seemingly out of nowhere came an eight-inch brookie that darted in front of the lunker's nose and snatched the floating fly. Up out of the water he came, glistening wet, arching, diving down again and shaking his head, trying to throw the hook. With a deep sigh Ranger McIntyre reeled him in, held him underwater while he wiggled the hook from his jaw, and released him again.

Target. Big fish interested. Small fish takes it. Blue Spruce Lake. Maybe, just maybe, there was a big fish going after Frye's Small Delights and a smaller fish wanted to snatch it first. Maybe he'd need to do a little diplomatic snooping, provided that Supervisor Nicholson's patience with him held out long enough.

Speaking of Nick Nicholson . . . McIntyre took a careful look around the meadow and began taking his fly rod apart.

"Brownie, up!" he said. "Time we were doing our ranger stuff."

We? Brownie knew the word, but her half of "we" had no intention of doing ranger stuff. Her half of "we" wanted to head back to the Fall River station, be rid of her saddle, and have a double scoop of oats.

McIntyre turned Brownie loose in the corral, poured oats into her feed bucket, and checked the water trough. From behind the ranger cabin came a noise like a hammer or heavy wrench pounding on metal. Investigating, he came upon a pair of boots sticking out from underneath the NPS pickup truck. They were recently polished and the trousers tucked into them had a crease; therefore he knew it wasn't Ranger Nevis.

"Frame? Is that you under there?"

"Yessir!"

Ranger Russ Frame wriggled out from under the truck and stood up, dusting sand and gravel from his trousers. He was holding a monkey wrench.

"Fixing my truck?" McIntyre asked.

"Just a little. Charlie drove me over from the barracks. We need to borrow your truck. While I was waiting for you I noticed the hand-brake cable was loose and needed adjusting. One of the machine screws holding the carburetor was loose, too. But I tightened it pretty good."

"Oh," McIntyre said.

"Reason we need the truck is, we found two of the missing trash barrels. Well, the real truth is that a fisherman found them. Almost a half mile upstream of Fall River Lodge. Somebody must have chucked them in the river just for fun. Kids, maybe. Charlie and me thought we'd haul them to the shop and have the road crew clean and paint them."

"Good idea," McIntyre said. "You know your way around cars and trucks and engines, do you?"

"Since I was a kid," Frame said. "Every car my dad ever owned, I took it apart."

"Guns, too? Know anything about fixing guns?"

"Not a whole lot, no. I can shoot and that's about it."

"I heard you own a fancy rifle," McIntyre said.

"Yeah, I do. A .303 Savage. It was a going-away present from my dad and mom. Charlie Nevis shot it a few times and offered to buy it from me, but I couldn't sell it. Sentimental, you know."

"Like to see it," McIntyre said.

"Sure. It's over at the barracks."

"Speaking of which, you'd better be moving if you hope to retrieve those trash barrels before quitting time. Maybe bring the truck back after supper, if you can?"

"You bet," Frame said. "See you later."

Ranger McIntyre walked to the entrance station kiosk where he asked the duty attendant, a summer hire from town, about the day's traffic count. McIntyre checked to see that there were enough park maps and brochures for the coming week. With a sigh of bored resignation, he went into the little office across the road from the kiosk to catch up on his paperwork. He was filling out the last of the reports—number and locations of all stalled automobile assists in the past thirty days—when the summer hire boy came in.

"Done for the day?" McIntyre said.

"Yup," the boy said. "Here's the cashbox. I put up the 'No Attendant on Duty' sign."

"Before you climb on your bike to go home," McIntyre said, locking the cashbox in the desk drawer, "have you heard anything of four men in town, riding around in a long sedan?"

"You mean the Chicago mob. That's what people call them. We think they've got machine guns and hand grenades in the trunk of their car. My pals say they're either hiding out from another gangster mob or else they're looking for somebody they need to kill."

"You must have been reading the same novels as the girl at the telephone exchange. That's all the men in the sedan do? Drive around?"

"Yeah. They're real good customers at the gas station where my pal works. He says that according to the one in the cloth cap, they been on every road around here. Even out to Maguire's place, and that's a long ways. Once they asked him—my pal, I mean—where they could buy moonshine liquor. And they wanted to know where's the local poker action."

"Nothing illegal in asking, I guess. And anyway, as long as they stay outside the park, it's nothing to do with us, right?"

"Right!" the boy said. "Well, see you!"

"See you," McIntyre said.

Speaking of driving around—there were two NPS pickups at the shop area next to the barracks, plus the two-ton Dodge truck. Why did Ranger Frame come all the way over to the Fall River entrance station to borrow his?

John Frye woke at his usual early hour while the Small Delights Lodge was still slumbering in the dark shadows of night, and was surprised to discover that his wife, Hattie, was already up. She had been up long enough, in fact, to fire up the stove and set the coffee pot boiling.

"What are you doing, woman?" he said, pulling up his gaiters and combing his hair with his fingers. "You never climb outa bed this early."

"John, I hardly slept. I was that worried. All night, worry, worry, worry. First, I heard a sound outside like the trash cans being rattled. And I thought I smelled smoke."

"Not again! Dammit, Hattie, I've told you. The cabins have woodstoves, we got the fireplace, Grand Harbor Lodge is upwind of us, usually, and they got wood fires. Of course you smell smoke. How could you not smell smoke?"

"You know how afraid I can be," she said. "Can't we buy fire protection for the place? I was thinking of a water tank, on stilts, with a fire hose coming from it for emergencies. Or maybe a gasoline pump down at the lake and a fire hose running up here. It's just that the forest is awful dry. Yesterday I saw one of the guests smoking out there under the tall pine tree, standing on those dry pine needles and smoking. And down at Cabin Four, they have an outdoor campfire nearly every night."

"And they fill up the garbage can with ashes, too," John said. "More work for me, lugging their damn ashes. But first of all, the forest isn't that dry. Plenty of rain this summer. Second, we can't afford no fancy fire-hose system. Probably be a good thing if the place did burn to the ground. We'd collect the insurance and move to the city. Tired of bein' stuck here playin' nursemaid to a buncha tourists all the time. In the city, I could find me an eight-to-five job, easy. I could come home and stop worryin' about everything at work. Around here the worryin' don't never stop. Pour me a cup of coffee."

Hattie brought his coffee and set it before him on the table. She lovingly ran her hand through his thinning hair. *Poor man,* she thought. *Trying to make our fortune with this place has turned him into a sour old grouch.*

"John," she said, as she began slicing bread, "what about those city fellows? Surely their offer to buy us out is good enough for us to move to the city."

"Listen to me," he said. "You don't know how these things work, see? Ol' Catherine Croker, she wants to bid on this place, too. Only she don't know what they've offered. We're in the catbird seat, see? Oh, yeah! They want it, she wants it, and whichever one puts up the most money and buys us out, they've bought themselves leverage over the other one."

Finished with the bread, Hattie turned to cracking eggs into a mixing bowl. The morning breakfast special was going to be her "own recipe" French toast.

"I think I understand, dear," she said. "But I don't see what they want Small Delights for. Surely those city fellows can't run a lodge! And Catherine has her hands full with her own place."

"Don't matter," he said. "It don't matter. What does matter is we ain't tipped our hand that we want out, see? And what else matters more is that they both want it. All we gotta do is sit tight and make 'em pay through the nose. We keep 'em thinking the only way they'll be able to buy Small Delights is if we're both of us carried outa here in pine boxes."

CHAPTER 6
BAD BRAKES AND A GOOD RIFLE

The new biscuit shooter at the Pioneer Inn had a knack with waffles and knew his sausages but it was his bacon that McIntyre liked best. For McIntyre's money, the man turned out the best rasher of bacon west of the Mississippi. Maybe east of the Mississippi as well. The cook had arrived in late April, bringing with him some kitchen equipment from a café he once owned. Two of those machines immediately won McIntyre's approval: a gadget for slicing potatoes into hash browns and a patented deluxe bacon slicer. The slicer turned out bacon of ideal thickness—no thin spots to scorch, no thick ones to turn rubbery—and the cook paid his respects to his machine by feeding it only the best lean bacon meat available.

Among McIntyre's indulgences was what he liked to call his "rest ups." In order to afford a "rest up" he would trick himself into saving money each week, putting it into an old pipe tobacco humidor. He thought of it as "found" cash—the change from his pocket, any coin he happened to find on the ground, any little unexpected amount that came his way. He wasn't above picking up empty soda pop bottles and turning them in for the deposit. His crude budget system consisted of a collection of envelopes in the back of a drawer. These were labeled "car" (for the automobile he hoped to purchase someday), "clothes," "fishing" (for that new reel), "food," and so forth. Each month each envelope received a few dollars, and it added up. If there was a dollar or even a half dollar left over after he had divided his pay into the envelopes, it went into the humidor.

For a rest up, McIntyre invariably chose the Pioneer Inn in the village, where the management gave him a government discount on a small, airy room, breakfasts included. The luxury of a different bed, crisp sheets, and a full breakfast prepared by someone other than himself refreshed his mind and readjusted his perspective. It helped him be a better ranger: in fact, he had once said as much to Supervisor Nicholson and suggested that the RMNP should pay for his "rest ups" once a month. In rebuttal Supervisor Nicholson suggested that the RMNP should charge McIntyre for the fuel and time he spent traveling to and from the Fall River entrance station.

Every summer morning in the village looked the same. From his favorite table by the window overlooking the houses with a view of the granite peaks and snowfields of the Front Range beyond, McIntyre saw a cloudless sky of blue crystal as pure as an archangel's soul. He breathed the best air in the world and smiled in deep contentment at how tidy the village looked against the mass of peaks and cliffs. Coffee had a richer taste here. The aromas wafting from the kitchen were nearly a meal in themselves. The only thing that kept a "rest up" breakfast from being perfect was the absence of a companion.

"Companions," she had said when she was alive. Her flawless lips pouted at him as she pronounced it: "Companion. Do you know it is from the old French, that word? From the word for bread? Companion, it is one with whom you break bread!"

Never again to break bread with him. Not this side of heaven, anyway, and McIntyre was pretty sure that his afterlife travel plans would take him in the other direction.

He was nearly finished with his breakfast when, through the window, he saw a young lad in knickerbockers hurrying toward the inn. It was Bud, Dottie's other boy. That's how most people in town knew the young scamp—her "other" boy, the one who was forever finding himself in mischief. Bud was the apple-swiping bicycle daredevil, the catapult wielding boy whom every dull businessman wished he could be again.

Bud entered the dining room, came to McIntyre's table, and plopped down in the empty chair. He had been running. He looked wistfully at the empty bacon and egg plates and settled for swiping the remaining triangle of toast, which he smeared liberally with jam from the pot.

"Mom got a call for you," he said with his mouth full of toast and jam. "Sent me to tell you."

"Who from?"

"Dunno. You're to come to the office. She don't like bothering the people at the inn with phone calls for you all the time. Says it's a darn nuisance for the desk clerk, she says. You gonna order anything else to eat, maybe? I could help you eat it."

"Sorry, Bud. Duty calls. Or your mother, which amounts to the same thing."

Ranger McIntyre removed his flat ranger hat and stood before Dottie's desk like a schoolboy volunteering to dust the erasers.

"Tim," she said, "I wish you'd sit down when you come in. When you're standing there, you seem to fill up the room. Besides, I have to crane my neck to look at you."

He sat down.

"Now," she said, "my morning began with the phone ringing off the hook. And you're the fellow who's going to deal with it. First, that lovely Polly lady phoned from Small Delights Lodge. She asked for you in particular. She's sweet on you."

"Fudge," McIntyre said.

"She claims there has been another attempt to hurt or kill her uncle, Mr. Frye. She says when you come, you are to bring her a two-inch machine bolt, one-quarter inch by twenty, whatever that means. Second, her aunt phoned. She smelled smoke again. She has been reading U.S. Forest Service brochures about building 'fire perimeters' around residences and she wants the NPS to do the same for her lodge. She believes we should station a fire pump at Blue Spruce Lake. The supervisor says for you to go talk to her about it."

"Yes, ma'am."

"And don't be a smart aleck. Catherine Croker also phoned to say that Grand Harbor Lodge ran out of RMNP maps and brochures and wants you to bring more. I put them in that box over there on the table for you. And she's complaining about the fact that John Frye hauled that burnt-out garbage truck to the main road and left it there where her guests see it every time they use her approach road."

"Okay," Ranger McIntyre said. "I'll see what I can do. I'll try to find the state highway boys and see if they'll haul that truck away. If they don't, we might have to spring for a tow truck to do it."

"And one more thing," Dottie said.

"Yes?"

"Your yummy friend phoned."

"Yummy?"

"You know. The gal with the great legs and fantastic clothes? The FBI secretary you can't stop talking about? Lipstick, elbow-length gloves, cloche? Am I ringing any bells for you?"

"Vi Coteau called, in other words."

"Clever fella, you. Yes. You're to call her after working hours. At her place. Here's the number. And Tim?"

"Yes?"

"Use your own dime this time."

Ranger McIntyre turned at the sign saying "Small Delights Lodge" and started up John Frye's approach road. He hadn't gotten very far when he saw John's car sitting on the side of the road with a pair of legs sticking out from underneath.

Second time in two days I've seen legs sticking out from under a vehicle, McIntyre thought. *Is that what they call déjà vu?*

Polly Sheldon's hands appeared from under the truck; she grabbed the running board, and, in a moment, was standing in front of the ranger dusting herself off. She took the quarter-inch bolt he offered and dropped it into her trouser pocket.

"Thanks," she said. "I'll keep it as a spare. Found the original back down the road a ways. Had to scrounge up a nut and washers, but I got it fixed."

"Got what fixed?" McIntyre asked.

"Brake cable swing arm."

She knelt down and used the handle of her monkey wrench to draw a diagram in the dirt.

"The brake cable, it starts at the brake pedal and goes to this triangle-shaped thing, see? I think they call it a swing arm. From there it operates two more cables, one for the front brakes and one for the rear. Some clever johnny unscrewed the nut holding that thing. After the car hit a few bumps the bolt fell out and the brakes wouldn't work."

"You can't be sure it was done deliberately, though," McIntyre said. "Bolts come loose all the time."

"I'm pretty sure it didn't do it by itself. When I got under the car I noticed that the old dirty grease on the bracket was marked up like somebody had put a wrench on it. The head of the bolt, too, it had the grease knocked off. The way it fell out of the bracket is suspicious, too. Uncle John hit a bump just before he lost the brakes. Well, your swing arm thing sits on top of the bracket and the bolt goes down through it, see? If the nut did work itself off, gravity would still hold the bolt in the hole. I'm pretty sure our suspect took the bolt loose and turned it over. That way it would drop out. Maybe he put the nut back on, but real loose."

"Lucky thing it happened before John came to the long slope down to the main road," McIntyre said.

"Absolutely. Or he could have been on the main road doing thirty, forty miles an hour and had a deer walk out in front of him. Just lucky for him he was mad again. Real foul mood. He went slamming out of the lodge, hopped in the car, tore off down the road. What saved him was hitting that bump hard enough to knock the brake bolt loose."

"I guess I'd better go talk to him," McIntyre said.

"He won't be in for a while. Took the boat and a fishing pole. He needed to be alone and he needed to kill something. He rowed out into the lake to slaughter the fish."

"Oh, okay. What else is going on? Dottie said your aunt had been scared again."

"Personally, I think it's those Chicago thugs. You know the ones. I've seen their car over at Grand Harbor any number of times. Once I saw them up by the old garbage truck, talking with that other ranger."

"Which one? Ranger Frame? Tall, neat, and tidy?"

"No, the other one. The one who wheezes. He and those city boys were having quite a talk. Arms waving, fingers pointing. They didn't see me. But I saw them all right."

"Think they sabotaged the car?"

"I do. I think they're the ones trying to scare Aunt Hattie."

"How's that?"

"Aunt Hattie, she never hesitates to let everybody know she's scared of fire. She's got a regular fire-o-phobia about it. And any kind of sound in the night makes her jumpy. But everyone knows about the fire thing, you, the grocer, Catherine Croker, her foreman, everybody. It only stands to reason that the Chicago boys learned about it. All they need to do is build a smoky fire upwind of the lodge. There's a couple of old campsites in that stand of lodgepoles. Easy to build a little fire in one of the old fire circles. I've got a theory about it."

"And what's your theory?"

"They take a trash can, see? They put twigs and pine needles in it, carry it to a spot in the woods where the smoke will drift toward Small Delights, set fire to it. When they're done, they put the lid on the can and carry it away again. No evidence. Got it?"

"You seem to be pretty crafty at all this, Miss Sheldon. I mean, you not only spot bits of evidence and figure what it means, but you seem to think like a saboteur. Hope you don't mind me saying so."

"I'm flattered," she said. "I've read nearly everything by Mister Conan Doyle. All of his cases for Sherlock Holmes, all of his logical deductions, it all . . . what's the word I want? It all resonates with me."

Ranger McIntyre's interview with Hattie Frye took most of what remained of the morning. She persuaded him to have a mug of coffee and help himself to the breakfast pastry tray while she told him how much she and John would like to quit the lodge business and move to a city where the trees didn't seem to be crowding in on a person. And fireproof brick buildings. She mentioned her fear of fire a dozen times, each time protesting that she didn't want to make a major issue of it. She showed McIntyre a brochure from the U.S. Forest Service about maintaining a fire-safe zone around forest cabins and how the USFS would help interested cabin owners with advice and help.

"That's why I called you," she said, "to see if the park service has the same kind of program. What I mean is, with all your equipment and men you should be able to help us thin out the trees and brush, see?"

"I do see your need, I really do," McIntyre said. "But we're not in the tree cutting business the way the forest service is.

Their mission is to utilize forest resources. They're the ones who oversee the logging operations and do the tree thinning. The park's job is to preserve and protect the park."

"Well," she said, helping herself to one of the donuts from the tray, "that brings up my next request. Protection. With two lodges on the lake, and a third one coming, you'd think the NPS would have a fire plan for us. A gasoline pump at the lake, or back there on the river, with hoses coming to the various buildings in case of fire. You could teach the men around here how to use it, kind of like a volunteer fire department. Or if you wanted to keep a fire truck here, we would volunteer to build a shed for it and keep it in tip-top running condition."

"Wait a minute," McIntyre said. "Did you say a third lodge was coming? Not possible."

"Oh, it's all the gossip," Hattie said. "Catherine Croker says it will help her business but she's afraid it will ruin ours. She's quite concerned for us, you know."

McIntyre knew better. Catherine Croker had never been concerned for anyone except herself.

"It's those gentlemen from back east," Hattie continued. "They hope to buy a little bit of our land, the part we never use, and add it to a little acre or two from Catherine's place and create a posh resort. Beach on the lake, swimming pool, tennis court, all that kind of stuff. They made John an offer, but he won't tell me for how much."

"But they wouldn't have any access to it, unless they used Croker's road or yours."

"I don't know about all that. I assumed they could just build a drive through the lodgepoles straight to the main road. But I don't know much about how those things work."

She kept talking for the better part of three cups of coffee, two donuts and a bear-claw sweet roll, and when Hattie was finished explaining all her ideas for fire prevention and her plans for moving to the city, she felt better.

"Well," said McIntyre, standing up and putting his notebook back in his pocket, "this has been nice, but I need to talk with Catherine and then drive back to the station. But tell me: does John own a rifle?"

"He has that shotgun. I think there's a old rifle hanging in his room. Yes, I know there is. Belonged to his father."

"It's too old to be a .303, probably," McIntyre said.

"A what?" Hattie asked.

"Never mind. I'll check with you again in a few days, okay?"

Catherine Croker seated herself on a couch opposite McIntyre's chair, crossed her ankles demurely, and nudged the plate of dry cookies across the coffee table toward him.

"Thanks, but I'll pass," he said. "I'm trying to cut down. The coffee will be plenty for me."

Truth to tell, McIntyre had a deep dislike for cookies. They were usually dry and sugary and they left crumbs everywhere.

"The S.O. secretary tells me you phoned the office?" he said.

"S.O.? Oh, the supervisor's office. Yes. First of all, thank you for bringing the brochures. It slipped my mind to pick them up while in town. What I really phoned about is that burned-up garbage truck. John Frye had no business towing it out to the main road, and there it sits where my guests must see it. I would like the park to remove it."

"Well," McIntyre said, "technically, it's not our road and not our problem. As you know, the park boundary runs along the state road right-of-way. Your approach road, and Frye's, is national park land. But not the main road. However, I'll see what I can do about it. Maybe have a word with the state police."

"Thank you."

"In return, maybe you can help shed light on all these troubles that John Frye seems to be having. Has anything happened at Grand Harbor that seems suspicious? Any strangers lurking around that you know of?"

"The garbage incident, that has been very inconvenient. You know Thad Muggins, my manager. He's been using his own pickup truck to haul our garbage to the dump, but it takes up much of his time and is rather costly in terms of fuel and wages. Two guests who went for a hike reported seeing a brown bear in the woods, but they didn't feel threatened by it. I told them it was very unusual to see a bear, especially around here and in this season. I used to do quite a lot of hiking, you know, before I was married. We were raised, my brother and I, on a small farm holding right next to a forest in Pennsylvania. When our father moved the family to a little town outside of Colorado Springs, we kids had the run of the mountains."

Interesting, McIntyre thought. *Anyone who knows her thinks of Catherine Croker as a grasping, shrewd kind of hard woman such as you'd be more likely to find in the city. Maybe losing her husband had turned her into the money-driven, self-serving person that she was.*

"Are you sure you won't have a cookie with your coffee?"

"No, thanks. Tell me what you know about these four men in a black sedan."

"I know one of them is called 'the boss' and one is called 'Dink' for some reason. They are spending the summer looking for investment properties, at least that's what they told me. They came here to see if I wanted to sell Grand Harbor Lodge."

"From what I've heard, they don't seem the innkeeper type," McIntyre said. He was looking around the lounge of the Grand Harbor at the leather couches and armchairs, the polished cocktail tables, the impressive stone fireplace, and wondering what the place would be worth.

"I had the same feeling," she said. "If they bought a place, such as this or Small Delights, I imagine they'd bring in a professional hotel staff to manage it. But I really don't know their intentions."

She knows more than she's telling, McIntyre thought. *And I'd bet my bottom dollar that they didn't just go away after she turned down their first offer.*

"Just one more thing," McIntyre said, "and I'll be out of your hair. Has another ranger been here, maybe asking questions about your place? Like how much land you have, whether you live here all winter, things like that? He might be . . . well, another lodge owner described him as kind of scruffy. A little rumpled, maybe?"

"No," she said. "Nobody like that. Maybe he spoke to Mr. Muggins. I could ask him when I see him."

"That would be good, thanks," McIntyre replied, standing up and reaching for his hat. "I've been noticing the rifle you have hanging over the fireplace. Beautiful weapon."

"Take it down and look at it, if you wish," she said. "It was my husband's. There are bullets for it in that carved box on the mantel. I believe it was made in England."

The lettering engraved on the rifle's receiver showed it to be a Westley Richards firearm, a British brand of gun that McIntyre had heard of but could never afford. Slender, long, and graceful, from the silk-smooth bolt action receiver to the hand-polished walnut stock, it was pure quality. He turned it in the light in order to make out the lettering on the barrel. Caliber .318, not .303. He hung it back on the pegs and set his hat on his head.

"Thanks again. I'll see about that garbage truck. Maybe I can have it towed to the ranger station as evidence of criminal sabotage."

He couldn't be certain, but it almost seemed as though his little joke had caused Catherine Croker to turn a bit pale. He watched her like she was a trout eyeing a floating dry fly.

"Yes," he continued, "I'm accumulating quite a pile of evidence at the station. Rope and wire from that deadfall that nearly clobbered your car. Bullet from the tree, a shell casing, electric wire, photos of the brake assembly from John Frye's car, that kind of thing. I might as well add a garbage truck, huh?"

Now he was certain. Catherine continued to smile, probably because he was smiling, but her eyes betrayed concern.

The drive back to town was a torture of temptations for poor Ranger McIntyre. If he kept the pickup moving right along, he would easily make it back to the S.O. before quitting time, which meant he could phone Vi Coteau at the Denver FBI office and indulge in the secret pleasure of hearing her voice. But he had missed lunch and the road would lead past no fewer than three places where he might stop and buy a sandwich. And worst of all, the road ran alongside a creek where the trout were jumping, the late afternoon rise that every fly fisherman dreams about.

The urge to hear Vi Coteau's creamy voice won out over hunger and fishing: he arrived back at the S.O. without having made a single stop along the way.

There was a small office in the new headquarters building, furnished with desk and chair and telephone but otherwise standing empty until such time as Washington would inform the supervisor that he needed an assistant supervisor. Dottie let McIntyre use the empty office for his private phone call. She emphasized the word "private" and instructed him to ask the operator for the charges when he was finished. She would deduct the call from his wages.

He sat his hat on the desk and his rear end in the swivel chair, briefly considered putting his feet on the desk, and then thought better of it—it wasn't quite quitting time yet. He'd bet-

ter not look too casual in case somebody looked in the door—
and picked up the earpiece.

"Number please?"

"Jane? That you?"

"Ranger McIntyre. Yes, it's me. I drew the three-to-ten shift.
Again."

"Are things keeping busy at the exchange?"

"No, not too busy. I'm knitting a sweater, in fact. Twice a
week there's a long-distance call to Chicago, always at the same
time on the same day, so that's interesting. And there's the
mystery buzz, as we girls call it."

"Mystery buzz?"

"Somebody on the Blue Spruce Lake party line. It's only
happened four or five times. Whoever it is will buzz the exchange
and use a funny voice and ask to be connected to the national
park barracks number. But when we ring the number, the caller
hangs right up. It usually—no, always—happens late in the last
shift, toward ten o'clock at night. It's sort of like they're sending
a signal to somebody at the barracks."

"That is interesting," the ranger said. "You can't tell who the
caller is?"

"Nope. There's eight phones on the Blue Spruce Lake party
line, plus a public phone at Tiny's store. Could be anybody, using any one of them."

"You know," McIntyre said, "you might keep a log of them, if
any more happen. Time and date. If it doesn't break any phone
company rules."

"Will do," Jane said. "Now can I connect a number for you?"

"Yes," McIntyre said. "I need to call the FBI office in Denver.
Just a second . . . I've got the number here in my notebook."

"Will this be station to station or person to person?"

"Person to person is more expensive, right?"

"That's right."

"Make it station to station. I'll need to know the charges when I'm finished."

"Okey-dokey. I'm ready for the number when you are."

CHAPTER 7
A PICNIC WITH THE FBI

"Federal Bureau of Investigation. Violet Coteau speaking."

"This is the National Park Service. We've had reports of garbage can damage. We need you to come to the park and fingerprint our bears."

"And when I come I'll just ask for Ranger McBlarney?"

"Hello, Miss Coteau. Keeping busy fighting crime down there in Denver?"

"We raided two speakeasies and arrested a hooch merchant. Broke up a counterfeiting ring. Resolved a kidnapping satisfactorily. What about you? Are you earning my tax dollars? Or are you spending them on breakfasts and fishing rods? Anything important going on at Rocky Mountain?"

"Oh, just a few cases of attempted murder. Or harassment. Arson, that kind of stuff."

"Nothing major?"

"Well," he said, "I'm looking into an important case here. Significant investigation."

"Like what kind of investigation?" she said.

"Well," he said again, "you know those signs we have along the roads, the ones that say 'Deer Crossing'? We've had reports of certain deer who are crossing in other places. They don't use the designated crossings. Jaywalking deer. As an enforcement officer, I need to learn the identity of these animals and slap a fine on them."

"Couldn't you just move the signs?"

"Hadn't thought of that," he said.

"Obviously," she said. "Did you call because you're feeling silly, or did you want something? It's nearly quitting time."

"I just wanted to hear your voice again," McIntyre said, using his best imitation of Valentino.

"Horsefeathers," Vi said. He decided to try again.

"I'm returning your call," he said.

"Which call would that be?"

"Pick one," he said.

"More horsefeathers," Vi said. "What do you want, Ranger?"

"Okay. I was wondering if you had been able to measure the caliber of that bullet we dug out of the tree at Small Delights Lodge."

"That's a fascinating name for a resort," Vi said. "It makes me want to rent a room there. But what's the place in town called? The one where the rangers all live?"

"Just one ranger, and not all the time. The others are on visitor information duty. They need to live at the barracks near the entrance stations. Plus, other rangers don't need a place where they can concentrate their minds on important law cases. It's called the Pioneer Inn, if you need to know."

"I do, actually," she said.

Her voice was like a cat purring as it settled into your lap.

"Oh?"

"I have a few days' vacation time coming to me," she explained, "and it's very warm here in Denver. I think I'll come to see you with my information about the bullet. Maybe I'll help you clear up that backlog of jaywalking and harassment cases while I'm there. I'll drive up tomorrow. Why don't you do me a favor and reserve a room for me at your Pioneer Inn? Or if they have no vacancy, one of the hotels in town."

"Not at Small Delights?"

"When you know me better you'll know that I make my own

small delights. Now be a good little ranger. Save the FBI a long-distance nickel and rent me a room. I'll be arriving late afternoon."

"Great. And I've got a day off, day after tomorrow."

"I know that."

"Maybe we could take a picnic and go for a hike."

"I had already thought of that, too," she said. "See you tomorrow afternoon."

"You always drive this fast?" McIntyre asked.

"I like to go fast," Vi Coteau said. "Don't you?"

"If you don't slow this car down I'll have to write you a speeding ticket."

"You can't. You're out of uniform," she said, taking her eyes off the road for a moment to glance—again—at his white shirt, khaki jodhpurs, and Stetson hat. "Besides, you don't have your summons book with you, and besides even that, I've got my gun in my bag."

She patted the leather shoulder bag.

"I bet you don't have your gun," she said, teasing him.

"Heck no. Never need one. It's just one more thing to lug around. A man might as well carry a ball-peen hammer stuck in his belt. Hey, slow down now! That's the Beaver Point Store up ahead!"

"Aye, aye," she said. "By the way, I enjoyed supper and our stroll around town yesterday evening. But I was surprised when you left to go home. I thought you were living at the Pioneer."

"Only when I can afford it. Which isn't often. Okay, pull in here. I phoned Tiny and had him fix us a picnic lunch. Got another surprise for you, in the lunch."

At three hundred plus pounds, "Tiny" Brown had a perpetually cheerful full-moon face. He handed Ranger McIntyre the picnic box and two bottles of root beer, all the while grinning from dimple to dimple. He acted as if he found something infinitely amusing about the ranger in civilian clothes in the company of a strikingly pretty city lady.

"Behave yourself, now," Tiny whispered as he put the change in McIntyre's palm.

"I'll have to. She carries a gun," McIntyre whispered back.

"She might have the right idea, there," Tiny said. His chuckle made his three chins bounce up and down. "Nice meeting you, ma'am!"

"Likewise," Vi said. "I like your store. You have everything, don't you?"

"Pretty much. I always say 'if I don't have it, you don't need it.' "

"I see you've got a rifle hanging over the door. For sale?"

"Oh, no. A fella traded that to me for groceries last summer. I like how it feels to me. As large as I am, lots of rifles don't fit me too good. But that's a pretty heavy one. And it's long in the stock. One of these days I'll get around to ordering bullets for it, maybe go up in the park and shoot an elk."

He glanced slyly at the ranger. The ranger wagged his finger at the fat man.

"None of that, now," McIntyre said. "If any venison sandwiches show up on your menu you'd better look out."

Back in the heavy roadster, Vi put her foot down and they exited the parking area in a spray of dirt and gravel. McIntyre held on to the door handle.

"Nice car!" he said over the loud thrumming of the engine.

"Thanks!" Vi said.

"I'm saving up to buy my own car," he said, hoping she'd slow down a little in order to carry on a conversation. "But I don't think I can afford anything this powerful!"

"No, I don't think you could!" she said.

She laughed and he loved the way she laughed.

"Unless you come work for the bureau instead of the park service," she said. "We take much better bribes, you see!"

They stopped at the Thompson River Entrance where Vi dutifully displayed her season pass to the college kid who was manning the gate. They drove on a ways at a slightly reduced speed until McIntyre pointed to an almost invisible dirt track ahead on the left.

"Turn in there," he said.

The side road was little more than two parallel ruts that curved back and forth through a very dark, very shady forest of lodgepole pine. It took them a quarter of a mile until it came to a locked steel gate; McIntyre got out of the Marmon and used his RMNP keys to open the padlock. He waited for her to drive through and he shut the gate behind the car.

The dirt track emerged from the trees into an open meadow bordered with willow where a mountain creek bubbled and hushed over rocks and roots. The road turned and went upstream, curved around a low rise of woods, and stopped at a tiny jewel of a lake. The only evidence of people was a square wooden box, slightly larger than an icebox, perched on the low dam that created the little lake.

"Campground water supply," McIntyre explained. "There's a pipe from that box all the way down to Aspenglade."

"Beautiful spot!" Vi said. "Oh, look, there's even a little sand beach! You should have told me, and I'd have brought my swimming costume."

One problem with having Scots blood in one's veins: at certain suggestions, it tends to rush to the surface of the pale skin and turn the face the hue of a freshly boiled lobster.

"Water supply," McIntyre stammered. "No swimming."

"Pooh on you," Vi said. "Well, spoilsport, bring the car robe

out of the trunk and we'll have our picnic. This truly is a beautiful place!"

The surprise in the picnic lunch that McIntyre had arranged
was one of Tiny's special specialties and one of the three things
Vi Coteau said she found impossible to resist: egg salad
sandwiches. She took two bites before holding her sandwich out
to McIntyre as if offering him a sample. The white bread showed
where her teeth had left a dainty semicircle, tinged with red
lipstick.

"This is absolutely the best I have ever had!" she said.
"Homemade bread? And these have to be fresh eggs. Does he
make his own mayonnaise? Fantastic! The man is wasting his
time running a roadside store. He should be working as a chef
in the city!"

"No," McIntyre said. "Tiny's doing exactly what he wants to
do. It gives him all he needs and he's happy."

They finished the sandwiches and chips, the pickles and
olives, the root beer and homemade cookies. Overhead a few
cotton ball clouds came drifting over the Front Range, heading
in the direction of Kansas. A hawk flew in an unhurried circle
over the meadow. A few brook trout rose in the pond. McIntyre
decided to pop the question.

"Did you find out the caliber of that bullet?"

Vi Coteau looked at Ranger McIntyre with slightly parted
red lips and undisguised curiosity. Here she was, sitting on a
blanket beside a little mountain lake in a setting worthy of
Eden. The sun was giving luster to her dark hair; her legs were
tucked under her but showing considerable silk stocking.

"You haven't had much experience with women, have you?"
she asked.

Here came the blood to his skin again.

"Matter of fact?" he said. "Yes. Pretty darn happy experience, too. Until she died.”

“Oh,” Vi said. “I’m very sorry. Let’s drop the topic.”

She dug around in her shoulder bag and brought forth a little envelope.

“Here’s your bullet,” she said. “Our lab couldn’t determine the caliber, other than to say it’s about thirty or thereabouts. Hitting the tree mashed it pretty good.”

“Well, that’s that.” He put the envelope in his pocket.

“Not so fast,” Vi said. “Whenever are you going to learn not to underestimate me?”

“Why? What did you find out about it?”

“How much it weighs. I had them weigh it.”

“No kidding.”

“I wouldn’t kid you, kid,” she said. “See? I wrote the weight on the envelope. That bit of lead, even distorted and mangled, weighs almost exactly two-hundred and fifty grains.”

“I see.”

“Not yet, you don’t. I looked it up in our ballistics books. The heaviest bullet made for a .303 Savage weighs in at only one-hundred and ninety grains. In other words, that lead you have in your hand could not have come from a .303 Savage.”

“Maybe a .30-06 rifle?”

“Not likely, although I did think of that. Guess what? A .30-06 only goes up to two-hundred and twenty grains, and even that is pretty rare. Are you sure we’re out of egg salad sandwiches?”

“Absolutely sure,” he said. “What kind of gun do you think fired that slug? And why did I find a .303 shell casing at the scene?”

“That’s where my time expires,” Vi said. “It’s up to you to figure out.”

“Sure. All I need to do is examine every rifle in the whole region. Shouldn’t take more than two, three years.”

"Well," Vi said, "if that's the way you want to do it."

"What way would you do it?"

"I would ask the local outfitters store, where they sell ammunition. Find out who buys bullets that heavy."

"Miss Coteau?" Ranger McIntyre said.

"Yes?"

"Have another pickle. And if you want to go wading in the water supply, you go right ahead."

"Okay," she said. "Maybe later."

She stretched out full length on the blanket with her ankles crossed and one arm beneath her head.

"Tell me about your attempted murder case," she said.

McIntyre took out his pocket knife and began whittling at a piece of wood he had found. He described the shooting incident in the early morning dark, the botched electrocution booby trap, the way a bear had been released at Small Delights' back door, the brake bolt that had been tampered with. He told her about the sabotaged garbage truck, although it didn't seem to count as an attempt to hurt anyone. He said the details were the puzzling part of the whole thing. All these attempts to make the Fryes want to sell out, they seemed random. Amateurish. They didn't fit together.

"What about this Polly person? Does she seem, you know, mentally stable?"

"I hadn't thought about it, but yes. You mean because she's always been at the scene. She's very capable, too. I suppose she could have gone to the barracks late at night where the bear trap was and could've driven it away. I haven't seen a rifle around Small Delights, but that doesn't mean there isn't one. John Frye keeps a shotgun handy. I don't think . . ."

McIntyre had a thought that stopped him in mid-sentence.

"What?" Vi asked.

"Oh, I just remembered a rifle. A short walk through the

woods and you come to Grand Harbor Lodge. Catherine Croker's place. There's an English-made rifle hanging over their
fireplace. And the door is never locked. They keep the ammunition right there on the mantel. It would be easy to take the gun,
shoot over John Frye's head, drop a .303 casing on the ground,
and put the gun back again. I wonder if Polly Sheldon is the
type to cause all this mischief."

"She might surprise you, Mister Ranger. In any case, I think
that what you call 'random' incidents were done by somebody
who's very organized and very mechanical. That .303 shell casing they conveniently left behind, the electric wire they left
hanging, the tire tracks of the bear trap, the loose bolt on the
brakes? If he was your average nervous amateur perpetrator he
would have cleaned up at least one of those pieces of evidence.
No, I think he's very deliberate. And I think he's trying to point
you toward suspecting someone else. Only you haven't gotten
that far yet. I think they want you to say 'hmmm, there's only
one person who could do all this' and spend your time watching that person."

"Well," he said, "I did think about Catherine Croker, the
widow of Grand Harbor Lodge. She has a manager named Thad
Muggins. He's plenty capable. But I think he's honest, deep
down inside. I considered those four guys in the black sedan
with Denver license plates, too."

"They're from Chicago," Vi said, tossing the pickle stem away
into the grass and daintily licking the tips of her forefinger and
thumb. "They borrowed that car from some local Denver thugs."

"You know about them?"

"Sure. We've had our eye on them ever since they got off the
train at Union Station. They're connected with bootlegging,
gambling, and racketeering, in case you hadn't guessed. Agent
Canilly's theory is that they're looking around for a resort to
take over. Legally, of course, but a place to set up a liquor and

gambling establishment. As a matter of fact . . ."

"Yes?"

"Can I trust you, Ranger Timothy McIntyre?"

He looked at her lying there on the car robe, the sun deep in her dark hair, her skirt draped over the outline of her legs. What was the word he wanted? Throughout the long winter nights at the Fall River station he read a lot of dime novels in which heroines were often described as lounging "languidly" or was it "languorously"? Either way, Vi Coteau smiling on the car robe was a living, breathing pinup picture. Could she trust him?

"Yes," he said.

"Well, phooey and darn," she said.

"What are we talking about?" he asked.

"Oh, gangsters, I guess," she said. "Part of my reason for spending a few days at Rocky Mountain National Park is to observe our Chicago friends and maybe find out what they're up to. In fact, tomorrow morning I'm going to check out of the Pioneer Inn and into the Small Delights Lodge. I'll stroll over to Grand Harbor, too. You know, a single lady looking around."

"I see," the ranger said.

Vi Coteau's trip to the mountains wasn't all about him after all. He felt a little pang of disappointment, but at the same time he felt a slight sense of relief. Given his experiences over the past couple of years, romance was like a jigsaw puzzle, only one where several pieces had gotten lost under the rug. Or where the pieces of two different puzzles had been mixed up together and there was no box with a picture to show what it was supposed to look like when it was finished.

"These gangs, they have a pretty predictable pattern," Vi continued. "All the way from the Catskills to California. What they like to do is to find a remote hotel or lodge or cabin camp located in an area where the law enforcement is weak. Maybe at the outer edge of a county sheriff's jurisdiction, a sheriff with a tight budget."

"Like Abe Crowell, our sheriff. He can't afford the gas to send a man here on patrol except two or three times a year."

"Like that," she said.

She sat up and brushed her skirt.

"The gangs set up a private resort with drinking and gambling and prostitution. They might also use it to distribute the hard stuff, heroin and cocaine. There's an awful lot of money involved. And tell me something: if a place like Grand Harbor wanted to set up a telegraph wire, could they keep you and your rangers from noticing?"

"Sure. They've already got telephone wires and electric wires. And sitting on the edge of the national park like they do, what's a wire strung on a few poles got to do with us?"

"Then your gambling crowd could set up a wire for bookmaking. They would make it look legitimate, like a poolroom or billiard parlor. In the past, we've heard of them making generous cash offers to the owners of such places. But when an offer is too generous, the owner figures his place must be worth more than he thinks and he holds out for even more. That's when the intimidations start."

"A lot more money involved?"

"Mister Ranger, you have no idea! The bureau busted up an operation in Nevada near a little town called Virginia City. The gamblers had rented themselves a tent commodious enough to hold half a dozen pool tables. They paid forty thousand dollars a year rent on it. On a tent."

McIntyre puckered his lips and whistled. With forty thousand smackers, he could quit rangering and go fishing for the rest of his life.

"Those are high stakes," he said. "No wonder they're willing to start taking shots at people, interrupting trash collection, things like that."

"You got it. Only, they don't dirty their own hands, see? They find themselves a local dupe, usually a town bully who thinks he's gangster material. Or maybe a local businessman who thinks he can do the dirty work and make a bundle out of it and nobody will know the difference. The gang gives this local guy money and a sense of importance. And, of course, they do it all on the sly. They'll use a go-between to give him orders, or coded messages, or both. Probably they'll leave payoff money for him somehow. In the agency, we call it a 'drop' where the local picks up his bundle of cash without seeing any of the gang."

"Maybe I need to be looking for this local character," McIntyre said. "And investigate for coded message systems and money drops. You do know, don't you, that my usual law enforcement chores mainly include poaching and trespass? Oh, and don't forget illegal parking."

She laughed. He loved making her laugh.

"It's high time you turned detective," she said. "You see, even if you did find out who shot the bullet and did the sabotage, you'd only have a local case of criminal mischief."

Vi Coteau stood up and shook pine needles and grass from the car robe before folding it neatly to replace it in the trunk of her Marmon roadster.

"Thank you for the picnic," she said. "It's a beautiful spot, and very thoughtful of you to order those sandwiches. Now, would you have time to take the long way back to the village and show me more of your national park? There's plenty of gas in the Marmon."

"Sure, I've got time. Except the way you drive, I don't think you'll see much of the scenery."

"But I told you I like to go fast," she said again. "Don't you?"

CHAPTER 8
RANGER McINTYRE GOES FOR A SWIM

Two days went by, then three. McIntyre went about his duties like a donkey on a treadmill, his body reporting to work while his mind went on vacation. He would be ticketing a car for illegal parking or issuing a warning for a hazardous campfire and would find his brain wandering off in the direction of Blue Spruce Lake. Trying to keep his mind on the job was like trying to teach a three-year-old to tie shoelaces while playing with a kitten. When he drove to town to ask shopkeepers whether they had sold any .318 ammunition, he caught his brain looking around for a glimpse of the Marmon roadster. When he went to the telephone exchange to ask Jane whether she had heard anything he was tempted to go into the phone booth on the front porch and place a call to the Small Delights Lodge.

The next day was his day off. Although he tried his level best to make it like every other day off, he couldn't stop thinking about Blue Spruce Lake. He bagged his laundry, packed a lunch, collected his fly rod and creel, tucked his grocery list into his shirt pocket, and left the Fall River station full of good intentions. His first task, dropping off his laundry with Mrs. Jones, went okay. But his brain rebelled again and convinced him that groceries could wait. That the trout would be rising in that little mountain stream that ran into Blue Spruce Lake. Therefore, instead of going to the grocery, he pulled into the filling station, paid for two bucks' worth of gas out of his own pocket since he was on his own time, and headed out of town.

It was a twenty-minute drive and the road was virtually free of traffic. McIntyre's shoulders relaxed. His thoughts relaxed, too. He mentally arranged the pieces of the Small Delights jigsaw puzzle. On the one hand, there was the .303 casing and the tracks left by the bear trap, like someone was trying to incriminate the new ranger, Russ Frame. On the other hand, he had big-city gangsters who, for all he knew, had hired Russ Frame to frame himself and help "persuade" the Fryes to sell Small Delights to them and leave town. He had Catherine Croker, who would want Small Delights because she could see a huge profit in it. She had a manager who could help her with sabotage. Last, but too large to be considered least, was the chubby young woman named Polly dashing about pretending to be Sherlock Holmes. Polly seemed to be able to explain all the evidence, and she had a stake in Small Delights. She, too, would undoubtedly profit from the sale of the place.

Ranger Russ Frame.

McIntyre hadn't spent much time with Ranger Frame, since Supervisor Nicholson had assigned him to visitor information. Dottie said he did a bang-up job of organizing the brochures and maps, not just at the S.O. but at all the ranger stations and entrance stations. He was a whiz at making trail signs that made sense, too, so Nicholson told him to hike the backcountry and organize the trail markers, which meant that Frame camped out for days at a time. Frame owned an expensive .303 rifle. He drove a nearly new car. He seemed to spend a lot of time and money on his clothing. He always looked neat and clean and freshly pressed, which was a complete reverse from the other new man, Charlie Nevis.

Charlie Nevis was a mystery all to himself. He seemed almost sloth-like when he moved, yet never seemed to have time to talk, never stood still long enough to have a conversation with anyone. The supervisor had told McIntyre to have a word with

Nevis about shaping up his personal appearance. McIntyre delegated the job to his assistant ranger, Jamie Ogg.

"When you see Nevis over at the barracks," he said to Jamie, "tell him he's to go see Mrs. Jones at the laundry and have her alter those uniform pants and that tunic of his. They look like hand-me-downs from an older brother. Help him fix a hat press to put his hat in overnight. And that's an order from the S.O., not from me."

"Yes, sir," Jamie had replied. "I'll see what I can do to square him away. Anything else?"

"If—and only if—you see a chance to bring it up, try to find out why he's been interested in whether any locals want to sell their property. I'd love to know what duties have been taking him from one end of the park to the other all the time, but don't question him about it. I'll ask Dottie to look into it. Maybe he turns in a weekly logbook."

"Unlike yourself," Jamie said with a grin.

McIntyre slowed the truck as he neared Blue Spruce Lake. *Here's an idea,* he thought: *what if those Chicago mobsters actually hired Nevis to cause mischief, like the bear and the garbage truck, and set it up to where the blame would land on him instead of themselves? Maybe they told him to ask around about lodges that might be for sale just to make him look suspicious. Maybe they planted clues to look like Nevis's carelessness, like leaving the .303 casing and the trailer tracks. The rifle shell didn't make sense, however. How would the Chicago thugs know that Nevis had access to Ranger Frame's .303 Savage rifle?*

None of the pieces of this puzzle would click. McIntyre was beginning to think that the puzzle itself was a waste of his time.

His plan was to drive on past the turnoff to Grand Harbor and then drive on past the turnoff to Small Delights. There was a third road. Just inside the park boundary this third road forked: the left-hand fork went to a half-dozen summer cottages while the right fork ended up at a small parking area and trail-head. From there the trail went around the head of the lake and up alongside Blue Spruce Creek. There weren't any large fish in that creek, but plenty of fry-pan-sized brookies. Or a man might take the road to the summer cottages and fish Rainbow Creek, which also held plenty of brookies.

That was the idea, to cruise on past Small Delights and spend his time fishing. However, the moment he came around a curve and saw the Small Delights sign his entire scheme went awry. As in Robert Burns's poem, where "the best-laid plans of mice and men gang aft agley." Upon seeing the sign, his traitorous brain flashed him a picture, like a magic lantern slide. It was of Vi Coteau in a meadow, lying in the sun on a car robe. His hands on the steering wheel took over and without knowing that he wanted to, he turned off onto the Small Delights road and headed for the lodge.

And wasn't it Vi herself who came running toward the truck as soon as she heard him approaching? This time she was in tan jodhpurs and laced boots and her white blouse was doing wonderful things as she ran to him.

McIntyre jammed on the brakes and slid to a stop.

"It's Hattie!" Vi cried. "Out in the lake! Hurry!"

They ran to the boat dock, where Polly Sheldon was strug-gling to unlace her high boots. Out in the lake Hattie Frye was hanging onto the bow of the nearly submerged rowboat and screaming for dear life.

McIntyre dropped his jacket and hat and pulled off his brogues and trousers. In what seemed like an instant he was diving off the end of the dock, swimming strongly for the sink-ing boat. John Frye came running with the red and white life ring he had managed to find back in the trees, but the rope tied to it wasn't even a tenth of the length needed. All he could do was stand beside Vi Coteau with his shoulders slumped, looking helpless.

McIntyre swam with his head up to keep the victim in sight. He fought against the drag of his shirt and socks and did his best to ignore the icy chill of the water. He kept going, keeping a steady pace, staying calm. By the time he reached where Hattie was clinging to the half-sunk boat, he was almost as relaxed as if he was just out for a bracing swim in the lake. She stopped yelling as he drew near. He stopped just out of arm's reach, treading water.

"Hiya, Hattie!" the ranger said cheerily. "You okay?"

"Not really!" she replied. "I'm freezing!"

"Can you swim?"

"Yes, a little. But not that far. And my clothes are really weighing me down."

"Okay," he said. "Let's see what we've got to work with here. I don't think the boat will sink any further. Made out of wood. What else is in the boat? No life preserver, I don't suppose."

"Nothing. Just the oars."

"There's an idea," he said. "Hang on, just like you've been doing. I'll be right back."

McIntyre went underwater and pulled himself hand over hand along the rowboat gunwales until he came to the first oarlock. He pulled the metal pin and the oar went floating to the surface. Reaching over the boat, he did the same on the other side.

He bobbed up next to Hattie.

"Now we need something to fasten them together," he said.

Fortunately, whoever had tied the rowboat's painter to the bow ring had done a sloppy job of it; McIntyre was able to slip it loose and retrieve the rope, which he used to lash the two oars together.

"There we go," he said. "Now drape your arms over the oars on that end over there, and I'll do the same on this end. Got it?

Now all we have to do is kick our way back to shore."

They had made a few yards when Hattie said she couldn't do any more. Her boots were weighing her down too much. McIntyre drifted back far enough to undo her laces and tug the boots loose.

"That's better!" she said.

He tipped the water out of the boots and upended them in the hope that they would float long enough to be retrieved. He put his arms over the lashed-together oars next to hers and they continued kicking toward the shore. John Frye had found another length of light rope to bend onto the one tied to the life ring. He waded out into the lake until the water was up to his waist and threw the ring in the direction of the two swimmers. For the next few minutes it looked as though they were hardly moving and would never reach it, but reach it they did. All that remained was for John and Polly and Vi Coteau to pull the victim and her rescuer to shore.

Polly hustled up to the lodge to find some blankets. McIntyre and Hattie stood shivering and shaking on the beach.

"What happened, dear?" John Frye asked. The words sounded almost funny to McIntyre, who had never heard Frye express concern for anyone.

"That damn plug, that's what happened! That damn drain plug you put in, it popped out when I was all the way out there! I nearly drowned!"

"Hattie," John said, "I hammered that drain plug in with a mallet, just like I do every spring. I hammered it in good. No way it could slip out again."

"What were you doing out there, anyway?" McIntyre asked.

"Fire!" Hattie said. "I had finished cleaning up after breakfast and went back to our room to fix my hair and I could smell gasoline. Strong smell of gasoline. All I could think was they were about to torch the place and we had to run away because all that dry wood would go up like a Roman candle. I shouted for John and shouted for him but he was nowhere around. All I could think to do was push the boat out into the lake where I'd be safe and I was rowing when I saw that damn plug pop out and water was coming in and I couldn't put the plug back and oh! God! I'm glad you came along!"

Polly arrived with the blankets. She led her shivering aunt up the hill toward the lodge.

Vi draped a blanket over McIntyre's shoulders and stood behind him massaging his shoulders.

"Good job, Ranger," she said. "Where'd you learn to do water rescue?"

"Air Corps, of course," he replied. "Down in Texas, where it's so dry that the armadillos carry canteens. First, they trucked us to a pond, but later took us to the gulf shore for water rescue training. Ironically, the next place they sent us to was France, where the only way you could drown was if you made a crash landing in a wine vat. That's our government for you."

"Good job, anyway," she said.

"The job's not over," he said. "I want to borrow a canoe from Grand Harbor and see if I can tow that rowboat back to shore. Maybe I can retrieve Hattie's boots, too."

"Would you need a bow paddler?"

"I'd love one," he said.

"Okay," she replied, "but only if you put your trousers back on."

Polly Sheldon was not terribly pleased at the sight of the slender and capable Vi Coteau sharing a canoe with Ranger McIntyre, even though she grudgingly admitted that Coteau handled a paddle with practiced ease. She noticed how the other woman's weight balanced with McIntyre's, making the canoe ride level on the water. Her own weight would probably make the canoe plow water. She waited dutifully at the dock to help haul the waterlogged rowboat onto the sand.

"How's Hattie?" McIntyre shouted as they neared the shore.

"Fine," Polly called back. "Uncle John is taking care of her. Chilly and wet, but otherwise fine."

Once they had secured the canoe, the three of them pulled and jerked at the rope tied to the rowboat until they had it halfway out of the water. More muscle, or maybe a truck, would be required to drag it any further, since it was still full of water.

"Polly," McIntyre said, "do you know . . . where was the boat when your aunt decided to take it out onto the lake? Do you remember where it was? Tied to the dock, or what?"

"No. Uncle John likes to keep it dry for guests. It was on the sand. With the front end pointing toward the water."

"That's what I thought," McIntyre said. He reached into his pocket and handed Vi Coteau the large cork John Frye used as a plug for the boat's drain hole. The ranger had found it floating near the half-sunk boat. "Smell that."

"Ooof!" Vi said, recoiling from the scent. "Naphtha soap!"

"It's an old trick you learn at Boy Scout summer camp," he explained. "While the boat's sitting there high and dry you take a rock and hammer the drain plug loose. You take a chunk of hard soap and your pocket knife and shave three or four wedges. You put the plug back and the soap wedges hold the plug in place until the soap slowly softens and dissolves in the water, and down goes your buddy into the drink."

"Do you mean . . ." Polly said, "do you mean they tried to drown my aunt? Who would do such a thing?"

"I don't think they meant it for anybody in particular. That would be too hard to arrange. No, the spilled gasoline under her window was supposed to terrify her, and it did, but the joker couldn't have foreseen that she'd jump into the boat and row into the lake. No, he just wanted a guest or John, or anybody, to have another so-called accident."

"Horrible man!" Polly said. "Well, maybe this time he made another mistake."

"How do you mean?" Vi asked.

"Soap!" Polly said. "What if we find a bar of naphtha soap and it's been shaved with a knife? Evidence, you see? Better yet, I think I will devise a kind of ruse, maybe a little package tied up with string and a very hard knot, and ask each man I encounter if I can borrow his pocket knife to cut the string. The knife of the perpetrator will smell of naphtha soap, you see."

"Worth a try, I guess," McIntyre said. "Let me know if you find out anything."

"But, by the way," Polly said, "what brings you to our neck of the woods, anyway? And out of uniform."

"Day off," McIntyre said. "I thought I'd go for a swim in your lake. No, seriously, my plan was to hike up one of the creeks and catch a few brookies. And mull over these accidents, of course."

He added the last part about the accidents just in case Polly might accuse him of not showing enough concern for the Small Delights situation.

"Would you like to come up to the lodge for a cup of coffee?" she asked sweetly, giving no indication whether the invitation would include Vi Coteau. "You might like to talk to Aunt Hattie, find out if she's all right now."

"I don't know," McIntyre said. "She'd only start in on me, again, about needing the park service to provide her with a fire pump and alarm system and all that. No, I seem to be more or less dry now, I think I'll just stroll up the creek and catch my dinner."

"Fine," Polly said. "Well, if you would like to stay, I'm sure the cook would be more than happy to cook your trout for you. Perhaps offer you a twice-baked potato and vegetable to go with it. No wine, I'm afraid. Prohibition?"

"Nice offer," McIntyre said. "I'll think about it, I promise. While I'm up the creek."

"Without a paddle?" Vi Coteau said sweetly.

He felt the warmth of the blood rising to his face and knew he was blushing. But he didn't know why. Exactly.

If it had been December or January, Rocky Mountain National Park would have been muffled and chilly under winter's heavy blanket. Ranger McIntyre would have been snowbound in his cabin. He would take his most challenging jigsaw puzzle from the shelf and spread it out on the card table, putting all the cardboard pieces into place with his hands while his mind shuffled the suspects and evidence in the Blue Spruce Lake affair. But it was warm summer when the streams of the mountains ran clear and full among the green willows, when McIntyre's method for thinking through a problem was to take his fly rod to a slow-moving stretch of creek and annoy the trout.

Over on the opposite bank of the stream where a half-submerged boulder sheltered a deep hole was an obvious hiding place for brookies. A Number Fourteen Ginger Quill drifting with the current around the rock should bring one of the brookies out. With a flick of his rod he tried it. Sure enough, a fish charged for the Ginger Quill, but with a laugh the ranger jerked the fly away before the little trout could have it.

That was too easy, McIntyre thought. *Too obvious. Like picking Polly Sheldon as the one who was doing all the sabotage herself in order to cause her aunt and uncle to move and sell Small Delights. That way she'd have her investment back, plus interest, and she could see her aunt and uncle settled in Denver. But she's just not that kind of person. If she was desperate for money she'd be trying to sell that airplane she's keeping in a farmer's garage.*

I think I'll try that fast-moving riffle in midstream, McIntyre thought, *in case there's a trout on its feeding station at the bottom. It looks like there might be a good-size rock down there for one to hide behind.*

One cast, the line quartering across the current. Nothing. Not a sign of a trout. A second cast, the dry fly bobbing down the center of the riffle. Again nothing. Make the same cast once more, or try a different place? If there was a big one lying in that riffle he might not be feeding, just resting there. Sometimes a large fish like that won't rise because he's not hungry. But once in a while he'll attack a dry fly out of annoyance. McIntyre flipped an S-shaped cast of the line and let the fly drop exactly where it had before. Nothing that time, but when he did it once again he saw a dark shape come muscling up out of the current to attack. He set the hook. The fish put up a pretty good fight and was a decent size. He released it unharmed because it was still early in the day. There would be others he could take home for supper. Or to the lodge dining room.

Those four city guys in the sedan, he thought. *Maybe I could work them up, make them seriously annoyed and see what happens. I wonder if I could goad them into doing something illegal, without hurting anybody?*

McIntyre moved upstream to a fresh spot. But with his first cast he got careless; as the line sailed gracefully out behind him in the arching S-shape, the tiny dry fly caught on a leaf or twig of the willows and stopped the line momentarily before tearing loose. Fly, line, and leader landed on the stream in a noisy, splashing snarl. A regular mess. Reminded him of Ranger Charlie Nevis. Did Nevis do the mischief, or was he too careless? Could he manage anything requiring timing and meticulous method?

McIntyre reeled in his line, pinching it between thumb and forefinger to force the twist out of it and straighten it out for the next cast. *Maybe,* he thought, *maybe a guy ought to take Charlie Nevis in hand and straighten him out. Make him look good and act right, and then the perpetrator wouldn't find it as easy to blame things on him. Charlie would make a tempting scapegoat for our actual villain. He moves around the park a lot, people tend to either avoid him or ignore him, he looks like he needs money, and he seems to know his woodcraft and guns and tracking well enough. He's an obvious suspect, but a little too obvious.*

"Having any luck?"

The female voice came from behind him. He knew who it was without turning around.

"Not until now," he replied.

It was a terrible flirty bit of dialogue, one he stole from a romantic movie, but it was the first thing he thought of. Vi Coteau rewarded him with that laugh that always brought the blood into his face. How could a simple thing like a woman laughing make him feel like he was blushing?

He finished reeling in his line and waded back to the bank where he sat down beside her.

"You always wade in your brogues?" she asked. "And wearing only one sock? What's that for? Good luck?"

"Lost the other one in the lake," he said. "I thought about throwing this one in after it, but I thought I might keep it just in case."

"Ranger," Vi said, "you never cease to interest me. What kind of man keeps one worn-out sock just in case he might need it? And doesn't the water ruin your shoes?"

"Nah. I'm in the water more often than you'd think. I keep them slathered in neatsfoot oil. One September, cold as heck, we had to relocate a beaver colony. I worked in the water all day long until my legs turned blue. At first, I tried rubber boots, but they always snagged on something and filled up with water. I eventually gave up and oiled my shoes and used them. Been fishing in them ever since. Anyway, how are you doing at Small Delights?"

"I'm learning a few things about our four Chicago friends with the long sedan. And I'm beginning to like John and Hattie Frye very much. They remind me of my own family. I keep trying to find them a way out of their dilemma, this idea that they have to stay here and keep the lodge open because they have no other options. In fact, there's an apartment for rent not far from where I live. Or I have a small rental house. My tenants said they might be moving, although they can't say when."

"What about Polly Sheldon? Are you two girls being nice to each other?"

"Oddly enough, yes. We're definitely two different types, though. She becomes interested in something and goes after it like a terrier digging for a gopher. She told me. She also said that she tends to lose interest after a while and begins chasing a new idea. Did you know she once bought an airplane? She was all eager to be a pilot, but now it's sitting in a farmer's garage."

"She told me about that. It's a Curtiss Jenny. I learned to fly one in Army pilot training. What about our friends with the black sedan? What are they up to?"

"They spend their time mostly sleeping and playing cards, my informant tells me. The man at the gas station said that they've made at least two trips to Denver. They're still at the hotel in town, but every day they drive out to Grand Harbor Lodge where they sit on the porch playing cards or checkers. Except for the one they call 'Dink.' He's nervous, restless. He takes walks in the woods or else he tinkers with the car. Catherine said he likes to borrow that rifle—the one over the fireplace?—and prowl around in the woods hoping to shoot at a porcupine or mountain lion. I heard him telling his boss that they ought to buy a speedboat to put on the lake."

"No," Ranger McIntyre said. "Park rules. No motors. Not

even a sailboat. Nobody knows you're from the FBI?"

"Nope. As far as the Fryes know, and Catherine Croker, I'm a well-paid, well-educated executive secretary in a downtown office in Denver. Which is true. And my company does a lot of industrial research. Which is true. I'm rather spoiled and lazy, which is why I stroll over to Grand Harbor a lot and sit on their porch reading their magazines. Catherine doesn't have any vacancies at the moment, so that gives me an excuse to stay with the Fryes but buy my suppers at Grand Harbor. Catherine likes to sit and gossip with me."

"I can see why," McIntyre said. "I bet she's jealous of your clothes and the way you look. If you don't mind my saying it, you're the kind of modern woman that she would like to be."

"How is your investigation going?" she asked.

"Nothing I could take to court, that's for sure. A bilge plug that smells like naphtha soap, a shell casing, a chunk of lead, a piece of wire, and a blurry photo of wheel tracks. What I need right now is to be standing with Sheriff Crowell and have our saboteur walk up to us and say 'I done all them things, I'm the man you want.' "

"That could happen," she said. "Maybe if you caught him red-handed and shoved your .45 revolver in his ribs."

"Sure," McIntyre said. "Whereupon he hauls out his own .45 automatic and offers to ventilate my tunic. I try to avoid those situations. Arresting a man should be like landing an airplane: you try to do it with as little excitement as possible."

Vi Coteau stood and brushed a few leaves and bits of grass from her pleated skirt.

"Time for the vacationing spoiled girl to wander back to the lodge," she said. "But do come and visit sometime. Come for breakfast. I understand it's your favorite meal of the day."

"Don't be surprised if I do!" he said.

"Ranger McIntyre," she said, "I make it a point to let nothing surprise me. Well . . . except things like seeing a man wearing only one wet sock."

Chapter 9
A Bullet in the Back

McIntyre wanted the whole Blue Spruce Lake thing to be over with. He knew himself well enough to know that when he had something he wanted finished, he would push and pry at it until something broke. During the war, he was assigned to locate a camouflaged German machine gun. He flew for hour after hour, searching the same places over and over again, going back to the aerodrome for refueling, searching the desolated landscapes until his eyes felt as though they had sand in them. Frustrated, he abandoned all caution: he dropped down to what would be treetop level, had there been any trees left after the shelling and bombardments, and sent the Nieuport roaring back and forth over the battlefield.

It was too much temptation for the Germans. They tore away the camouflage netting and began firing their machine gun at him.

"Gotcha," he said, cocking his own machine gun and banking the Nieuport into a steep U-turn.

Besides knowing that he wanted the Small Delights situation resolved, and knowing he was liable to do something rash in order to bring it about, McIntyre knew that he wanted more time to spend with Vi Coteau. After being with Vi, he found anything else dull and boring: if he couldn't spend more time with her, then he needed to either take a long solo camping trip or throw himself into the case and stir things up. Having depleted his vacation time, he opted for stirring things up.

McIntyre began to hover over the Blue Spruce Lake situation like a hawk watching a nest of field mice. He visited the hotel where the Chicago boys were staying. He interviewed hotel staff, the man at the gasoline station, the grocer, the laundry woman, anyone who might have had dealings with them. He phoned Catherine Croker nearly every day and asked questions about her boats and her guests and her rifle. He enlisted Dottie and Jamie to keep tabs on the comings and goings of the two new rangers, Nevis and Frame.

On Friday afternoon, he learned that the Chicago foursome had checked out of the hotel in the village, leaving their rooms in a mess.

"It's okay, though," one of the cleaners told him, "they left a large tip."

For a few hours McIntyre indulged himself in a feeling of self-satisfaction; it seemed as if his harassment had worked and the four were giving up and going back to Denver or Chicago or wherever. But when he rang up the Grand Harbor Lodge to ask Catherine Croker some questions about her foreman, Thad Muggins, she informed him that two of her cottages became vacant and the four men with the sedan had rented them. They paid two weeks in advance.

"I see," McIntyre said. "Well, business is business, right?"

"I'll admit to you that I'm pretty ambivalent about it," Catherine said. "On the one hand, yes, they paid two weeks' worth of rent in advance plus gratuity for the help. But, on the other hand, whether they are sitting and smoking on the boat dock or shooting pool in the billiard room or lounging on the front porch, they have an intimidating look about them. Now they will be here all the time. Other guests find it difficult to relax with those men in suits hanging around."

"Maybe I need to drop in. Make Grand Harbor part of my patrol route. Keep an eye on them for you."

"No need," Catherine said. "Ranger Nevis said he will talk with them about making people nervous. He also said that he would come by to check on it from time to time. To make sure the guests aren't feeling uncomfortable, you know. He's a good boy, such a gentleman."

"Nevis? Okay. I'll take your word for it. Talk to you later."

McIntyre did not like the idea of the pinstripe quartet living within a stone's throw of Small Delights, but for the moment there wasn't much he could do about it except to keep on talking to people about them and making sure they knew he was watching them. He wished they would just go back to Chicago and report that building a liquor and gambling joint at Rocky Mountain National Park wasn't a good idea. "There's this damn ranger, see . . ."

Sunday morning. For McIntyre, the weekly church service was a quiet hour of reflection and remembrance. The rituals such as singing the doxology or reciting the Lord's Prayer, the old familiar hymns, even the sometimes familiar sermons always put him back in touch with his childhood church and his grandparents. After the close of services, the week's hustle and frustrations lost their urgency as he joined the socializing, standing around talking with people while sipping weak coffee and nibbling tiny sandwiches. For those few minutes there were no puzzles, no crime, no hurrying to do anything. There was only the milling around, hands being shaken, smiles being freely given, backs being slapped, hats being tipped to ladies attired in their Sunday-go-to-meeting clothes. Mothers sometimes dragged their eligible daughters over to where the tall forest ranger was standing to see if he might be free for supper some evening.

On this particular Sunday morning both hymns happened to be in McIntyre's key and he sang with enthusiasm. The small choir delivered the anthem with heartfelt sincerity. The minister offered his interpretation of certain passages from the Book of Job; McIntyre felt that the man of the cloth had skirted certain key issues about whether God had any responsibility toward Job. Both the sermon and the pastoral prayer seemed overly long, making McIntyre think back to the hard pews in his grandfather's church and the drone of the old minister.

As the ranger filed out with the rest of the congregation he heard someone call his name. He turned and saw the retired Englishman coming toward him, the gentleman who owned a .303 Enfield rifle.

"Good morning!" McIntyre said it with a friendly smile as if he actually remembered the man's name.

" 'Morning, Ranger," said the Englishman. "Need a bit of a word, if you've the time?"

"Certainly," McIntyre said.

The two men stepped away from the departing worshippers.

"What can I do for you?" McIntyre asked.

"Major J. Lee Angel, retired. I wish to report sounds of shooting in the national park," the Englishman said. "Just this week past. Out beyond our bungalow at Blue Spruce Lake, you know. Near the Rainbow Creek Road. High-powered gun, almost assuredly a heavy rifle. Sometimes a single shot, sometimes as many as three shots in a row. Naturally we are concerned. Not hunting season, you know. Not even legal in the park, what? Definitely coming from the park, which puts it in your bailiwick."

"I see," McIntyre said. "Were you able to locate the shooter more exactly?"

"I did," the Englishman said. "Wish I had my map with me. I drew a map listening to the shots, you know. Rather like locating a sniper during the war. You know the Owl Creek layout.

115

Creek comes down off the mountain, cuts through a clearing, joins into the river after that. That's where the bugger does his shooting. There's marmots in there, around that clearing, might be shooting them. Deer, too, of course. The man's a damn nuisance, whatever he's after. Much obliged if you'd look into it. As I said, a heavy rifle by the sound of it. Got no business firing it off in the national park like that. Stray shot could hit the bungalow. Makes a fellow nervous."

"Thank you for the information, sir," McIntyre said politely. "I think I already know who it might be and I'll certainly look into it. First thing tomorrow, I'll make a mounted patrol of the area and report what I find."

"Good show, Ranger. Knew I could count on you. Then perhaps we'll talk tomorrow."

"Tomorrow," McIntyre agreed.

Sunday afternoon would be spent at the Fall River station. He had nothing else to do. There were no invitations to Sunday dinner, no picnic rendezvous with Vi Coteau and her Marmon Roadster. Following a lunch of leftovers, he would exercise Brownie and work on teaching her another command. He also needed to give her a good grooming. After that, he should grease the wheel bearings on the horse trailer and make sure it was set to go the next morning. For supper, he decided to boil a couple of potatoes to go with some ham, which he would eat while studying the station's S.O.P. manual to see what the procedure was for arresting people for target shooting inside the park. He already knew the first item of the procedure: "Rule 1: Approach any armed person with extreme caution."

Thank God for the Washington, D.C., desk wranglers. Without their helpful standard operating procedures, he might forget to exercise caution when approaching a man holding a gun. McIntyre smiled to himself; maybe he needed to follow that same S.O.P. when approaching Vi Coteau, the lady with the gun in her bag.

Monday morning. As soon as the clock showed six and he knew the telephone exchange would be open, Ranger McIntyre phoned Grand Harbor Lodge. He expected Catherine Croker to answer, since she would probably be in the kitchen oversee-ing the breakfast preparations, telling the cook how to crack eggs and showing the waitresses how to pour orange juice. He was surprised to hear the raspy voice of Thad Muggins on the line.

"Manager," Muggins growled.

"This is Ranger McIntyre. Mrs. Croker, is she around?"

"She's busy."

"Oh. Well, maybe you can tell me. Got a couple of questions. People have reported hearing gunshots, like a heavy rifle."

"Yeah, but a long ways off. It's okay. It's that hood from Chicago, the one they call Dink. He's taken a shine to Catherine's husband's old rifle, the English job. She lets him shoot it. He calls it 'hunting' but what he really likes is to walk around carrying it. He'll shoot at rocks, pine cones, anything."

"Using up her ammo, is he?"

"Bought himself a box. Ordered it out of Denver. A greasy-looking kid in a fast coupe brought it to him."

"He doesn't shoot around the lodge?"

"Nah. His boss told him off about shootin' too close to the place, told him to take a long hike. The clown thinks he's a woodsman, a regular Davy Crockett type. Talks about how far he hiked, how many deer he coulda killed except it meant drag-gin' 'em all the way back again. Yesterday he bragged how he brought down a deer but it was too heavy to haul out by himself. If ya ask me, I think he's been readin' too many Boy Scout books. I don't think he'd know how to gut and quarter a deer even if he did kill one."

"Okay," McIntyre said. "Next question. Mind if I park my pickup and horse trailer behind the lodge for a day, maybe two?"

"Nah," Muggins said again. "We don't mind."

"Okay, thanks. Tell Mrs. Croker, will you, that I'll be out there today."

"Yeah," Muggins said. And rang off.

Duty, McIntyre thought. *Duty. At times it can be damn hard.*

He put his foot to the stirrup and swung his leg over Brownie, trying hard to ignore the marvelous smells coming from the Grand Harbor Lodge kitchen. Bacon, pancakes, coffee . . . he thought he could even smell the orange juice. He looked down at his uniform and badge as if to remind himself that today he was a mounted policeman. He didn't even have his fly rod with him. Just the .45 service revolver in its shiny holster, his shiny badge, his shiny boots, and his shiny handcuffs.

One of the pretty serving girls came out of the kitchen's back door to scrape a plate over the garbage pail. She smiled, and smiled beautifully, at the sight of the tall uniform and flat hat atop the handsome brown mare.

McIntyre smiled back. Breakfast and a pretty girl to pour coffee. He gave a long sigh and put his heels to Brownie's ribs.

"Let's go, girl," he said. "Up the trail. We need to reconnoiter that clearing before Mr. Daniel Boone arrives with his rifle."

Trotting away from the lodge, McIntyre was hit with a flash of realization: if the rifle shooter was one of the four Chicago men and was staying at Grand Harbor, he wouldn't miss seeing the NPS truck and trailer. Brownie's hoofprints would show they had gone in the direction of the clearing. If the man wanted to avoid a ranger, he'd stay put at the lodge and not go plinking in the park. On the other hand, if he was in the mood to take potshots at a uniform, the clearing might be exactly where he would want to go.

McIntyre was not paranoid by nature; in fact, he tended to be trusting and optimistic. Now, however, maybe he should look at the situation as if he was a paranoid. What if a city hoodlum thought somebody was trying to make trouble for him, trying to spoil his racket? If the thug felt like he could get away with murder, what would he do? It might be like Dottie's other boy, Bud, who would steal an apple or write his name on a fence because he knew he wouldn't be caught.

Judging by newspaper stories McIntyre had read, a gangster would be likely to lure the judge, or cop, or detective or whatever to a rundown garage or dark alley, where the body would be found riddled with Tommy gun bullets. The Chicago Four had invested a month or more exploring a place to establish their liquor and gambling "resort." Would they walk away from the project because a park ranger began asking questions? Paranoid McIntyre didn't think they would.

This Dink character, maybe in cahoots with Thad Muggins, seemed to want him to investigate that certain spot in the woods. Otherwise why go all that way and do all that shooting where he knew the major or some other summer resident would hear it and complain? And why keep going back to the same spot? On the other hand, maybe Dink had simply discovered a secluded place to shoot off Catherine Croker's rifle. Whatever Dink's motives were, it was McIntyre's duty to investigate shooting in the national park. There wouldn't be any harm in doing it suspiciously, and with caution.

The game trail from Grand Harbor to the clearing ascended a long gentle hill through the ponderosas. It skirted a rock formation, then crossed a shallow creek before emerging into the open. McIntyre stopped after they had waded across the creek and had a consultation with Brownie.

119

"We'd better do a careful recon, partner. It's no good riding straight out into the open. That's what some sniper would like for us to do. Let's ride around in the woods and make sure there's nobody hiding. C'mon, let's look around a bit."

It meant that Brownie had to step over fallen logs and make detours around thickets and boulders, but she and McIntyre made a wide circuit of the meadow clearing without leaving the protection of the trees. Satisfied that they were alone, they stepped out into the open and, staying close to the timber, made the circuit again. McIntyre studied the ground. From time to time he stopped and looked around to assess the terrain.

"You weren't there," he told Brownie, "but during the war, pilots sometimes made forced landings in farm fields. If they could stay airborne long enough, they'd circle around and make a few passes just to be sure they weren't going to hit a ditch or a stump or a dead animal when they landed. So, let's just check out this clearing and . . . hello?"

A gleam in the grass caught his eye. Dismounting, McIntyre found two brass cartridge cases. They were .318 caliber and head-stamped "WR" for Westley Richards. The rifle from the Grand Harbor Lodge.

"Look at these," McIntyre said, although Brownie wasn't listening. She was snacking on fresh grass. "Maybe he stood here and took a couple of shots. At what, I wonder?"

At first, he saw nothing that a plinker would be tempted to shoot at. McIntyre's eyes, however, kept coming back to one particularly large ponderosa pine tree across the clearing. He put the cartridge cases in his pocket and mounted up again. He and Brownie reconnoitered the perimeter again, going in and out of the trees, dodging branches, methodically forming a clear picture of the layout. When they came to the matriarch ponderosa it was as McIntyre had expected: the tree's trunk was riddled with bullet holes, ten or twelve of them, all bleeding with pitch running down the bark.

They were about to continue on when Brownie flared her nostrils and went rigid. She stood smelling the air with her eyes wide and her ears pointing forward. McIntyre smelled it, too.

It was a dead deer, a dry doe lying behind a currant bush. The animal had been shot through the shoulder, in the haunch, and through the heart. The thug with the rifle must have arrived at the clearing to do his shooting and saw the doe grazing near the ponderosa. His first shot broke her shoulder. The deer must have turned and began hobbling away into the trees. He shot again and hit her in the rump. Probably would have knocked her down. A .318 slug was heavy enough to do that. The shooter walked up and fired a third one through the heart. The powder burns could still be seen on the hair around the bullet hole.

"That cuts it," McIntyre said to Brownie. "Illegal kill, a kill without a license, a loaded firearm inside a national park, killing a deer out of season, not to mention damage to government property when he shot holes in the tree. If this city clown shows up today, we'll take him and arrest him. Armed or not."

McIntyre drew his Colt .45 service revolver and checked the cylinder. He studied the clearing for a few minutes and explained his strategy to Brownie.

"He's been coming out of the woods the same place we did. He shot the tree and the deer from there. He thinks he has the range. He's familiar with shooting from that spot. Even if he suspects that we're here, he'll still go there. He'll be sneaky, but that's where he'll go. He'll feel confident shooting from that point. I'll bet you a measure of oats that he'll do it again. So, let's set up a surprise for him. If he doesn't show, we haven't lost anything except a little time. If he does show up, we'll take him back in handcuffs. That ought to irritate the Chicago mobsters."

McIntyre mused awhile longer, imagining himself in the role of a shooter standing where the trail entered the open field. Then he decided what to do.

"You're gonna think what I'm about to do is corny as heck," McIntyre told Brownie. Brownie had learned long ago not to be surprised by anything the ranger might do. "But why not do it?"

The ranger dismounted. He removed his green tunic and put his Sam Brown belt and holster back on over his shirt. He arranged the tunic over the currant bush and set his hat on it: from across the clearing, the bush and tunic could be taken for a man in uniform kneeling down to examine the dead deer. He took out his sheath knife and cut away any branches that might spoil the decoy's effect.

Next, he led Brownie back through the trees to the rock formation near where the trail crossed the creek and entered the clearing. From there, if Dink came up the trail and into the open, McIntyre could get behind him. A grove of aspen crowded the rock formation: white aspen trunks would help hide his white shirt while affording a clear view of where the trail entered the clearing. He sat down against an aspen and made himself comfortable. Brownie was content to stay behind the rocks where the grass was tender and damp with dew.

McIntyre had almost dozed off when he heard the crunch and scuffle of someone walking up the trail.

"Brownie!" he whispered. "Hide."

The mare obediently lay down in the grass and stretched out on her side.

Revolver in hand, the ranger stayed low behind an aspen tree and watched as Dink reached the edge of the trees and began to look around. Dink was being very cautious. Probably saw the fresh horse tracks on the trail.

Checking to be sure Brownie was hidden, McIntyre froze and

watched what would happen next.

Dink may have fancied himself a rugged woodsman, but in his cloth cap and short Mackinaw jacket he looked more like a cab driver. He had been carrying the rifle in the crook of his arm, rugged woodsman style; spotting the dark green tunic in the trees across the clearing he went into a dramatic half-crouch and brought the gun up into the "ready" position across his chest. It was painfully obvious that Dink did not know how to handle a hunting rifle. In Chicago, he might have been quite the lad with an automatic pistol or a short-barreled shotgun, but out here in the wild he clutched the English weapon like a nervous bachelor holding a newborn baby.

Dink appeared to be weighing his options. Shooting a ranger, any ranger, would sure put the cat among the pigeons. Make the tree cops think twice before sticking their noses into gang business. One shot, and who'd know who did it? Damn rangers probably would suspect the gang, but couldn't prove anything. Way out here in the woods, nobody around.

Dink assumed the kind of shooter's stance you might see in a magazine ad for an outdoorsman's brand of pipe tobacco. He pulled the trigger on an empty chamber: another greenhorn mistake. Flustered, he jerked open the receiver bolt and loaded a live round. This time the sharp report of the rifle went echoing through the woods. Dink apparently failed to register the fact that the "ranger" had not fallen over after the first shot. Maybe he thought he had missed. He worked the bolt action to chamber another round and fired again.

With the blast of his two heavy shots ringing his ears, Dink didn't hear McIntyre come out of the brush behind him, didn't suspect anyone was there until he felt a gun jammed into his ribs. A hand reached around him to seize the rifle by the barrel.

McIntyre, however, had underestimated Dink's strength. Instead of letting go of the gun, the gangster twisted this way and that, forcing the ranger off-balance, using his leverage try-ing to force the gun free. McIntyre brought up his revolver and struck Dink a pretty good crack to the head, but, despite the blow, Dink stayed on his feet and kept twisting and jerking to pull the rifle out of McIntyre's grip. He twisted his body around, grabbing McIntyre's wrist. They were locked in a face-to-face trial of strength, neither one willing to let loose of his weapon, boots digging at the ground trying to shove the opponent off-balance.

From the corner of his eye McIntyre saw movement in the bushes and realized that Brownie was watching them. She had evidently heard the commotion and, figuring there was no longer any need to "hide Brownie," she decided to come see how her master was doing. It looked like he was dancing with that other man, but didn't seem to be enjoying it.

"Brownie!" McIntyre shouted. "Break it up!"

She knew the command. The ranger had taught it to her. But he had never said it when he was part of the struggle himself. In her training, it involved two or three park laborers or other volunteers who pretended to be rioters or people struggling with one another. Having her ranger be one of them, that was a new thing.

"Brownie!" he shouted again. "Break it up!"

Okay. Orders is orders.

Brownie rushed the two men at high speed, her neck arched and her head held high, smashing into them with her broad chest, knocking each man backward into the grass. And knock-ing the breath out of them in the bargain. She planted all four feet, stopped, then wheeled around, ready to do it again.

McIntyre shook off the shock and jumped to his feet. He was holding the rifle by the barrel, and he still had his revolver.

"That's it," he said. "All over! Onto your knees. Put your hands up. Do it or I'll have her knock you down and stand on top of you."

The ranger emptied the rifle and threw it down before reaching for his handcuffs.

But Dink wasn't ready to be arrested, not yet. The gangster had gone to his knees but now he stood up, stared around for a moment considering which way to go, and took off at a dead run for the shelter of the trees.

"Stop!" McIntyre called.

Dink kept running.

"Dammit," McIntyre said. He fired a warning shot from his revolver, but Dink kept running. He reached the shadows now and, in a moment, he'd be sprinting down the path that twisted through the woods.

"Dammit," McIntyre repeated. He took aim, squeezed the trigger, and sent a .45 slug slamming into Dink's shoulder.

Like McIntyre had told him . . . it was over.

Hauling the Chicago tough guy back to Small Delights Lodge was no picnic, but it was the nearest place where he could patch him up and phone for the county sheriff without interference from his Chicago cohorts. It was late afternoon by the time the sheriff arrived to take him off McIntyre's hands.

"He'll live, I guess. You'll have to come down to the county seat and fill out paperwork," Sheriff Abe Crowell told McIntyre. "I'll phone you when we want you to come. Meanwhile, you need to write up a detailed report. Find a notary public and sign it in front of him. It wouldn't hurt to take photos of the deer and recover the slugs that killed it, either. And save that tunic with the bullet holes in it. I'm going to take this rifle and lock it up as evidence."

"I appreciate you coming for him," McIntyre said. "His buddies will probably try to bail him out when they learn about it. But they won't learn about it from me. I'm going to ride back to Grand Harbor Lodge, put Brownie in her trailer, and drive away without talking to anybody about anything. Maybe they'll go search for Dink and wander around the woods all night, but that's no problem of mine."

"That's up to you," Abe said. "I don't care whether you tell anybody or not. The doc will dig your bullet out of his arm. If your man lives through it, we'll let him call a lawyer or anybody he wants to. In a day or two. So, I'm off now."

"See you," McIntyre said.

The ranger was tired to the bone. His stomach was empty and audibly complaining about it. There would be a couple of hours, however, before he could clean up and eat and rest. First, he needed to take Brownie back to the ranger station and give her the rubdown and extra oats that she had earned.

CHAPTER 10
NEW ORDERS AND A SHARED MEMORY

The next few days were routine for Ranger McIntyre. He apprehended a pair of teens who were stealing a trail sign, cited a cabin owner for an illegal open fire pit, helped old Mrs. McReedy fill out her annual access road agreement, and put tickets on the windscreens of cars parked on a meadow. He made a point of ignoring anything to do with Blue Spruce Lake; however, Polly phoned the S.O. at least twice a day to report to Dottie that she hadn't seen the "gangsters" or their black sedan at Grand Harbor Lodge. It was as if she expected them to wreak horrendous revenge for the wounding and arrest of their compatriot.

"After she tells me that she hasn't seen them, she always has a reason to talk to you," Dottie told McIntyre. "First she wanted your advice on storing firewood. Next, she had a question about her airplane. She even wondered if you could come to Small Delights and give the guests an evening fireside talk about the park."

"Tell her to contact the boys in visitor information. The supervisor has me on enforcement."

"Which reminds me," Dottie said. "This requisition for a new tunic? Can't you take your old one to the tailor shop and have them re-weave the bullet holes?"

"Well," McIntyre said, "those holes might be evidence. I'm thinking I could order a new one and when the case is settled I'd repair the old one and use it for every day, save the new one

127

for special occasions."

Dottie shook her head and signed the paper. From past experience in arguing with McIntyre, usually about his personal use of the park service pickup truck or telephone, she had learned that he could stand and debate for hours. She smiled patiently as she handed him the requisition form.

"Is it true what they say," she said, "that you either need to agree with a Scotsman or kill him?"

"Och, no!" was his grinning reply. "That's not true at all!"

Sheriff Abe Crowell phoned. He, too, wanted to keep the park service informed about "those mobsters." The latest development was that they had taken up residence in a boarding house a few blocks from the county courthouse and the Boss visited Dink at the jail at least once a day. He called for a big-time lawyer to come bail him out: however, the judge thought it more prudent to keep the man jailed. Shooting at a federal officer might not seem serious back in Chicago, the judge explained, but out here in the West it was not taken lightly. Not very many years prior, irate citizens would have lynched the shooter on the spot. Westerners tend to respect their lawmen and have no use for outlaws. The judge denied bail: first, there was every possibility that the accused would grab the first train out of town; second, if he didn't leave town, friends of Ranger McIntyre might come looking for him.

"In fact," the judge said, "one of the ranger's friends, a man who runs a livery up there near the village, he phoned to tell me they would like to invite Mr. Dink to hang around awhile at the Beam-and-Rope Café."

Back in the little village the four tough-looking men referred to locally as "the Mob" were noticeable by their absence. Rumors about them still remained, rumors that this owner or that owner had been offered a fortune for his resort property, or that the Mob had bought the cooperation of the local moonshiner to stockpile illegal booze for them. But these were only rumors; the general atmosphere of village and park slipped easily into its normal relaxed state. Even Hattie Frye out at Blue Spruce Lake seemed to relax. She went an entire week without shaking John awake in order to ask him if he could smell smoke.

On one of these relaxed afternoons, Ranger Tim McIntyre discovered that he had finished every single blessed chore on his list an hour before quitting time. It was too late in the afternoon to drive a patrol around the park. Which is why he was sitting in his cabin listening to the radio and tying a dry fly when the door opened and Supervisor Nicholson walked in. McIntyre jumped to his feet, bumping the fly-tying table, nearly spilling the spools of thread, boxes of hooks, bundles of feathers, and scraps of chenille. His hands flew to his throat to adjust his necktie, but his necktie was draped over the back of the chair. Caught. Busted. He wondered how the fly fishing, and breakfasts, would be in Death Valley.

Supervisor Nicholson waved McIntyre back to his chair and pulled up another chair for himself. He leaned in to look closely at the artificial bug clamped in the fly-tying vise.

"That a new pattern?" he asked.

"Yessir," the ranger said. "They call it a Western Bee. Supposed to look like a small honeybee. You use yellow chenille for the body. Wings are breast feathers from a wood duck."

"Why don't you make me one or two while you're at it," Nicholson said. "I never heard of a trout rising to take a honeybee, but I'll give it a try."

"Sure."

"Any news on that bear?"

"No," McIntyre replied. "Russ Frame and Jamie had a good look around but there's no sign of it. Probably headed for the high country."

There followed a long silence, and it was awkward. The supervisor poked around in McIntyre's fly-tying materials, then picked up a few finished dry flies to examine while McIntyre sat wondering what had brought the boss all the way out to the Fall River station that late in the day. Maybe to tell him he was to be reassigned to Death Valley for shooting that Dink character.

"I still don't like this Blue Spruce Lake situation, Tim."

"Oh?" McIntyre said. "I thought things had calmed down out there."

"That's kind of what has me worried. Too calm. And believe you me, I've got plenty of other things to be worried about. The bank, for instance. You recall the bank, don't you? That funny-looking square little building where other rangers have savings accounts?"

"Sure," McIntyre said. "I was in there just a few days ago to have them notarize my written report for the judge. Nice place. Well, kind of cold. Formal, if you know what I mean. I like their free calendars."

"I was talking to the banker this morning," Nicholson said. "John Frye, up at Small Delights Lodge, he needs a new boiler for his hot water supply. Has needed a new one for a couple of years now. Maybe you've seen it, that rusty steel tank out in the woods? Oil-fired."

"Looks like a forest fire waiting to happen?"

"That's the number. Frye went to the bank for a loan to buy a new boiler. Less than twenty-four hours later, that boss of the Mob proceeds to threaten Dave Kersey if he gives Frye the loan. How he knew about it, I couldn't say. Or how he knew the boiler could break down and spoil Frye's business. And before you say it isn't a national park matter, I'm going to say you're right. But when you shot his henchman you more or less dealt us into the game. Abe Crowell's boys are spread awful thin throughout the county. On the other hand, it looks like my own enforcement people have time to sit around tying dry flies during duty hours. Tim, I've got two semi-unofficial requests for you. One, finish getting this Blue Spruce Lake thing off my back. And I mean Frye complaining about Grand Harbor and Catherine Croker bitching about Small Delights and mobsters running around intimidating bankers. Two, contact Abe Crowell and see if he'll deputize you, at least temporarily, so you can act outside of the park boundaries."

"You want the black sedan crew to pack it up and go back to Chicago or wherever they're from."

"Exactly. They need to lose interest in Blue Spruce Lake. In the whole region, for that matter. Whatever plan you come up with, whatever you want to do to discourage them, we keep it to ourselves. Just you and me. Except for the one who poached the deer and tried to shoot you, we have no legal cause to keep them out of the park. We need to keep it quiet, whatever you decide to do. I don't want Dottie or any of the rangers or staff involved in stuff that might not be official park business. Unless absolutely necessary. The less they know, the safer their jobs will be."

"Whereas *my* job . . ." McIntyre said.

"Thanks for volunteering," Nicholson said.

"You're welcome."

The sound of Nicholson's coupe faded away and the deep mountain silence returned to the Fall River station. Ranger McIntyre lit the oil lamp on his desk and went back to wrapping black thread over the yellow chenille of the Western Bee. One of the interesting things about fly tying was how ordinary materials like chenille and feathers would magically turn into lifelike details. A few wraps of plain black sewing thread plus a little glue and the eye of the hook would become the head of an insect. A tiny feather tied on behind the head looked like nothing until you put a couple of turns of thread to separate it into two little wings. A few more turns over the center to divide the yellow chenille and presto! A honeybee.

The ranger chuckled, mostly to himself; thinking about fooling trout with a bunch of thread and feathers had made him think of how he had fooled Dink with that empty-coat-over-a-bush gag. Straight out of the movies, just like the cowboy who sticks his empty hat up over the rock to draw fire from the outlaw.

What would have happened, McIntyre wondered, if Dink or one of the other mobsters had succeeded in killing him? Back in the city they would probably have police and city attorneys on their payroll and could bribe or intimidate their way out of a murder charge. They could bluff it out, in the city, and probably go on with their business. But way out here in the national park it would be a different story. The county sheriff would investigate and because it was federal property, the FBI would start an investigation.

Rangers and deputies would maybe go gunning for the gangsters, too, and not because McIntyre was a popular and well-liked character. They just didn't tolerate lawbreaking outsiders. Didn't like them, and didn't cut them any slack whatever. Local citizens often helped hunt down criminals in the valley. It was the West, after all, where every man and most women knew how to handle a gun and wouldn't hesitate to pull the trigger on any stranger who stole horses, burned houses, or fouled a water supply. Or shot a ranger. It was probably a good thing that McIntyre had hurried Dink out of town and had him safely lodged at the county seat. Otherwise a posse of citizens might have been arguing whether to use hemp or manila.

McIntyre took the finished Western Bee from the vise and placed it on the cotton pad. He struck a match and lit the ceiling lamp; there was still daylight left outside, but inside the cabin it always became dark along toward suppertime. He wasn't ready to fix supper; he clamped another bare hook in the vice and began tying another Bee.

If I'd been shot and killed, McIntyre thought, *everything would go back to the way it was. Things would get so hot for those mobsters that they'd be out of the park as quick as you can say "Jack Robinson" and they wouldn't look back. One problem solved, but there would still be that trouble between the Fryes and Catherine Croker.*

McIntyre dipped the glue brush into the bottle and found it nearly empty. He would need to buy some at the outfitter's store next time he was in town. While he was at it, he had better lay in a winter's supply of glue, yarn, hooks, and anything else he'd need to tie flies. Once the snow hit and the outfitter closed for the season there wouldn't be anywhere to find fly-tying stuff this side of Denver. Same thing applied to groceries. Better start stocking up now, just in case the blizzards began in early October and made it hard to get to the store.

He woke before daybreak the next morning. He couldn't say why, but abruptly he was wide awake and staring into the darkness thinking about crazy, random little things. He knew he would never get back to sleep. With a heavy sigh, he threw back the blankets and swung his feet to the floor. There were mornings when the simple act of hauling his body upright seemed downright heroic.

In his BVDs and bare feet he went out the back door of the cabin and into the stable where he fumbled around filling a measure of grain for Brownie. He opened the gate to let her into the fenced grazing meadow and went back inside. The cabin seemed more gloomy and confining than usual. He lit two of the oil lamps, built up the fire in the stove and set the coffee pot on, and then sat down to polish his boots while waiting for the water to boil. He was hungry, but he didn't feel like cooking breakfast. Strange mood he was in and he didn't know why until he happened to look at the calendar and saw the day's date circled in black.

He knew what he had to do. Blue Spruce Lake and winter provisions be damned. Duty be damned, too.

When the water was hot McIntyre shaved and washed. He brushed his hair and put on his uniform. He closed the damper on the cookstove, put out the lamps, latched the cabin door, started the park service pickup truck, and drove up the road to Fall River Lodge.

Minnie March had been expecting him. The dining room was empty this early; it wouldn't open for guests for another hour. Minnie had prepared the table in the corner, the table with a view out across the willow-fringed park and the creek and pond. It was the table she had always shared with Mike March before he died. There were four chairs at the table, but rather than set his flat hat on an empty chair, McIntyre walked to the dining room door to hang it on the pegs. He sat down. Minnie brought orange juice and sat down. They raised their glasses in a silent toast.

"To those who can't be here," she said.

"The same," McIntyre said.

They sat in silence awhile, each one finding in the other that special quiet feeling of comfort that comes from knowing that somebody understands. No words can express it.

Minnie gave McIntyre a sad tight-lipped smile and rose to fetch their breakfast, which would be the ham and egg special, the same as it was the morning of the day Mike had died. And the day McIntyre's one real love had died. She and McIntyre had come to the lodge for breakfast that morning. It was the start of their long day's drive over Fall River Pass. They had shared the table overlooking the willow meadow and the four had laughed together and teased one another. And by afternoon

Mike's heart had given up beating forever and McIntyre's heart lay, broken and mangled, in a torture of twisted metal at the bottom of Fall River Gorge.

"I sometimes wonder," Minnie said.

"What about?" McIntyre asked.

"Why you're still here. Me, I've got this pile of logs and boards to look after and no way to make a living without it. But I'd have thought you'd move on. You know, away from the memories."

The ranger sipped his coffee and looked out of the window at the stream meandering through the willows, the deer grazing the meadow, the snow-tipped peaks beyond.

"This is where I am," he said. "This is where everything kind of comes together in a complete picture for me. Until one of the pieces goes missing."

"Speaking of which, let's change the subject. I heard you were a life saver the other day, rescuing Hattie from the lake."

"How'd you hear about it?"

"It was that other ranger, Charlie Nevis. He seems to know everything that goes on over at Blue Spruce Lake. Yes, he was here the next day. He said he was on his patrol route and needed to check our fences to make sure our horses can't stray. Said he didn't want a fence to break and let the livery string loose in the park. He told me to be careful with the little rowboat we keep on our pond because the one Hattie was using sprung a leak and she nearly drowned. That Nevis, he's a cheerful earful, isn't he? I wish he'd lose weight and press his uniform once in a while. You know how people like to take your picture? My guests never want his picture. They don't even like to talk to Nevis because he looks so sloppy."

"Strictly speaking," McIntyre said, "your lodge isn't his responsibility. He's supposed to keep an eye on campgrounds and picnic areas along the Elk Park Road. Twice a week he's supposed to do a horseback patrol up the Cascade Creek trail."

"In that case, you might mention to him that he doesn't need to be nosing around here. One guest said Nevis was asking about whether they had been offered any bootleg hooch during their stay, or if they knew where there was any gambling action."

"That's strange," McIntyre said.

"Weird, is what it is," Minnie said. "You know, Tim, every once in a while, I have a guest who wants to know what the place is worth. They ask me 'what would you take for it' and 'have you ever considered selling' and that kind of stuff. Some of them suggest that I might have my own speakeasy hidden away. Or a gambling room. Mostly I laugh at them, but your creepy ranger talks like that, with his wheezy voice and all, he gives me the shivers."

"I'll have a word with him," McIntyre said. "Meanwhile, I need to say thanks for breakfast and go back to work. This Blue Spruce Lake thing is taking up way too much of my time. I agree with Nick Nicholson: it would be great if the whole thing just went away."

"Thanks for coming to share the morning with me, Tim," Minnie said. "It means a lot. Gives me a feeling like, well, like I can put the grief back on the shelf for another year. Know what I mean? Kind of like washing a special serving dish after a party and putting it away. I'll still see it every day, I'll know where it is, but I'll be able to work around it."

"I know what you mean," McIntyre said. "Say, did I tell you that I'm starting to look around for a car to buy? A personal car of my own? I haven't had one since . . ."

"Yeah," Minnie said, "I know."

"It's time," McIntyre said.

"Well, that's great! A step forward! Good on you. What kind do you think you'll buy?"

"I'd been thinking about a pickup truck. There's a guy down on the Little Thompson who has a three-quarter-ton Dodge that I like. He said he might sell it."

"And what do you do if you meet a nice young lady and set out to court her? You expect her to ride in a drafty pickup truck? No, Tim, you'd better get yourself a classy little runabout if you're ever going to drive around with a pretty woman beside you."

"I see your point. I'll think about it," the ranger said. "See you later."

On the drive back to the Fall River station, he did think about it. Minnie had summed up his entire dilemma, the largest unresolved issue in his life. Most rangers would be thinking about possible promotions, or transfers to better assignments, or about marrying and having kids, maybe going back into the military. Or, like one of his pals, quitting the park service to take a job with a commercial logging and forestry outfit. But Ranger McIntyre was happy enough where he was. Plenty of freedom to be alone, or to go hiking or fishing, and the only thing that would make it better would be his own vehicle so he wouldn't feel guilty about using the government truck all the time.

Was he a pickup kind of guy, or a sporty runabout kind of guy? With a pickup, he could tow a horse trailer. On his days off he could help friends haul a piece of furniture or some firewood. And hunting: when he went out for his winter supply of venison, it would be really handy to have a pickup to bring it home. But Minnie was right. If Vi Coteau came to visit him again, she would prefer a nimble little two-seater. Besides, if he had a little runabout it would impress the young ladies in town. And he could always borrow a park service pickup if he needed to haul anything. It was a dilemma.

Brownie was looking over the fence when he pulled into the station and parked next to the horse corral. McIntyre climbed out of the pickup and pushed the door shut with a clang that made the mare raise her ears at him. He went over to where she was standing and scratched her forehead.

"What kind of car I buy doesn't have anything to do with anybody else, does it, Brownie? I don't need to impress anybody, do I?" the ranger said. "It just depends on who I think I am, right? I mean, who am I?"

Brownie regarded him with her solemn brown eyes as if to say, "you're the human who's going to fork some of that fresh hay over the fence to me, that's who you are."

CHAPTER 11
AN EXPLOSION AND A NICE LUNCH

He was throwing the last forkful of hay over the fence to Brownie when the phone began to ring. McIntyre wanted to ignore it but knew he shouldn't. Maybe if he took his time answering, it would stop ringing. No such luck, however; the darn thing kept up its insistent ding-dong noise as he took his own sweet time walking around to the door. He sat down at the desk and picked up the earpiece.

"Fall River station," he said.

"*There* you are!" It was Dottie at the supervisor's office.

"Good morning."

"Not from where I'm sitting, it isn't. You'd better come down here. At once."

"Okay, I'm on my way. Nick wants to see me, does he?"

"No, Supervisor Nicholson does not want to see you. You are probably the last person he wants to see. He wants you to put a lid on this Blue Spruce Lake thing, that's what he wants."

"Why? What's happened?"

"You're to go straight to the medical clinic. Polly Sheldon is there. She won't calm down until she talks to you. She keeps telling the nurse to phone us and I keep trying to phone you and the quicker you talk to her the sooner we can all go back to work."

"What's she doing at the clinic?"

"I told you. Screaming for you. Apparently, she was standing too close to the boiler at Small Delights when it blew up."

139

"The boiler blew up?"

"Yes, Ranger, the boiler blew. And Supervisor Nicholson says you're to look into it and find out how it happened and resolve everything at Blue Spruce Lake and do nothing else until it is all taken care of and if he even as much as thinks you are looking at a fly rod . . ."

"I know," McIntyre said. "I know. He'll transfer me to Death Valley. I'm on my way."

The nurse ushered him into the tiny room in the back corner of the little clinic, where Polly Sheldon lay in the bed, propped up on pillows. Her skull was covered in a white bandage that also covered one eye; a cast enveloped one wrist; her bare arm and shoulder showed nasty-looking red splotches like sunburn.

"What the heck?" McIntyre said.

"Broken wrist, I'm afraid," the nurse said. "She's been burned, too. Well, scalded, really. And a piece of flying metal or wood left a nasty long gash in her side and along one leg. She won't let us give her a sedative until she talks to you."

"I can hear you, you know!" Polly Sheldon said. "Now leave! And shut the door."

"What happened?" McIntyre asked.

"Take notes," she said. "We'll need to go over it again later. My head hurts like heck right now. I think I'm deaf in one ear."

McIntyre took out his notebook and pencil.

"Go ahead," he said.

"Uncle John was feeling a little under the weather this morning. He woke me up early and asked if I'd do the morning chores for him. I got up and stoked the cookstove, dumped the kitchen garbage, opened up the dining room windows and all that. I hiked up to the boiler like he does every morning to make sure the coal bin is full enough and the self-stoker chute is working right. The sun wasn't up yet, but there was enough light to see by."

"Okay," McIntyre said. "What happened?"

"The burner was roaring like crazy when I got there. The draft had been cranked wide open and the damper as well. I looked up at the tank and you know what?"

"What?"

"I saw a piece of wire twisted around the safety valve. Odd-looking wire. It was blue. Up high on the boiler tank, there's a blow-off valve. It's probably gone now, after the explosion, but I'll swear in court that there was a piece of blue wire wrapped around the handle to keep the safety valve from opening."

"And it blew up."

"Yes. Lucky for me I went into a panic and did the wrong thing. What I should have done was go up to the burner and shut the draft and the damper, cut off the heat. If I had gone ahead and tried it I would have been blown to kingdom come. As it was, some dumb part of my stupid brain told me to look around for a long stick and try to knock the wire off the safety valve. I turned. I stepped away from the boiler just as it blew up. Next thing I knew I was lying on the back seat of a sedan, heading for the clinic."

"You in much pain now?"

"Head hurts. And my leg. But don't leave. We need to talk."

"Okay," McIntyre said, drawing a chair to the bedside and sitting down.

"First off," Polly said, "need to find that blue wire. Long shot, but might be evidence. Maybe marks from pliers on it and we could find the pliers. Something like that. Look around for footprints or maybe where somebody stood in the woods and smoked a cigarette. You know the kind of thing. Little details. Gotta find the guy who did this. We got to."

She sure is a determined little gal, McIntyre thought. *She's gone through all this and still wants to stick around and find out who's causing all the trouble.* He sat and listened while she rattled on about the time of day when the boiler would be used the most, when would be the best opportunity to tamper with it without being seen, what kind of man would know how to sabotage a boiler like that, and what kind of "evidence" might be found near the scene. The nurse came in with Polly's sedative and McIntyre rose from the chair.

"Try to sleep," he said. "But before I leave, do you have any idea what the next target might be, if there is one? If your aunt and uncle don't go away, I mean. What would the saboteur do next, do you think?"

"Hmmm," Polly said. "Hmmm. I see what you're thinking, Ranger. If you knew where they might attack next you could lay a trap. Well, let me think. Uncle John figures they're always spying on Small Delights. They see opportunities, you understand? I mean, they don't just go in and hope to cause mischief. It's as if they had been watching the place for a way to make an accident happen. When you think about it, that's what seems to be the deal."

McIntyre did think about it. And Polly Sheldon was right, or else it was her uncle, John Frye, who figured it out: somebody had witnessed Hattie's fear of fire. They saw her when she took the boat out into the lake; no doubt it was the same person who had observed John's habit of standing by the back door of the lodge in the early morning. They studied the layout well enough to figure out how the trailer could back down the alley and release the bear. They realized that the bumps and potholes in the approach road could loosen a truck's fuel line. Or a brake cable.

He went away from the clinic still thinking about it. His mind was in high gear putting the pieces together like a jigsaw puzzle, taking them apart, trying different connections. He started up the pickup and drove to the grocery to pick up a few provisions but his brain was still teasing at the puzzle.

The sidewalk in front of the grocery was almost completely blocked by empty boxes and crates. Egg crates, apple boxes, orange crates, all sizes of cardboard boxes. The grocer's boy came out of the store to add another crate to the pile when McIntyre approached.

"What's going on?" McIntyre asked.

"Clean-out day," the boy said. "Gonna haul all these away, clear out the storeroom. There's a winter shipment comin' and we need the room."

McIntyre looked at the pile of crates and boxes. A man never knows when he might need a good apple box. And then he had an idea.

"If you're throwing them out," he told the boy, "why don't you go ahead and pile as many as you can into my truck. Maybe it'll save you one trip to the dump."

He drove more slowly than usual on his way out to Blue Spruce Lake: although the load of boxes and crates was securely tied down with rope, McIntyre knew it would take only one wrong bounce or an abrupt swerve to tumble them out onto the road. He was glad when he made it to the Small Delights approach road and pulled up behind the lodge. John Frye came out to greet him.

"Where the hell you been?" Frye demanded. "You oughta be over there to Grand Harbor arrestin' that damn Catherine Croker and her henchman, that Thad Muggins. While you're at it, round up them Chicago thugs and throw 'em in jail with their pal."

"Good morning to you, too, John," McIntyre said. "Or maybe it's afternoon. Anyway, I've just come from seeing Polly at the medical clinic."

"Well?"

"Well what?"

"Well how the hell is she? What the hell did you think I meant? She still alive? Damn clinic, they don't phone to tell a man nuthin'. You'd think we didn't even exist out here. You talk to her, did you?"

"Yes, John," McIntyre said evenly. "She's got a broken wrist and a headache, plus numerous burns and bruises, but she's lively as can be."

"I'm the one found 'er after the explosion," John said. "She was really hurtin' but she kept yakkin' about seein' the safety valve wired down on that old boiler. Damn Grand Harbor outfit. I'd of gone over there and shot the lot of 'em, except I hadda take care of Polly. Polly was about outa her mind. That and plus them gangsters probably got Tommy guns and hand grenades. But I'll figure a way to fix 'em. You'll see."

"She told me about the wire wrapped around the valve handle," McIntyre said.

"I s'pose you wanna waste time lookin' at what's left of the boiler, instead of arresting them crooks," John Frye said. "That's the way you government types operate, ain't it."

"Calm yourself down a notch, John," McIntyre said. "You and I both know that old boiler was ready to fall apart. Still, I don't doubt Polly for a single moment. Somebody caused that thing to blow up and they darn near killed her in the process. It's high time we put a stop to this whole business. Let's you and me go see the scene of the crime. You lead the way. And wave your arms around a lot, like you're explaining it all to me."

"What the . . ."

"Just walk, John. There's one thing I need to see before we unload my truck."

"Fat lot of good a bunch of boxes is for," John said. "But

hell, I'll play your dumb game. Okay, come on this way with me."

The two of them went through a pantomime of searching the ground around the exploded boiler, picking up various pieces of wreckage and debris, consulting with one another, gesturing toward the forest as if they were trying to determine which way a bit of pipe or boiler plate had flown. After five minutes, however, John Frye's patience began to wear thin. He went stomping over to where the ranger was standing and handed him a length of twisted wire. Bits of blue insulation were still visible.

"Here's your damn evidence, not that I need anythin' to tell me it was that damn crowd at Grand Harbor who done it. Shouldn't be no wire like this anywheres around here. It ain't fence wire. Looks more like dynamite wire to me. You about finished with your stupid investigation?"

McIntyre was finished. Besides finding the wire, he had seen what he thought he might see, a flash of reflected sunlight coming from the direction of Grand Harbor. He saw it three times and each time it moved slightly. He and John were under observation by a person with binoculars standing on an upper balcony of Grand Harbor Lodge. What he had earlier realized was that the front of the upper floor of the lodge could be seen from nearly anywhere on the Small Delights property. Which in turn meant that anybody with a telescope or pair of artillery binoculars mounted on a tripod could pretty much keep track of anything happening at Small Delights.

"We're finished," he told John. "Let's look at that storage building of yours."

When they got to McIntyre's truck, the ranger told John to pick up an empty crate as if it was full.

"Just pretend we're taking a couple of these crates into the storage shack," he said.

145

John Frye grumbled and made several uncomplimentary remarks about government employees and their possible relationship to long-eared members of the equine species, but McIntyre just laughed. When they got inside the small building, McIntyre looked around.

"Good," he said. "This place looks like I thought it would. Those bed frames, what are they doing here?"

"Just old bed frames. Too narrow to suit most people. We replaced 'em."

McIntyre saw a couple of dressers, one with a broken leg and the other with a shattered mirror, numerous broken or torn chairs, a few boxes that looked like they might contain old books and china, a rocking horse with a rocker missing, and all the other debris of a man who lives in the hope that, one day, junk will become needed for spare parts.

"Okay," McIntyre said. "This'll do. I just need to be really clear on one or two points. Number one, you and Hattie would really like to be rid of this place, right?"

"Hell, yes. I even told her brother, down in Denver, I'd take the job he offered me, if only we could unload this property for a good high price. Got loans to pay off. I never put up a 'For Sale' sign on account of it'd keep customers away. But I got me a price in mind."

"Where would you live, though?"

"There's a problem," Frye said. "I need t' be here the whole damn day, ten days a week, can't go traipsing down to Denver lookin' for a house. Don't even know as they'll loan me the money for one."

"Well, John," McIntyre said, "I've got a kind of a plan. If it works, we'll take care of your problem and mine at the same time."

"What if it don't work?"

"I haven't got that far yet. Meanwhile, let's start by stacking the rest of those empty boxes into the storage shed. Over the next few days, I want you to come pick up a box, take it to the lodge, bring it back again."

"What the hell for?"

"Ever hunt antelope, John?"

"Who's got time to hunt?"

"Out on the open prairie, antelope can see a hunter for miles. What you do is, you tie a white piece of cloth to your rifle barrel and you hide behind a sagebrush or in a gully and you wave it. Maybe you change location and do it again. After a while Mister Pronghorn just has to come see what the heck it is and you've got him. What I'm asking you to do is move these crates back and forth as though you're taking stuff from the lodge and storing it in the shed. Make it look like you're stockpiling supplies out there. You do it enough and I guarantee that our antelope is going to get real curious. Real curious."

"Know what, Ranger?" John Frye said. "I'm gonna do it, but mainly just because I'm real curious t' see what you're up to. Once in a while when you're not eatin' free breakfast or poaching government trout, you can be downright entertaining."

Ranger McIntyre drove back to the medical clinic where he explained his plan to Polly. When she heard the details, she was ready to climb out of bed and go help her aunt and uncle set the trap. McIntyre, however, wasn't quite ready to do it, not yet.

"Gotta go to Denver first, see," he said. "Right now, I need to go to the supervisor's office before he heads home for the night. You rest, and if you think of anything we've overlooked, phone it in to the office."

"One thing," Polly said, wincing from the headache she still had. "What if your fire flares up and jumps out of control and into the forest?"

"I thought of that," McIntyre said. "I'm going to let the bad guys worry about it."

At the office, McIntyre found Dottie and Supervisor Nicholson in the front reception area studying a stack of paperwork.

"Don't have much time to talk, Tim," Nicholson said. "Got a new batch of stuff from Washington to look over and file away. God help us if we put an order or memo in the wrong place where we can't find it again."

"That's fine," McIntyre said. "Nothing to report anyway. I just wanted your okay to drive to Denver."

"What for?"

"I need to arrange for a house where John and Hattie Frye can stay. Just until he finds a new job and they can look around for a permanent place to live."

"And how does this qualify as national park business?"

"You can bill the trip to law enforcement. Call it 'protecting witnesses' or 'precautionary procedures' or whatever you can think of. I want them out of the way while I catch whoever's trying to force them into selling out."

"Mr. Nicholson," Dottie said, "maybe Tim could pick up those office supplies while he's in Denver. I'd like to stock up on things before winter hits. I can make out the requisition real quick."

"Fine. Sure, whatever you need to do, Tim. Stay in touch if you can."

"Will do. Which reminds me, Dottie. Can I use your phone to call Denver?"

The number rang through and his heart made a little jump beneath his tunic when he heard the soft and throaty voice on the other end.

"Federal Bureau of Investigation, Denver," she said. "Vi Coteau speaking."

"Vi? Tim McIntyre, up at Rocky Mountain National Park. How are you?"

"I'm bored and ready to quit for the day, if you must know. What's up, up there? Have you found more bullets? Or another lovely spot for a picnic?"

"No, dang it. I've got two reasons for calling you. One is, you said you might know a place in Denver where John and Hattie Frye could stay. An apartment? And didn't you say something about a rental house you own? If your tenants left?"

"That's three things, Ranger."

It was the way she never hurried, that's what got to him every time. He'd say something, she would say something, and there would be this quiet pause before she said it. It made him hold his breath a little waiting for it. It was awfully distracting.

"And?"

"Yes to all three," she said. "I know about an apartment. However, my tenants have left. He found a better job across town, so I'd be glad to let them have the rental house."

"Fine. Now for another thing."

The little pause.

"You've already had three," she said.

"Smart aleck," he said. "Another thing is, if I drove to Denver tomorrow, could I meet with Agent Canilly for a few minutes? And maybe yourself? I need a bit of professional law enforcement advice."

"Can't do it over the phone?" she said. "Certainly. We'll be here in the office all day. I imagine you'd arrive about lunch time?"

McIntyre ignored the insinuation.

"Probably eleven or thereabouts. I need to pick up office supplies and drive back up the canyon before dark. The lights on my truck aren't any too good."

"See you tomorrow. Bye!"

At the Denver office of the Bureau, FBI Agent Canilly listened carefully to McIntyre's plan for resolving the Blue Spruce Lake issue. He asked a few questions: he packed his pipe with tobacco, lit it, and went to look out the window while he smoked. It was several minutes before he replied.

"I'm not a lawyer," Canilly began, "you have to keep that in mind. But we've had similar situations. As far as putting the storage shed under observation goes, that would be legal. Given previous incidents of vandalism at the resort you would naturally suspect that the same perpetrator might try to steal or destroy the stored supplies. I'd suggest, however, that you be very cautious about how you spread the word that the Fryes have stored supplies there. It could be called entrapment, see?"

"Right," McIntyre said. "If I don't tell anyone, directly, that there's supplies and stuff stored there . . . ?"

"That's the idea. Let them come up with the idea all by themselves. Whoever you're talking to about it, if you do talk about it, be sure there's another person there as a witness. Make sure to know their name."

"I see what you mean. What about the other part of my scheme? What do you think about that?"

"Could be tough on you if it went to a court trial with lawyers and such. There again, you don't want to be accused of deliberately tempting a man to commit a crime. In this case, you could be accused of lying about what you found at a crime scene. A lawyer would argue that you did it in order to trick his client into criminal activity, see? Not that we haven't done it ourselves."

Vi Coteau laughed.

"Mr. Canilly is talking about me," she told McIntyre. "We had a kidnapping case where the felon went across state lines. He had lost a hat that had his initials in it. I found it on the street but I told friends of his that I found it in the victim's room and was keeping it in my desk. He broke into the office to retrieve it and we arrested him."

"That's what I mean, see?" Agent Canilly said. "Let the suspect jump to conclusions on his own, if you can."

"Okay," McIntyre said. "I guess I've got a way to do that. Yeah, I see a way to do it."

An hour later McIntyre was satisfied that he had answers to his questions about legality. He told Agent Canilly about tricking Dink into shooting at a dummy.

"I'm surprised he hit it," Canilly said. "Dink is the worst shot of the bunch. Everybody knows that. That's why he favors a sawed-off shotgun. Probably why he was out there in the forest practicing. To make people stop talking about it. The Boss, on the other hand, is an expert. Especially with the Thompson submachine gun. Have you fired a Tommy gun, Ranger?"

"No," McIntyre said, "can't say I have. In the war I saw guys carrying them but I never had any occasion to shoot one. With the park service, I don't have any need for an automatic weapon. Most of the time I don't even carry my revolver. I try to keep tourists and chipmunks in line without threatening to shoot them. I'll have to admit, though, that I'd like to try shooting a Tommy gun."

"Take a few days off and come down to Denver," Canilly said. "Miss Vi here can take you out to the police range and show you the basics. When it comes to the Thompson, she can shoot circles around anybody. You ought to see her fire a full magazine into a moving target. Forty rounds just like that."

He snapped his fingers.

"I bet that's a sight to see, for sure," McIntyre agreed.

Vi Coteau raised an eyebrow at him. His little embarrassed grin made her laugh as she led the way out of Canilly's office. And the way she laughed . . . her way of laughing gave McIntyre's heart a thump. That's how he would describe it. Just a thump or two, the sort of heart thump that makes you look around to see if anyone heard it.

She covered her typewriter, selected a plum-colored cloche from the hat tree, threw a filmy shawl over her shoulders, and took McIntyre's arm.

"C'mon. Lunch is on me today. A little walk and a little lunch will do you good. Before you have to drive home, I mean."

As they went down the steps and out of the building, McIntyre asked her a question.

"Hat, shawl, arm," he said. "Tell me, do you do everything in threes like that? I noticed it in the office, too. Three chairs, three pictures, three things on your desk. What's that about?"

"It's just how I am," she said. "Everything seems nice and orderly that way. Under control. Or, I just like doing things in threes."

"Then I guess," McIntyre said slowly, "we have a walk, we eat lunch, and then we . . . ?"

"There you go," she said. "Maybe the 'and then' part is up to you, Ranger."

McIntyre expected that they would go to Woolworths, like last time, where Vi Coteau found the egg salad sandwiches irresistible. He had yet to learn not to anticipate anything when it involved the FBI secretary. She steered him by the arm into a stream of lunchtime pedestrians. After two blocks, they turned up a narrow street where the hum and bustle of the city traffic faded away behind them; in five minutes, they were in a part of town where none of the buildings were more than two stories high and where people nodded and smiled when meeting one another on the sidewalks.

Vi halted in front of a nondescript doorway simply labeled "Verdi's Café" and allowed McIntyre to open the door for her. As his eyes adjusted to the light, or lack of it, he saw that they were in a small restaurant where the walls were decorated with travel posters and framed photographs of family groups and landscapes. The tables, all small, were mismatched as were the wooden chairs that surrounded them. Each had a checkered tablecloth, in the center of which stood a wax-encrusted wine bottle, evidently from the pre-prohibition days, holding a single candle. The place reminded McIntyre of the little village cafés in France, at least the ones that the war had left intact.

Vi led the way past four tables to one of the booths against the back wall. The owner—head chef, waiter, busboy, and dishwasher all in one rotund and cheerful frame—greeted her by name. He took two glasses of water and a pitcher from his tray and set them down and apologized for having no wine to offer.

"This prohibition, you know," he said.

"A great shame, Señor Verdi," Vi said. "But it cannot be helped. Two of the daily specials?"

"Sí," he said. "Coming right on up."

Vi Coteau turned sideways, leaned back against the wall, and stretched her legs along the bench.

"I hope this doesn't look unladylike," she said. "But it's wonderfully relaxing. Do you mind?"

"Not a bit."

"Now," she said, picking at the candle wax hardened on the neck of the Chianti bottle candleholder, "let's talk."

"Okay," McIntyre said. "What about?"

"Romance."

Which was his cue to take a large swallow of water from his glass, and to refill his glass from the pitcher.

"Ah?"

It was the most brilliant reply he could come up with.

"While I was staying at Small Delights, Polly Sheldon and I had lots of girl chat. We got on quite famously, in fact. You do know that she has a crush on you?"

"Not really."

"Yes, really. She's a very sensible girl, and she's been raised right. She would never make the first move with a man. But all of her detective work, all her talk about developing Small Delights into a money-making resort, that's mostly about making an impression on a certain park ranger. I didn't want to bring this up in front of Agent Canilly, but in this entrapment scheme of yours, what's going to happen with poor Polly?"

"I hadn't thought about it. Good thing I have a long drive home this afternoon to think it over. This idea of her being sweet on me, that's not fresh news. Supervisor Nicholson and Dottie sprung it on me first time I was assigned to look into what was happening out at Blue Spruce Lake. They thought it was pretty funny."

"You be careful with her," Vi said. "I mean it. Her feelings."

"Sure. I know how to behave. It's not my first time, you know. I've been down this trail before. Even in high school there was a girl who chased me around. Other kids ribbed me about it. Usually, once a girl finds out that my idea of fun is a ten-mile hike to go fishing in a high-country lake, or that I'm out of bed and dressed before sunrise to go have breakfast, she tends to lose interest. Maybe not all of them. Like that young lady last summer? The photographer? She actually enjoyed having breakfast at dawn and riding in my bouncy old pickup truck."

"But she turned out to be a murderer," Vi said.

"Yeah," McIntyre said. "She did kill that girl. And she tried to kill that other guy. And looked like she might kill me, too. I had to hold all that against her. I suppose every relationship has its problems, though."

Despite the lack of wine, the meal of lasagna and bread and salad was probably the best McIntyre ever had. Real Italian home cooking. As they ate, Vi Coteau talked about Polly Sheldon and John and Hattie Frye and how much happier they would be once they got settled in Denver. Ranger McIntyre found it difficult to concentrate on anything Vi Coteau might be saying. It might have been because of the cozy booth with the checkered tablecloth and the candle in a wax-covered Chianti bottle; or, it might have been the red lipstick and the way her fork brought those precisely carved little squares of lasagna to her mouth. It may only have been the soft tone of her voice. Whatever it was, as he sat across from her in Verdi's Café, everything about Polly Sheldon and the Blue Spruce Lake problem faded into insignificance, including his plan for trapping the saboteurs.

"Ho finito!" Vi said, delicately dabbing her lips with the napkin.

McIntyre finished up the last scraps of his lasagna. He watched Vi open a large round compact and apply fresh lipstick. *Any other woman,* he thought, *might look vulgar if she applied her makeup in public. Women with Vi Coteau's poise and classiness, however, made it look natural, even artistic. A man could take a photograph of her putting on lipstick and hang it on his wall.*

"Time for me to wander back to work," she said, snapping the compact shut and putting it in her purse. "And you had better head for the mountains if you don't want to be driving in the dark. Pity you can't stay a few days. We could take in a movie or go to a concert."

"I don't think the park service would approve of me charging a hotel room in order to go see a moving picture," he said with a smile.

"You wouldn't need a hotel. I have a guest room."

She said it sweetly and she left it like that. The idea of spending the night in her house and having breakfast together the next morning hung in the air like smoke-drift from an extinguished candle.

CHAPTER 12
McIntyre and Polly Conspire

Ranger McIntyre pulled into the parking area at Grand Harbor Lodge. He turned off the ignition and heaved an audible sigh. It was a beautiful summer's day in the Colorado Rockies; there was a light scent of pine in the air, trout were rising in the lake, and all was quiet. The lodge with its shingled roofs and log walls, its stone foundations and wide veranda, fitted into the forest setting as if it had grown there and had been there forever. Guests lounging on the boat dock and on the covered porch and strolling among the trees were part of the peacefulness. In such an idyllic setting, why did there need to be all this friction and contention and greed? The widow Croker wanted Small Delight's property; the shady characters from Chicago wanted both her lodge and Small Delight; sometimes it seemed like somebody—and the ranger was determined to discover who— only wanted to keep harassing people.

McIntyre watched the trout making leaps and leaving circles of silver in the lake. He inhaled the blend of delicious aromas drifting out from the lodge kitchen—waffles, bacon, coffee— and thought about his own predawn breakfast of oatmeal and toast. With another sigh, he opened the door of the pickup, stepped out, squared his official ranger hat on his head, and started up the stone steps to talk to Catherine Croker.

The desk clerk said he should go up to her living quarters, which took up a corner of the second floor. She was holding a folder of papers and giving instructions to a housemaid, whom

156

she dismissed with a wave of her hand when the ranger knocked on the open door. She did not greet him at once, but rather waved him into the room as she had waved out the housemaid. She took the folder to her desk and ignored McIntyre while she examined whatever was in it.

McIntyre strolled around the room. From her windows, the view of the lake was like a picture-postcard. The walls were decorated with enlarged photographs of scenes from Rocky Mountain National Park; he recognized the Keyboard of the Winds, the Little Matterhorn, the sheer face of Hallett Peak. He could even identify the photo of a rushing mountain stream, having fished it often. On the other wall, behind an uncomfortable-looking couch, he saw an assortment of mounted documents. There were a couple of framed letters of appreciation from previous guests, presumably people whom Catherine thought were important. Another frame held her late husband's military commission. Next to it, a picture of a man and Catherine standing together. He assumed the man was her husband. There was also someone in the background of the photo, someone who looked vaguely familiar.

On the wall next to a second photo of the happy couple was their marriage certificate, its ornate borders and official seal faded and its ink turning brown. McIntyre stopped and looked closely at the certificate, mostly out of curiosity to see when and where the Crokers had been married. It's always interesting to find out where people got married. But a detail other than the date and place of the marriage jumped out at him. A grin spread across the ranger's face like in a Felix the Cat cartoon where a light bulb appears above Felix's head. In making the ranger wait for her while she attended to more important things, Catherine Croker had made a mistake. She should not have let him get near enough to read that marriage certificate. A serious mistake.

She turned and gave him a look that conveyed disappointment.

"I thought you would have my rifle with you," she said. "To return to me."

"I'm afraid not," McIntyre said. "I thought I'd better come tell you. The judge needs to keep it as evidence until the case comes to trial. Or to a hearing, depending upon what he decides."

"Well, I would like to have it back."

"I understand. With all this sabotage going on. Oh, you'll be glad to know that Polly Sheldon is recovering. She's back at Small Delights."

"Terrible thing, that boiler blowing up like that," Catherine said. "Terrible accident."

"Yes," McIntyre said. "It's got John and Hattie pretty shook up."

"Oh?"

"Oh, yeah. In fact, John's upset enough that he's talking about closing down early this season. His nerves are about shot. I've been trying to help him, since he hasn't got many friends. I could only help him on my days off, of course. With the banker afraid to loan him the money for a new boiler he's just about out of business for now."

"Perhaps we could help?" Catherine said sweetly.

"Probably not," McIntyre said. "There's not that much to do. Moving stuff to the storage shed, that kind of thing."

"Ah!" she said, "I thought I noticed them moving boxes and crates."

Just happened to be looking through your high-powered binoculars, probably.

"Yes. You see, Hattie, she's still afraid of the lodge catching fire. That's her main fear. Keeps her awake at night. That's why I've been helping John. We've been moving most of his flammable inventory into that old storage shed. It's well away from the main lodge. All the summer supply of paper stuff—toilet paper, butcher paper, boxes of doilies for the dining room tables, his files and registration forms—plus a couple of five-gallon cans of cooking oil. And their whole supply of linens. Sheets, pillowcases. You know the kind of things it takes to run a place. Seems kind of silly to move it all that far away from the lodge, but it makes Hattie feel better."

"I once told the man that he ought to pull down that old storage building," Catherine said. "It's rather an eyesore. Good thing he didn't, I suppose. By the way, though, I have noticed your truck parked over at Small Delights. You seem to be there rather often."

Oh, oh. Think fast, McIntyre. If the plan is going to work, you'll need to be making regular visits to Blue Spruce Lake.

"Well . . . I'm looking into these incidents, of course. Somebody is causing mischief out there and I've been given the job of putting an end to it."

Weak excuse, he thought. *Got to do better than that.*

"And I guess you know the other reason," McIntyre said, looking down at his boots and fidgeting with the brim of his hat, which he was holding at his waist with both hands.

"Oh?"

"Well . . . Miss Sheldon is . . . that is, we seem to have a lot in common. If you know what I mean."

"I see," Catherine said. Her rouged lips tightened in a patronizing smile, a smile that was almost matronly. She had a little gleam in her eye as though she had just discovered a bit of information that could work to her advantage.

"I'm concerned about these men from Chicago," McIntyre said. "Are they still trying to buy Grand Harbor Lodge from you?"

"As a matter of fact, yes. But I've learned that they would

pay much, much more—more than double—if they could buy Small Delights at the same time. Speaking frankly, Ranger McIntyre, they do frighten me a little. They have a menacing air about them."

"Just between the two of us," McIntyre said, lowering his voice to convey a sense of confidentiality, "they're the ones who ought to be nervous. They threatened the banker and word got around. It's a tight little village and people don't take kindly to strangers trying to push people around. In fact, certain citizens—including a couple of summer residents—have talked about making up a posse to run the gangsters out of the valley. A posse of men armed with deer rifles. Chicago thugs might think they're pretty tough, with their Tommy guns and .45 automatic pistols, but they wouldn't have much of a show against a couple of our western boys hiding behind trees with deer rifles."

"Not even with a machine gun? I know for a fact that they have one."

"The thing about a Tommy gun," McIntyre explained, "is that it's only dangerous at very short range. Maybe two hundred feet. Same goes for a shotgun. On the other hand, a man with a deer rifle can pick you off at two hundred yards, if he knows what he's doing."

"I see," she said.

"I need to move along. I'll bring your rifle back when I can."

McIntyre started the pickup and headed for the approach road leading back to the main road, from which he would drive back into the woods again on the track to Small Delights. It would be easier if there were a connecting road between the two places. Such a road could be built, he reflected, but it would need to go right through that old storage building of John's.

He drove past the place where the falling log booby trap had been. That was a curious thing. They went to considerable trouble to set that trap, and yet there was no way it could have done any significant damage. The log was too small and the timing wasn't right. Maybe it was built by that character named Dink; he fancies himself to be quite the hunter and outdoorsman, but he's not very good at it. Or maybe the trap was ineffective because it was built by a man who was just naturally sloppy and inept. Maybe it wasn't supposed to do anything in the first place.

At Small Delights, he found Polly Sheldon in the dining room. Despite having her wrist in a cast and her arm in a sling, she was helping the waitress clear away the remains of lunch. There weren't that many tables to clean off, since all but three couples had checked out. Without the boiler, there was no heat in the rooms, and mountain nights are chilly. Nor was there any hot water in the rooms. Guests had to use the old central shower house behind the lodge where a woodstove kept a tank of water hot. For most of the paying customers it seemed too much like roughing it.

"Have you had lunch?" Polly asked McIntyre.

"Matter of fact, no," McIntyre said. "And I had an early breakfast. My stomach's threatening to end our relationship if I don't feed it real soon."

Polly laughed.

"Sit down," she said. "I'll whip up a couple of roast beef sandwiches. Or better yet, how about roast beef on toast, with brown gravy? Just take a minute."

"That would be grand!" McIntyre said. "I appreciate it."

She sat opposite him as he ate, sipping her cup of tea and indulging herself in a small helping of rhubarb cobbler. You couldn't grow much in the way of fruit when you lived in the mountains, but anybody could have a patch of rhubarb. Pie plant, the early gold miners called it.

"Well," McIntyre began, "I need your help. And I'm going to lay all my cards on the table. I'm hoping to see this whole Blue Spruce Lake affair wound up within the week. Everything settled, every piece in place so I can return to rangering."

"Shoot," she said.

"Pardon?"

"Go ahead. Lay out your cards."

"Oh. Okay. Well, the first thing you need to know is that you and I are becoming serious about each other. That's why my truck is frequently parked here. Or so Catherine Croker thinks. You're trying to impress me by playing detective and by showing me that you could take over the management of Small Delights, and I'm always making up excuses to drive out here."

"Sounds fun," she said. "Although if I really did set my cap for you, I think the FBI would probably step in. At least one particular FBI person."

"What?"

"Never mind. What else do you have to lay on the table?"

"For one thing, your aunt and uncle have friends we didn't know about. I've been canvassing the area, up and down the road, and came across a retired Englishman living in a cabin not too far from here, as the crow flies."

"That would be the major. Major J. Lee Angel. I've met him."

"Did you know that he and four or five other summer residents have a radio-telephone setup? Apparently, it's a hobby with them. These modern radio-telephones are quite the invention. No need to string wires from place to place. Their range is limited, but, according to Major Angel, this network of radio owners could raise a posse and come to our assistance on short notice."

"That's very nice to know," Polly said. "But why would we need assistance?"

Ranger McIntyre went on explaining his plan and how he

intended using the storage building and its "essential contents" as bait. If he had his villains figured right, his little decoy of boxes and crates would make an irresistible target. Catherine Croker must have been spying on Small Delights from her second-floor window; McIntyre was a hundred percent certain of it. And after seeing that marriage certificate on her wall he also knew who she was sharing information with.

"I think they'll try for it the next time we have a dark, rainy night. If I'm any judge of weather, that should be pretty soon. There's two more problems you could help with. Like I said, our saboteurs could decide to break into the storage shed and steal the supplies, in which case they'd find the boxes empty. I'd like you to help me and John fix up a yard light between here and the shed, and I'd like one of your upstairs rooms facing the shed where I could keep watch on it."

"All night? Every night until something happens?"

"Not all the time. My idea is to have a really dim light on in that room and rig my binoculars in the window sticking out between the curtains to make it look like someone is sitting behind it. I'll wake up every couple of hours and move things around."

"Then . . . you're going to use the storage shed as a trap, but want them to believe you're keeping it under surveillance. Won't that keep them from going inside?"

"Right. Exactly."

"How's that going to help?"

"Given their history up to this point? I think they'll try to sneak up to the far side of the shed, where it will be dark, and set fire to it."

"But that could start a forest fire! It could burn down both lodges!"

"Not if they pick a good rainy night. And we have rainy nights pretty often this time of year. But the idea of a fire brings up the second problem you could help with. We need to have John and Hattie gone. I want it to look like they're still here. If they're willing to go down to Denver for a few days, Vi Coteau has offered them a place. But we need to sneak them out of here and take them to Denver without anyone catching wise to what we're doing. And we need to leave their car here. We don't want anyone to suspect they've gone."

"Okay," Polly said. "Give me an hour to work on it. I'll telephone your Coteau friend and we'll hash out a plan. What's next on your scheme?"

"Next I need a reason to hang around here. Besides having a crush on you, I mean. With a crush on you, I'd be finding excuses to come here all the time. And I think I've got one. Excuse, I mean. Did you know that any owner of any private land within the borders of the national park is required to obtain a permit from the park supervisor before starting any major repairs, renovations, or additions?"

"I didn't know that, no."

"It's true. When the park was established, private land owners were allowed to keep their property but only if they signed an agreement not to make 'significant' changes. Our Chicago friends who are anxious to gain control of both Grand Harbor and Small Delights would probably tell us that they needed a connecting road. And that old storage building is sitting smack in the middle of the most obvious route."

"I understand. But how does that give you an excuse to 'hang around' Small Delights?"

"You need to arrange for a new boiler, and new plumbing for it," McIntyre explained, "which means that you need to ask the park for permission. To make a repair that extensive. We'd have to approve it for safety, see. I need to come out here a few afternoons and take measurements and study the options and evaluate the situation."

"Sounds reasonable."

"I think that the water well at Small Delights has been compromised, too."

"But it hasn't."

"We tell people that we think it has. We'll need to shut down the well while we have the water tested. But we don't want to hurt your business, so I'll lend you one of our fire-fighting trailers. Gasoline powered pumps on wheels, is what they are, with a hose reel. We'll put it down by your boat dock and use it to pump water from the lake to your water supply cistern. I'll need to be on hand to do that, since the pump is government property."

"And it will just happen to be there if the shed catches fire."

"You mean if the forest catches fire."

"Right. If the forest catches fire."

"I guess that's about all. You make the arrangements to have John and Hattie leave without being seen. I'll let the S.O. know what I'll be doing the next few days."

"Okay," Polly said. "I've got one of Vi Coteau's cards. I'll telephone her and see if she can sneak up here and collect Uncle John and Aunt Hattie. And I'll let her know that you'll be spending several nights with me because you and I are having this torrid love affair. I'm sure she'd want to know."

"Uh . . ."

Chapter 13
McIntyre Fires Charlie
and Takes Polly Fishing

"Here, lemme help you with that."

Coming out of the barracks on his way to the showers, Ranger Charlie Nevis saw Ranger McIntyre manhandling a fire trailer into position behind his pickup truck.

"Kinda hard for one man to move these things," Nevis said.

"Thanks for the help," McIntyre agreed.

Charlie got behind the trailer and pushed while McIntyre pulled from the front until the trailer tongue latched down on the truck's drawbar. McIntyre straightened his back and looked at the remaining three trailers.

"Are you doing anything today, Charlie, other than your patrol route?"

"No, I guess not."

"Why don't you organize these trailers. Line them up side by side so we can back a truck up to the one we need and hitch it on. It's a waste of time and effort to have to pull one out and lug it to the truck when we could just as well bring the truck to the trailer. See if you can have it done by the end of the day."

"You can't ask me to move those trailers on my own," Nevis whined in his high-pitched voice. "The work crew's been leavin' early these days. You gotta give me time. Don't know why I always got to do that kind of stuff. Anyway, where you goin' with this one?"

"Blue Spruce Lake."

"Oh? Why?"

"That boiler explosion messed up John Frye's plumbing system. Now he's got it into his head that they polluted his well, too. We're going to pump water from the lake up to his cistern. Plus, having this thing stationed at Small Delights might make Hattie less nervous about fire. Help calm things down."

"Okay," Charlie said. "Anyway, we got three more fire trailers. And if we ever have a fire out toward Blue Spruce Lake we'll already have a pump on hand out there."

He stopped and scanned the sky like an Indian medicine man looking into the future.

"Not much danger of fire anyway," he went on. "Looks like we're in for another week of afternoon rains."

McIntyre was inspecting Charlie as Charlie talked. The morning was quiet. They were alone outside the barracks. It seemed to McIntyre to be a good opportunity to take care of another duty, one that Nicholson had assigned to him but which he had been putting off.

"Where are you supposed to be patrolling today, Charlie?" McIntyre asked.

"Over at Bear Lake, I guess. Inspect the outhouses, walk the trail around the lake, check the trail to Dream Lake. Talk to tourists. Lot of walking. Wish I could take a horse."

"You're not that good on a horse, not around lots of people. You might kill an innocent pedestrian. But I want you to listen to me. Listen real hard. First off, I've had complaints from citizens that you waste government time hanging out at lodges, asking questions about problems they might have and whether they might want to sell their places. It's not our business, and you need to stop. Today you do visitor information and trash cleanup at Bear Lake after you rearrange these fire trailers. Got it?"

"Hey! You can't talk to me . . ."

"Shut up, Charlie."

McIntyre was getting into the swing of the thing. It was like he had been waiting all summer to give Charlie Nevis a dressing-down.

"Second thing is this: when you shave in the morning, stand closer to the razor. Sometimes I see you on duty when your face looks like you haven't shaved in three days. The other day you had enough five o'clock shadow that you looked like a hobo. And go have a haircut this week."

"Listen, I shave all the time. But my beard grows fast . . ."

"Shut up, Charlie. Just listen. You need to press your uniform before you put it on. It always looks like you slept in it. And your boots are a disgrace to the park service. Polish them. I hate to talk like this to anyone, but honest to God at times you look like such a slob that I think you ought to be in coveralls and picking up trash instead of acting like a uniformed ranger. No, I take that back. Even in coveralls the road crew looks better than you."

Charlie had his dander up. When a man doesn't give a damn about how he looks and doesn't want to go to any trouble to look decent, nothing irritates him more than having another person call attention to it. He took the towel he had been carrying in one hand and threw it around his neck. As he started toward the barracks he thrust out his arm to push McIntyre to one side.

"Outa my way, Tim," he said in a growl. "I don't take no orders from you."

"You watch who you're shoving, Nevis!" McIntyre said.

Charlie turned and gave McIntyre an even harder shove to the shoulder.

"Or else what?" Charlie snarled.

McIntyre's reply was to grip Charlie's wrist, hard, and twist his arm up behind his back. Holding the arm there and grabbing the back of Charlie's belt, McIntyre propelled him toward the barracks door.

"Frame!" McIntyre called out. "Russ Frame! Ranger!"

Ranger Russ Frame opened the door to see Charlie Nevis, cringing in great pain and bent over the stair rail.

"Russ," McIntyre said, "Charlie here, he's finished. Fired. Gone. I want you to help him pack and watch him leave. Search his foot locker and duffel bag to make sure he doesn't take any government property with him. Clear?"

"Yeah, but . . ."

"But nothing. You can drive him into town. Or throw him in the river, I don't care which. When I come back I want to see his locker empty and his mattress rolled up. I'll stop at the S.O. on my way through town and see what kind of paperwork we need to terminate him."

Ranger McIntyre did not drive directly to town. Towing the fire pump trailer behind the pickup, he drove up the main road and went past the Fall River station without stopping. He parked outside Fall River Lodge and stomped into the kitchen, where Minnie March found him sitting at the little white table with a cup of coffee steaming between his shaking hands.

"Damn, but I hate losing my temper," he said. He told her about his encounter with Charlie Nevis.

Minnie sat down and put a comforting hand on his arm.

"What's got you on edge, Tim?" she asked.

"Ah, darn near everything. I've got these Chicago thugs hovering around like vultures circling carrion, and Hattie afraid of her own shadow, and John who just wants to dump everything and run away. And meanwhile I'm trying to work out a trap to catch whoever's been sabotaging the Small Delights and I'm not even sure it's legal for me to do it and I feel like I'm all on my own in the whole darn mess. Thanks for the coffee."

"Any time," Minnie said. "You know you do have Polly to help."

"Yeah. There's another thing to keep me on edge. Somebody had the bright idea of making it look like she and I are a hot item to give me a reason to hang around Small Delights. I'll tell you what that's like. Two seasons ago we had to catch a rogue bear, an old grizzly? I hauled the bear trailer out to where he'd been seen and I baited it with a quarter of a half-rotten elk carcass. I dragged the bait around in the woods to spread the smell everywhere. But then I realized that I was covered in the stink myself. I was out there in the woods alone without a gun, smelling like a bear's lunch, and no way to clean off the smell. That's what it's like."

"In other words," Minnie said with an amused look, "even if you ignore Polly after it's all over, people will still think that you and her . . ."

"Right," McIntyre said with a growl.

"And that lovely FBI lady, Miss Coteau, she would think that you . . ."

"Right again," McIntyre said. "Is there any more coffee?"

Supervisor Nicholson leaned back in his chair and regarded Ranger McIntyre with an expression that could be described as entertainment mixed with disbelief. Dottie, standing beside the supervisor's desk, looked equally puzzled.

"You're telling me," Nicholson said, "that you fired Charlie Nevis? You fired him? Exactly who gave you authority to terminate any rangers? I know he goes around looking like a bum and he's been doing strange things lately, but I'm the one to fire him. Not you."

"He pushed me."

"You told him he's fired because he pushed you? Tim, I wish you rangers would learn to play nice with each other. I'm already walking a tightrope with the boys in Washington, trying to show them that we've got what it takes to keep this national park running smoothly while at the same time asking for more money and resources. And what happens? One of my 'resources' fires another one because he pushed him. I look around for a ranger and here's one of them off fishing and another one spending his time trying to make real estate deals with guest lodges. One fires the other one and right in the middle of tourist season I come up short one ranger. Because of you. And you're supposed to be making life easier for me by clearing up that mess out at Blue Spruce Lake, not fighting with other rangers. What the hell were you doing at the barracks anyway?"

"Picking up a fire pump."

"And if I'm not being too nosy about the national park I'm in charge of, what exactly is on fire? Where are you going with a fire pump?"

"I'm taking it out to Blue Spruce Lake."

"The lake is on fire? Or maybe the forest is burning down and you thought you'd stop by the office for a chat and 'oh, by the way, I fired Ranger Nevis.' "

"It's just a precaution, Nick," McIntyre said. "I think that our saboteur is going to set fire to John Frye's old storage shed."

"And why would he do that?"

"Or she."

"Or she. Why would she do that?"

"Because they think that all of John's supplies for Small Delights are stored in it. If they burn up, he'll be out of business."

"And why do they think that?" Nicholson asked.

"I guess it's because I told them."

A long and uncomfortable silence followed. Supervisor Nicholson stood up, walked to the window, walked back to the chair, and sat down again.

"Dottie," he said, "open McIntyre's file. Take out that sheet of paper where I listed all the reasons I should have him transferred to Death Valley. Do you spell 'entrapment' with one *p* or two? And add 'encouraging arson of private property on federal land.' You might as well keep the file open on your desk because I'm sure I'll soon have something else to add. Now, Ranger McIntyre, explain what's going on."

"Yessir," the ranger said. "You know how you're out there fly fishing, and you know there's a great trout hiding in a deep pool, but he's too smart to rise to a little dry fly? So maybe the thing to do is tie on a really large fly, like a Number Six Black Gnat, and keep flicking it over him until he's mad enough to attack it. He's not hungry, but that fly riles him up. Well, sir, I came across a missing piece of the puzzle the other day, and now I think I know who the culprit is. I think firing Charlie Nevis will make them just angry enough, or frustrated enough, to show their muscle. The logical thing would be for them to torch John Frye's supply shed. I plan to catch them at it."

"You expect me," Nicholson said, "you expect me to go along with this Nevis thing? When he comes storming in here and demands to know how the hell . . . excuse the language, Dottie . . . how the heck you have the authority to fire him, I'm expected to tell him you do have the authority and I can't stand in the way?"

"That's about it, yes."

"I suppose I'm also expected to approve of you sleeping and eating at Small Delights when the government provides you with a cabin and grocery allowance? Small Delights, I should add, where there's an unattached young female in residence?"

"Yessir."

"You're going to get both of us transferred to Death Valley. I hear that the fly fishing is really lousy there."

"Might be."

"All right," Nicholson said. "All right, let's fire Charlie Nevis. His performance hasn't been all that good, anyway. Just between you and me, I wasn't going to rehire him next season if he didn't shape up. Take your fire pump trailer. Go stay at Small Delights. Distribute cans of gasoline and handfuls of matches if you want to. Maybe both those damn lodges will burn to the ground and the forest along with them. That way Frye would be gone, Croker would be gone, the Chicago gangsters would be gone, and I could put you to work replanting the damn forest. All by yourself. Have at it. Go do it. Enjoy yourself. Get out of my office."

McIntyre put on his hat, carefully squared it to his head, came to attention, and gave his boss a smart military salute.

"Will comply," he said. "And thanks."

Dottie looked at Supervisor Nicholson. He shook his head. She shook her head. Together they watched the tall ranger walk out of the office and across the parking area to his pickup truck.

Polly stood over Ranger McIntyre. He was on his knees, clamping a brass tube onto the end of the fire pump hose. To Polly it looked like a giant nutmeg grater.

"What's that for?" she asked.

"Foot valve," he replied. "It keeps junk from getting into the hose. More important, it keeps water from running back down and into the lake after we turn the pump off. Otherwise we'd lose the prime and have to refill the hose by hand."

He dipped up buckets of water and poured them down the hose, connected the hose to the pump, and slid the end out into the lake.

"That ought to do it," he said.

He wound a rope around the starter wheel, gave it a hard pull, and the engine came alive with a throbbing roar. They watched the canvas hose swell up as water began to flow up to the storage tank at the lodge.

"I like this!" Polly shouted above the noise of the engine. "It really feels like we're doing something! Not just sitting around, really making things happen!"

She went up the hill to keep an eye on the rising water level in the tank, even though it would be tricky to climb the ladder with her arm in a sling. When the water reached the overflow pipe she waved to McIntyre to shut off the pump. Proud of herself, she used her good hand to drag the hose out of the tank and dropped it to the ground. The ranger came up with the fire nozzle as she was descending the ladder.

He screwed the nozzle onto the hose and brushed the dirt and sand from his hands.

"Good job," he said. "Now we wait. It looks like rain, too. Good."

"That is good," Polly said. "Now, what else do we need do so your 'visit' looks normal? If you were here because you're sweet on me, what would you do next?"

"Heck, I don't know."

"Well, would you leave and go straight back to your ranger station, for instance? If you were sweet on me, I mean."

McIntyre consulted his watch.

"Probably not," he confessed. "It's close to quitting time anyway. I suppose I'd figure out an excuse to take a walk with you. I guess I'd be hoping you'd ask me to stay to supper, too."

Polly laughed.

"You're very predictable, Mister Ranger! Have you ever had a romance that didn't involve food?"

"There's one thing that might look like I was planning to stay."

"What's that?"

"I've got my overnight kit in the truck."

"Say!" she said. "Let's go fishing! In the boat! It's not going to rain for a couple of hours yet. We'll row out far enough that they can see us from Grand Harbor Lodge. If they keep watching us it might distract them if Vi Coteau shows up to collect Uncle John and Aunt Hattie. You slide the boat into the water and bring it alongside the dock while I go borrow a couple of Uncle John's fishing rods."

It wasn't McIntyre's kind of fishing. He preferred stalking a mountain stream, staying concealed, spying out the most likely places where the trout would be feeding, planning each cast carefully, anticipating every little twig or branch that might snag his fly. Sitting in a boat with a fishing rod, however, there was nothing to do except sit there. You either used bait, in which case you just sat and sat and sat watching a red and white striped bobber, hoping it would vanish under the surface, or you used a lure. With an artificial lure, there was nothing to do but keep throwing it into the water. It would sink out of sight and you didn't know what it was doing down in the depths. There was always the chance that your next cast would snarl the line on the reel and you'd need to spend ten minutes untangling it.

Polly was enjoying herself. She slipped her arm out of the sling and used the hand with the cast on it to hold the rod while she operated the reel handle with the other. So far she had only snarled her casting reel once.

"The trick," she told McIntyre, "is to let your spoon sink all the way to the bottom. You retrieve it with quick little jerks to make it imitate a crippled minnow trying to swim to the surface."

"Great," McIntyre said unenthusiastically.

The lake was calm and there was no wind. Like a blue mirror, the water reflected the snow-tipped peaks and the tall spires of the spruce forest. Everything everywhere seemed dead still, resting quietly in the oddly pervasive silence that often precedes a rainstorm in the mountains. The skies were beginning to darken with gray clouds; in about two hours a rain shower would begin, soft at first, gradually becoming harder. The rising wind would drive the rain hard into the trees and against the walls of the buildings.

Polly reeled in, changed hands, lifted her rod tip, and with a nice flick of the wrist sent her lure flashing through the air again. McIntyre gave his own casting rod an unenthusiastic little twitch and slowly cranked the reel handle.

"Well," Polly said, "what about you and this gorgeous FBI lady, anyway?"

"What about it?" McIntyre said.

"She always asks about you. I think she's pretty interested."

"We like each other," McIntyre said. "Maybe she told you how we met. It was during that murder case? The one with the lady photographer? And a victim wearing only underpants? Vi was real helpful with that one. We worked together really well. She said I ought to apply to work for the FBI."

"In the city," Polly said.

"Yeah, I suppose."

"Not you," she said. "You, living in a city? You'd be the unhappiest man alive."

McIntyre thought he felt a tug on his line, but it was probably just the lure catching on a weed or rock. He looked at Polly. From the expectant expression on her face he guessed that she was waiting for an answer to an unasked question.

"Anyway," he said, "there's nothing serious going on with us. Plus, it always seems kind of pointless to talk about where a man might live and what he might do if this or that happened."

"You know what you ought to do?" she said. "If you can find a mental hospital or veteran's clinic that offers a self-report inventory test you should take one and find out what you have the most aptitude for and what you really want out of life. I took one when I was all at loose ends and it helped enormously."

"I'm not at loose ends. I like my job, I like this little village. I even like most of the people, most of the time."

"That's all right then. All I know is that I learned interesting things about myself when I took it. The test I took included a two-day course in the psychology of personality."

"I think you have a bite," McIntyre said, pointing at her bending rod tip.

Polly reeled in her line and released the eight-inch trout from the hook. McIntyre said nothing, but he was thinking that if they had been fly fishing on a stream they could have filled their limit by now. On a stream, you can avoid catching the little ones if you know what you're doing.

"For instance," Polly said, making another long cast into the lake, "we were told about this psychiatrist named Jung. Now, his theory about what you and I were talking about . . ."

"What were we talking about?" McIntyre asked.

"Your love life," Polly said.

"Oh, that."

"This Doctor Jung, his theory is that a person is attracted to a person of the opposite sex when that person is the kind of person that the first person would like to be if he or she were of that sex."

"Huh?"

"In other words, if you were a woman . . ."

"God help the world," McIntyre said.

"If you were a woman, you would want to be like Vi Coteau. That's why you're attracted to her. If you were female you'd want to be tall, very attractive, and extremely independent, have terrific taste in clothes, and have the kind of mind that loves to investigate problems and puzzles."

177

"Maybe I'd want to be like my friend Minnie March, who owns Fall River Lodge. She's comfortably chunky, she doesn't have to worry about latest fashions and makeup, works with people, has terrific breakfasts at her own little table, can take off and go fishing in a creek that runs past her door, very savvy about making money."

"Right," Polly said. "That might be you, too. If you were a girl. At least you see Doctor Jung's point, don't you?"

"Then," McIntyre said, "if you were a man, is there a man you'd like to be like?"

"What kind of man do you think I'd like to be? What do you think?" she countered.

"I think we'll turn this boat a little bit for a better view of Grand Harbor Lodge. That long black car just pulled up."

McIntyre made an easy sweep of the starboard oar and brought the rowboat around enough for Polly to see the lodge and the dark sedan. Two men got out of the front of the car and two others exited from the rear.

"I see four of them?" Polly said. "I thought the one who tried to shoot you was in jail."

"He is," McIntyre replied. "That fourth man ain't him. Unless I've read the clues all wrong, that fourth one is our troublemaker. That's Charlie Nevis."

The four men went up the steps to the porch. It looked like somebody had come out to meet them, although the porch was too shadowy to tell what was actually happening. From the way they were standing around on the porch, it looked like they were having a conference.

McIntyre turned and scrutinized the heavy clouds that had begun to gather above the mountain range.

"We'd best be heading back to the dock," he said.

He reeled in his line, hoping that no fish would grab the lure. He handed the rod to Polly and swung the oars out to begin rowing. Polly sat on the other seat watching him row while she took the lures from the lines and secured both fishing rods.

"How did you recognize Charlie Nevis?" she asked. "I couldn't see his face."

"His posture, for one thing. He hasn't got any. He probably bummed a ride with them. Charlie hasn't got a car."

"What do you suppose they're talking about over there?" Polly asked.

"Arson, I hope. It looks like it could rain tonight, which I think is what they've been waiting for. To burn up your Uncle John's 'supplies,' I mean, without setting fire to the forest. Catherine wouldn't approve of it if her scenery got spoiled."

"What are you saying? Am I hearing you correctly? Are you thinking that Charlie Nevis is working for those Chicago thugs? And he's working for Catherine Croker, too? You think Charlie sabotaged the garbage truck and set up the electric wire and released that bear and everything?"

"Yup. He even tried to incriminate Russ Frame by dropping the .303 Savage cartridge case in the woods behind Small Delights. He wanted me to think that Russ had moved the bear trap trailer, too, but it was pretty clear that Russ had nothing to do with it."

"You could tell? How?"

"Whoever returned the trailer left it sitting cockeyed. They put it back where the other utility trailers are, but didn't straighten it. Russ is a very fussy guy, very neat and organized. Russ would have parked it meticulously. Charlie would just stick it anywhere and leave it there. I didn't absolutely know it was Charlie, of course. You're the one who gave me another clue."

McIntyre went on rowing steadily. *Good exercise,* he thought. *I should do it more often.*

"I gave you a clue?"

179

"I ruled out Russ Frame. Everything was too sloppy to be his handiwork, from the electric grid and the lost cartridge case to the harmless deadfall. I was thinking it had to be one of the Chicago boys, except I couldn't figure out how they would learn that there was a bear in that trailer at the barracks. If it wasn't one of the gangsters and it wasn't a ranger, who the heck did it? That's when I remembered where I'd see the kind of wire that was used to rig the deadfall log. Black stovepipe wire. Very handy stuff. We keep a half-dozen spools of it at the barracks workshop."

"But you said I gave you a clue?"

"After you got hurt, you told me to look for the wire that had been twisted around the boiler's safety valve. Remember? You said it was blue wire. I looked around and found a piece of it near the boiler and you were right. Blue. It was blasting wire. Dynamite wire."

"So . . . ?"

"The construction crew has been blasting on the new Bear Lake Road project. Whenever you go up here, which for a ranger is at least once a week, you're apt to come across pieces of blasting wire. They run it from the dynamite charge to a safe place at a distance and set it off with an electric magneto box. After the blast, there's a hundred feet of wire half-buried in broken rock and rubble. When you're out hiking and see a length of it lying there you just naturally pick it up, coil it, put it in your pocket. It's just what a man does. I don't know any man who can resist picking up lengths of wire. Kind of a pack rat instinct."

They were coming close to the dock; Polly got the mooring line ready.

"And that's what made you certain it was Charlie Nevis?" she said.

"I never heard of the Chicago bunch going up to Bear Lake.

There's nothing up there that would interest them. But a ranger's up there every week."

"And my bit of wire convinced you that Charlie Nevis is involved in all this sabotage."

"No. What clinched it was a marriage license."

"A marriage license?"

"It was while I was snooping around Grand Harbor Lodge," McIntyre said. "I saw a marriage certificate Catherine has hung on her wall. It gives her maiden name as Catherine Nevis. Charlie's her brother. I'm convinced that Catherine and Charlie have been in cahoots the whole time because they wanted Small Delights. It would give them an exclusive monopoly on lodgings at Blue Spruce Lake. When those Chicago thugs showed up and offered huge amounts of money if they could take over both places, Catherine and Charlie probably figured they would be set for life once they forced John and Hattie to sell."

Polly steadied the boat while McIntyre stepped out onto the dock and tied off the mooring line. He held the boat with one hand and offered her the other as she disembarked. Just as she set foot on the dock, dark spots began speckling the wooden planks. Raindrops were dimpling the lake.

"Here comes the rain," he said. "Better make a dash for the lodge."

As they hurried up the hill, Polly kept talking.

"And if Catherine sold out to the Chicago men, or stayed there to run the operation for them, neither she nor Charlie would have to worry about money. Which is why he didn't seem to care about keeping his ranger job, right?"

"That's what I'm thinking," McIntyre said. "After they can get rid of John and Hattie, Catherine and Charlie are on Easy Street. It still made Charlie mad as hell to have me fire him, though."

CHAPTER 14
RANGER FRAME AND THE MAJOR DEAL THEMSELVES IN

The rain kept falling gently into the early evening hours while Ranger McIntyre and Polly Sheldon maintained their vigil from the upstairs room. Using a small flashlight, Polly went to the kitchen and brought back sandwiches and lukewarm coffee and they ate and waited. In a dark corner of the hallway a clock ticked off the minutes and then chimed the hour and still nothing happened.

"Why don't they come?" McIntyre said. "You'd think this was an ideal night for it."

"Maybe they were just tired and went to bed," Polly whispered.

"Maybe," McIntyre agreed. "Or maybe it's like fishing. Once in a while, you know the fish are there and the conditions are right and yet they just don't rise to the lure."

The clock softly chimed midnight and McIntyre needed to stretch his legs. He rose, took his rubber rain cape from the back of the chair, and felt his way out of the room, down the stairs, and outside into the inky damp blackness. He scanned the Grand Harbor Lodge with his binoculars, but at first there was nothing to see except for the black sedan parked under the single yard light and a bit of light coming from inside the lodge. Probably a night lamp at the reception desk.

After a minute or more he saw it: a shadow. A shadow moving behind the silhouette of the black sedan. Part of the car's silhouette changed as though the trunk lid had been opened.

Too far away to tell. Maybe one of the gangsters had gone to the car for a bottle. There was a little flare of light like a penlight might make, and after a couple of minutes, it flicked off. The sedan's silhouette no longer showed an open trunk lid. The moving shadow dissolved back into the dark.

Staying in the dark shadows of the spruce trees, McIntyre crept closer to the lake and lay down behind a log to scan the shoreline with his binoculars. The clouds had drifted off and the stars came out. There was enough mountain glow for him to see whatever might move between the glassy water and the shoreline. He saw a deer come down to drink from the lake. A few trout made splashing noises as they fed on night bugs, but otherwise all was quiet. Boring, uneventful, and quiet. After what seemed like at least two hours, the ranger had had enough of the damp cold: he decided to pack it in and catch a few hours' sleep.

Living alone, McIntyre was unaccustomed to being awakened by the smell of fresh coffee and frying bacon. It took him a moment to remember where he was. Polly must have gotten up at first light to make breakfast for the lodge's remaining guests. He looked out of the window and saw the old storage shed still standing in the distance. He checked it with the binoculars and could see nothing amiss, no footprints in the damp earth, nothing.

McIntyre shaved with cold water, put on his uniform, gave his boots a quick once-over, and went downstairs. Imagine his surprise when he walked into the dining room and saw himself already sitting at the small table next to the kitchen door. If it wasn't himself, it was practically a mirror image. Uniform, shined boots, military haircut—and a table fork poised above a steaming omelet.

"Frame?" McIntyre said.

"Guilty," said Ranger Russ Frame. "Can I make you an omelet? Won't take but a minute."

"Yeah, later. First, why don't you tell me what you're doing here?"

Polly came out of the kitchen with the coffee carafe and a white mug, which she set on the table across from Ranger Frame.

"Good morning, Tim," she said cheerily. "Sit down, have a cup. I'll bring your toast. Omelet?"

"Yeah, sure," McIntyre said.

"You look surprised," Frame said. "I guess I gotcha this time."

"I guess," McIntyre said.

"Well, sir," Frame continued, "I got to thinking about this whole situation with these guys from Chicago. And Polly being out here with nobody but John Frye to help her. And I got to thinking about Charlie Nevis. He's been acting really strange, been acting all palsy-walsy with Mrs. Croker and those guys in the long black car. Anyway, I was at the S.O. and asked Dottie where you were—I needed your signature on a requisition form—and she said you were out here at Blue Spruce Lake keeping an eye on things for a few days."

"And you volunteered to help? When you were in the Army, didn't you learn never to volunteer for anything?"

Frame laughed and took another bite of omelet.

"Sure," he said. "But things were more interesting when you volunteered."

"Did you drive out this morning?"

"Last night. I left my truck hidden beside the main road and walked in. I did a little snooping around Grand Harbor first."

"Maybe I saw you over there. With my binoculars, about midnight. Looked like somebody with a penlight?"

"Probably me. I thought I was being too sneaky for anybody to spot me. I was up to something I learned in the trenches, over in Europe: if you see a chance to reconnoiter the enemy's weaponry, take it. See, I figured that if Charlie was involved, mad as he was at you, they might come at you during the night. Beat you up, at least. Figured I'd look for that heavy artillery they're supposed to have in the trunk of that car. Rumor has it that their car trunk is crammed full of guns. After that I got myself into position where I'd be behind them if they tried anything, see?"

"Seems a little too imaginative, but okay," McIntyre said.

"Back a couple of weeks ago," Frame continued, "Charlie was bragging how he'd seen what his Chicago friends have in the trunk of that sedan. They had a double-bore shotgun and a Thompson submachine gun in there, he said."

"I knew about that."

"Well, sir, I figured it might be worth a try to spike their guns for them. In case any shooting broke out."

"You know what, Frame? You figure too much. I mean, I like how you always have a plan and all that, methodical and everything, but . . ."

"Hey, I can't help it. Anyway, last night I had a chance to look into that trunk and sure enough, there they were. See this?"

Russ Frame put his hand into the pocket of his tunic and brought out a handful of .45 cartridges, stubby, heavy things with polished brass casings and bright silver lead bullets that gleamed in the light. He put them on the table beside his plate and reached back in his pocket for a small wad of modeling clay.

"You swiped a few bullets," McIntyre said. "That should be a help. Those Tommy gun magazines hold . . . what? Twenty or thirty rounds?"

"Twenty." Ranger Frame chuckled and pushed the bullets around with his finger. "I didn't just swipe them. I replaced the first half-dozen, the ones on top. Oh, by the way, when I was getting ready to mess with their guns I needed to buy a box of .45 ammo. Supervisor Nicholson said he'd charge it against your salary, along with the gasoline you've been using to drive out here all the time."

McIntyre gave Ranger Frame a long searching look. He was a very calm, very methodical young man. Quiet and effective. McIntyre had seen the same characteristics in certain men during the war. During German air attacks on the aerodrome the steadiness of those men had meant the difference between chaos and order, even between life and death.

"So then," McIntyre said, "Nick knows you're here, too."

"Yup. Mostly he wants to know more about what you're up to, but he's kinda concerned over your safety. He figures this whole thing is going to bust open in the next few days. Oh, and there's another thing. While I was out there in the woods I ran into Major Angel."

"The British guy."

"Right. Complete with dark clothes, a face hood, and that Enfield .303 rifle. He thought he'd keep an eye on our Chicago friends for a few nights. From what he said, I think he's worried about Polly. Said she's about the same age as his daughter. He said he dealt himself into the game because things have been pretty boring lately."

McIntyre finished his coffee and reached for the carafe.

"Well, Ranger Frame," he said, "is there anybody else wandering around with guns that I might like to know about? FBI agents, maybe the Marines?"

"Nope, that's it. Oh, Supervisor Nicholson did tell me that David Kersey hadn't exactly told him the whole story about being threatened by the mob."

"The banker? Hardly a mob. With Dink in jail it's down to three men."

"Supervisor Nicholson assumed that the Chicago guys had come to the bank. But it was up at the Kersey house. Mr. Kersey came home from the bank one evening and found them in his living room, scaring the wits out of his wife and his little girl. That's where they told him not to loan any money to John Frye."

"In his own house, threatening his family," McIntyre said.

"Yup."

"And the major knows this?"

"Yup. The major doesn't hold with criminals walking into a man's home and intimidating his family. Besides which, Mr. Kersey's a friend of his. They play chess together. Another reason he's taking a personal interest in the Chicago bunch. Three or four of the other cabin owners have joined him. Did you hear about their shortwave radio club? If you ask me, I think those Chicago thugs will wish they'd stayed at the hotel in town. They might not make it out of Blue Spruce Lake alive."

After finishing his breakfast, McIntyre went to the front desk and phoned the S.O. Supervisor Nicholson harped on the same old string: restore things to normal at Blue Spruce Lake, and try to do it without killing anybody.

The next phone call was going to cost the park a long-distance charge, but McIntyre didn't care.

"FBI Denver, Vi Coteau speaking."

Hearing her voice was like a jolt of strong coffee, or like that first morning breath of outdoor mountain air that fills the chest and relaxes the shoulders.

"Good morning," he said. "This is the National Park Service. You were seen picking wildflowers and we're coming to arrest you."

"Bring your handcuffs," she said. "And bring that cute ranger, the one who doesn't do anything except eat breakfast and go fishing."

"Hi, Vi. It's me."

"Hi yourself. What's happening up there in your little mountain paradise?"

McIntyre briefed her on the situation and how he was still planning to use the old storage building as a trap to catch the culprits, whoever they might be, in the act of stealing or arson.

"Be careful," she suggested. "Those gangster types might not go down easy. You might wave your revolver at them and they'll just laugh and start shooting. You wouldn't believe the gun fights that happen in Chicago."

McIntyre asked her about the Fryes.

"Doing fine," she said. "John went looking for a job yesterday. He got two or three very good prospects in addition to the one that Hattie's brother offered him. Hattie's going to paint the kitchen and bedroom in my little rental house. They're both really happy. They even found out they can take the trolley from my house to the city park. But tell me how you're doing at Small Delights! Is it delightful even without me?"

McIntyre loved the way she always had a little note of fun in her voice, how she always seemed too classy, too smart to take everything seriously. He told how he was roughing it at the Small Delights Lodge, with no hot water or steam heat. Staying awake long hours to watch his "trap." And as he was talking about boilers and water and sabotage and all, a question struck him and popped out of his mouth before he could stop it.

"Why blow up the boiler?" he said.

"What?"

"If they want to take over Small Delights and run it as a speakeasy or gambling joint," he said, "why would they ruin the hot water supply? Wouldn't they be needing it?"

"Maybe they saw an opportunity to cause damage and push John closer to quitting."

"If that's the case, they're not thinking very far ahead," Mc-

Intyre said. "But I think they do plan ahead. Maybe I'll ring off for now and call you back later on. I need to mull this over in my mind."

"In your mind? Where else would you mull something? Can't you mull while talking to me?" she purred.

"Not a chance," he said.

"I'm glad! Talk to you later."

" 'Bye."

McIntyre got his fly rod from the pickup and walked out to the end of the boat dock, stopping to inspect the fire pump. The knife scratch on the fuel cap still lined up with the scratch on the tank and the bit of thread was still stuck to the drop of pine sap on the starting handle, which let him know that the pump hadn't been messed with since he tested it.

A few trout were breaking the surface of Blue Spruce Lake, most of them well beyond the reach of his fly line. A couple of six-inchers came up to take his Rio Grande King, but he flicked it away from them. He wasn't really there to catch trout anyway: to him, fly fishing was a necessary part of the thinking process, the only way to put his mind into the proper mode for puzzles. He had tried to explain this to Supervisor Nicholson when he caught him fishing on duty one day, but Nicholson wasn't buying it. "Goldbricking," he called it.

From the end of the dock the ranger could keep an eye on Grand Harbor Lodge as well as Small Delights and the storage shed in between, but he didn't think the mob would try to take the shed in broad daylight. But that boiler thing, that was what he needed to figure out. If Catherine Croker was in on the plot to take over Small Delights, she wouldn't want to destroy the hot water system. Didn't make sense. And it would be expensive to replace. McIntyre knew there was no one in the village equipped to do it. The village had one plumber who could take care of your septic tank or put new leathers in a pump, maybe run a water line from your well or cistern, but McIntyre was pretty sure he wouldn't be up to the task of installing a boiler system.

They would have to bring pipe fitters up from Denver to do that.

Or Chicago.

A mob connection? Tough guys who dig drainage ditches and handle heavy iron pipe? Guys who were handy with pick and shovel and blowtorches, and with their fists? An excuse to bring a small army up to the village?

McIntyre turned his back on Grand Harbor and practiced a few roll casts in the opposite direction. The end of the dock was a good place for roll casts, since there were no obstructions behind him or beside him that could snag the fly. Up came the tip of the long, supple bamboo fly rod to the eleven o'clock position. A snap of the wrist brought it down smartly, like an Air Corps salute, propelling a tall circle of line rolling across the water like a kid's hoop going down a sidewalk.

For a moment, his mind strayed back to a sunshine day of spontaneous laughter and giggles, the day when he had tried to teach her how to make a roll cast. They had hiked up to a certain small lake he knew about, a lake without a name, where they could be alone with one another and with the mountains.

"Look," he had said, as they stood side by side and knee-deep in the icy water, "imagine you have a little apple impaled on the end of the rod, okay?"

"I'm not fond of apples," she said, her eyes laughing, "how about an apricot?"

"Fine. Sure. An apricot. You have an apricot impaled on the tip of the rod. Now, you're going to bring the rod up, like this . . ." and he put his arms around her to demonstrate and it felt wonderful to feel her body pressed against him.

"You bring the rod tip up, and now you're going bring it down really fast and flick off the apple—I mean the apricot—and make it go sailing across the water, like you were skipping a stone."

"I can't do that."

"What?"

"Skip a stone. My brothers could do it, but I never could. They said it was because I throw like a girl."

"Are you going to try this cast or not?" McIntyre had said.

"I would hate to throw away a good apricot. Love apricots."

McIntyre made another rolling cast into Blue Spruce Lake and let the memory of love fade back off into the mountains. A formless idea began nagging at him, a piece of a picture that pulled him into the present moment. He raised the tip of the rod and did the cast again: again, the fly line formed a round loop that rolled across the water like the coil of a spring.

Like a coil.

An ol' coil. A copper coil.

He reeled in his line and secured the dry fly to the cork handle of the rod. If a gangster owned a remote lodge and cabins, and if he brought in pipe fitters and steamfitters to repair a hot water boiler, he wouldn't need permission from the national park or the county or anybody. To build a new setup from scratch he would need permits and the park would impose lots of safety restrictions because of fire danger and visitor safety. But a replacement would be just a replacement. Nobody would need to inspect it.

McIntyre walked back toward the lodge.

If gangsters had the right connections—and they would—they might just install a backup tank for hot water and include a coil in it. Build a sheltering wall around the whole shebang and presto! You've got yourself a neat little whiskey still right in your backyard.

"A tuppence for your thoughts, Ranger?"

McIntyre turned to see the major approaching, a comfortably portly gentleman wearing tweeds and a hunting cap and carrying a walking staff.

"Hello, Major," McIntyre said. "No rifle today?"

"Can't have the enemy thinking we're ready for 'em now, can we? Rest assured, however; the Enfield is close to hand. But let me ask again: why the deep reverie? You look awfully thoughtful for a young fellow."

"I was just thinking how simple it would be to build a hot water boiler that could be used to run off a few dozen gallons of moonshine, from time to time. Bathtub gin without the bathtub."

"Ah, the dear old gin," the major said. "How I do miss the authentic article, flavored with the juniper berries of your ancestral highlands. Have to make do with the local product . . . but perhaps I've said too much."

"You mean you buy your liquor from our boy up the hill from Moraine Park," McIntyre said.

"Have to admit it. I do find it curious that you ranger fellows turn a rather blind eye to his distilling operation."

"His stuff is harmless. He knows what he's doing, you see. Without him, there would be three or four locals who would try making their own and probably poison all their friends. Besides the fire hazard. Horseshoe Park is a safe place for it. Besides that, from his spot on the ridge he can keep an eye on a lot of territory for us. Forest fires, poachers, gold prospectors. He's like a volunteer fire warden. If he boils up a little juniper juice and sells it to buy his groceries, where's the harm?"

"Ranger," the major said, "you're a good sort. Now . . . the lads and I are wondering where things stand in regards to the heathen invaders."

"Do you know Helen Peters?"

"The high school girl? She of the ample upholstery? Works for that Catherine Croker woman? Oh, yes. She walks for exercise and her walks seem to bring her straight to my kitchen door. Has a weakness for jelly scones, you see."

"That's her. She walked into the Small Delights kitchen early this morning and told Polly Sheldon that the Chicago men are making life miserable at Grand Harbor, but that she had heard them talking about burning down John's storage building."

"Are they, by God!"

"Tonight, if her information is right."

"Ah! And a good moon for light! You'd like me and the lads to surround the buggers and you'll take 'em into custody, eh?"

"Not my plan."

"Oh? Perhaps we should take a stroll to someplace less conspicuous than here. The Croker woman can see us with her telescope, where we are."

"You know about that? No, that's fine. As long as she can't read lips. It would be good for her to watch us and suspect that you and I are making plans."

"Go ahead."

"I phoned headquarters and got them to send my assistant ranger, Jamie Ogg. Right now, he's busy with an axe and saw on the main road. I told him to make it look like he's thinning the dead timber. But he's actually making a deadfall that will shut down the main road to the north, toward the village, if necessary. I want to frighten our Chicago thugs into making a run for it, see? And I want them to go south. It's a long and dark road to Denver in that direction. They'll be at it most of the night, if I've got it figured right."

"And you think you can put the fear into them? By yourself?"

"Pretty much, yes. I've got myself an ace in the hole, you see."

"Excuse me? Ace in hole?"

"You don't play poker?"

"Never learned, no. Understand it's quite popular out West."

"One of these days we'll need to take care of that gap in your English education," McIntyre said. "Anyway, I think I can send them down that road and I doubt if they'll ever want to come back."

"Where do we come in? The summer resident posse, I mean."

"Did you ever hear how we beat your British army during the Revolution? Hiding, shooting from cover, using marksmen instead of massed troops with short-range rifles?"

"Disgusting manners, if you don't mind my saying it."

"This little gang of Chicago tough guys, they're armed with short-range guns. Pistols. A Tommy gun, which is noisy and deadly at close range, but worthless at a hundred yards. A shotgun, maybe two. Now, if your riflemen were to be stationed strategically along the south road ready to do a little creative sniping, it might just hurry our friends along. Don't want to kill anybody, or even disable the sedan. Just let them know you're shooting at them."

"I see!" said the major, his eyes bright with eagerness. "Perhaps a bullet through the bonnet, a few into the boot! Dark, winding road, potholes in it. We could do it, Ranger McIntyre! I'll wager that the lads and I could make those brigands think there was a whole army of sharpshooters in the black woods."

"That would be fine," McIntyre said. "Just one other thing. If you see a fire over here at Small Delights, don't come running. Stay in position. We can handle the fire."

"Roger. Situation understood. We'll hold position. I'll just stroll homeward now. Gather a few of the lads and reconnoiter for good sharpshooter positions. Give the hoodlums a lively little going-away party. Tah!"

McIntyre watched the major walk away and saw a new spring in the old boy's step.

The ranger entered the lodge lobby to find Polly Sheldon speaking on the phone. She handed him the receiver.

"It's the FBI for you," Polly said.

He told Vi what he suspected about the boiler, and how they had learned that tonight might be the night when the gang makes their next move.

"Darn!" Vi said. "I hope I'm there in time."

"You're coming up?"

"Wouldn't want to miss the fun. I think I'll bring our type-writer."

"Typewriter?" McIntyre said.

"The Tommy gun we keep in the closet," she explained. "It's what they're called sometimes. Slang term. On full automatic a Tommy gun sounds like you're typing real fast on a typewriter. Only really loud."

"Nice of you to offer firepower," McIntyre said, "but we've got plenty."

"Maybe not," Vi said. "I've been on the phone to the Bureau in Washington. That guy you call the Boss, the Bureau is one hundred percent certain that he was part of the machine gun massacre in Detroit. They're pretty sure he shot up an office in Cincinnati with his Tommy gun, killed a secretary. Apparently, he keeps low, stays calm all the time, fades into the crowd, acts really quiet until he goes off on a shooting rampage. That's when he goes out of control. Dangerous."

"I'll watch out for him."

"I've got more information for you, too," she said. "That Charlie Nevis character, he's no lamb. If he's the one the Bureau thinks he is, the Army wants him. During a battle in France he left an officer severely wounded and went AWOL. They think he was the one who shot the officer. He apparently lied about his veteran status to apply for a job at Yosemite, too, and later he was suspected of assaulting at least two women there. The

Bureau would like it if you could send them a good clear photograph of him and fingerprints if possible. If that Grand Harbor woman really is his sister they would like to know about her, too."

"Oh. Well, at the moment I don't think I'd have time to ask him to sit for his portrait."

"Be careful of him. Hey, I'm looking at the clock. I don't think I have time to get there. Tell me your whole plan. Maybe at least I can see where it might go wrong."

"This is a party line," he said. "Better not."

"Okay," Vi said. "Oh! One more thing. You might be right about the boiler thing. Agent Canilly is certain that the Chicago mob has a number of 'legitimate' shops here in Denver where they can recruit muscle when they need it. And one of them is a boilermaker. And the cherry on your sundae, Ranger, is that that very same boilermaker sold tanks and coils and burners to a known moonshiner here in the city."

"Thanks, Vi," he said. "It sounds like maybe they're planning to build a still in our backyard. I'd better ring off now. Lots to do. Including supper."

"McIntyre, you be careful. Like I said."

"Don't worry. I won't eat too much. But I'm pretty hungry."

"Idiot. I mean be very, very cautious dealing with those thugs. Don't leave anything to chance. I don't want anything to happen to you. I'm starting to like you."

He put the phone back on the desk and floated toward the dining room. She liked him! Knowing that, he knew that nothing could go wrong.

Chapter 15
McIntyre Draws Fire

The long mountain afternoon descended into evening. The green of the forests on the slope across the lake became darker and darker until becoming black shadow. Only the dark points of the tallest spruce trees could still be seen sticking up into a cobalt sky, reflected in the calm surface of Blue Spruce Lake.

Ranger Tim McIntyre relaxed in a deck chair on the porch of Small Delights Lodge, a cold mug of coffee on the little table next to his battery lantern. There was nothing going on either in the lodge or out in the woods. He was content to sit and watch the lingering alpenglow over the lake. He could see everything he needed to see, even the old storage shack that stood between Small Delights and Grand Harbor. His world was at peace. His sworn duty and the mission of the National Park Service was to preserve and protect that peace, that primal world, for future generations to enjoy; evenings such as these always renewed McIntyre's passion for that mission. Thanks to the park service and the rangers, young people a hundred years from now would have the same pristine mountains, forest, and lake. No houses, no roads, no telephone poles. Just the wilderness as it had always been.

During the war, he saw the French landscape blasted and torn by the battle-mad hand of man. It made him sick to look down from the cockpit of his Nieuport biplane and see charred stumps where a forest had once stood, or bomb and artillery craters filled with sodden muck and mud mingled with the blood of soldiers, mud where no grass grew. It was a no-man's-land that God had forgotten, that even the grass had forgotten. The war ended, he exchanged his Air Corps uniform for that of a park service ranger, but he did not forget what a ruined land looked like. Sometimes he would hike to a promontory or ride Brownie to a remote alpine lake where he would try to take in the entire wilderness at once, all the green beauty. He opened his arms as if to embrace it and he would feel recharged, ready to do whatever was needed in order to keep humans from destroying it. He was not known to his friends as a very serious man, but when it came to keeping part of the natural world as it is, he accepted the mission with solemn dedication.

The darkness deepened. A chilled breath of air drifted over the porch. McIntyre heard footsteps behind him, followed by the scrape of another chair being drawn closer to his.

"It's getting dark," Polly observed. "Looks like there's a full moon coming up on the other side of the lodge."

"Yeah," McIntyre said. "I guess everything's all set in case they make trouble tonight. Poor Jamie Ogg! He's a game kid, you know? Dead game. He's got his sleeping bag and his shelter half and he's going to camp on that roadblock until he's needed. I told him he might hear shots or see fire. If he does, he's supposed to block the road. Good kid, Jamie."

"This is getting exciting," Polly said.

"I saw a couple of lights moving in the woods," McIntyre told her. "Over there, a couple of minutes ago. Must be the major and his posse of summer residents. Now, have you got your part ready? All rehearsed? Got your flashlight?"

"Don't worry," Polly said. "If it goes like you've planned, you're going to see the best bit of hysterical acting you've ever seen. A regular Camille, that's me."

A mountain mist drifting on the night air floated up from the lake's edge, passed over the lodge porch, and went on.

"It's been a wet week," Polly said. "Low fire danger."

"Really low," the ranger said. "If you were camping out in the woods tonight, you'd have a heck of a time starting a campfire."

"How would you do that, exactly?" she asked. "If you had to, I mean."

"It's not easy," McIntye said. "A lot of people pile up a stack of pine needles and pine cones and try to light it, but damp needles don't burn unless you pour gasoline on them. The thing to do is find yourself a spruce tree or a fir tree, one of those with the branches that droop down and make a kind of umbrella."

"And gather dry tinder underneath it," Polly said. "That's a good idea."

"No," McIntyre said. "In weather like we've been having, anything on the ground will be too damp, even under the trees. No, you reach up the tree. Up in a spruce tree you'll find lots of small dry branches you can break off. Build your fire teepee out of those. Keep an eye open for any dry blobs of sap on the trees. Any tree, pine, anything. Sap makes a good fire starter. If you look around you'll probably find pitch pine—it only takes a few splinters. Or if you find a juniper tree, strip off a length of bark and pull off the fuzzy fibers underneath. They burn really good. Put your pitch and your fuzzy cedar bark under the twig teepee and you're ready to light it. Make sure to have it sheltered from the wind, like up against a rock face."

"You make it seem almost cozy."

"Can be. Do you like camping rough?"

"God, no. Sleeping on rocks? Washing in icy cold creeks? Trying to cook over an open fire with smoke in your face? Not my idea of fun."

The sound of footsteps on the gravel road startled them.

"Who's there?" McIntyre said.

"A ranger," came the reply from the dark. "Frame."

Ranger Russ Frame stepped onto the porch, where the light from the window showed he was in uniform, complete with Sam Brown belt and pistol holster, and holding a battery lantern. His prized rifle, the lever action .303 Savage, was slung over his shoulder on its leather strap.

"Supervisor Nicholson thought you might appreciate backup if the gangster thing goes down tonight. I'm going to be around. Think I'll take a little moonlight stroll along the lake in the direction of Grand Harbor. I'll check in with you later."

"Stay out of sight," McIntyre said.

"I will."

McIntyre watched Frame dissolve back into the shadows. If Nicholson and Frame both knew what he was up to, how many more people knew about his trap? Maybe Ranger Frame had told about it in the barracks, and the word got back to Ranger Charlie Nevis. Or maybe . . . McIntyre's mind went back to the beginning of all this when he had found the .303 shell in the woods . . . maybe Frame is our guy after all. But the question was not about the quarry: the main question was whether the trap would work. Had the culprits already discovered that the "supplies" in the shed were nothing but empty boxes and crates? Did they know that Hattie and John were safe in Denver?

With Ranger Frame gone, the silence of the dark mountains returned. The full moon had risen clear of the forest and mountaintops. A yard light over at Grand Harbor Lodge made a long yellow streak out onto the lake. John Frye had put another yard light between the shed and the lodge, but it was so weak that it scarcely illuminated the front of the shed. There were no other lights to be seen anywhere except on the Small Delights porch, where a dim pool of yellow spilled from one of the dining hall windows.

"I had a phone call from Vi Coteau," Polly whispered in the dark.

"Oh?"

"She's arranged a job interview for me next week. She seems very eager to have me move to Denver. Or away from Rocky Mountain National Park, anyway."

"I hope she didn't mention that your Uncle John and Aunt Hattie are down there, darn it. Anybody can be listening in on these party lines."

"She was discreet. But I think it's kinda sweet how she wants to keep single women away from her mountain ranger friend."

"Polly?"

"What?"

"Shut up."

Ranger McIntyre relaxed in his chair and watched the moon's reflection playing on the lake. If his saboteurs didn't strike tonight, the major's posse would be disgruntled over having lost sleep for nothing. They might not want to try it again if it didn't happen tonight. On the other hand, he was thinking, it wouldn't be his first colossal mistake. He smiled at the memory of his first season with the park when a brown bear came out of hibernation too early and went prowling the village for food. McIntyre was on his way to church when he spotted the bruin ambling in the same direction. Hurrying to the little white church, he persuaded the congregation that they could form a human circle around the bear and contain the animal until he could lasso it and get it into a pickup and take it away. But the bear went into the church instead, ate the sandwiches and cakes the ladies had prepared for an after-service lunch, and went to sleep behind the pulpit.

The sermon was delivered outdoors that Sunday. The Ladies Aide Society didn't speak to him for weeks after.

Or there was the time, the following spring, when McIntyre

heard shooting, quite a few shots, and rounded up local businessmen to make a posse and surround the poachers. The first foray yielded nothing. But on the following weekend he heard the same thing, collected the same men, who would have rather stayed home doing weekend chores, deployed them in the forest and closed in on the shooting only to surprise a very embarrassed young drugstore clerk giving marksmanship lessons to a buxom young woman, the wife of a local carpenter.

And tonight, McIntyre thought, *I've got a citizen militia of riflemen out there in the woods, plus a ranger sneaking around with a deer rifle, a rogue ranger who may or may not be the culprit, and three Chicago gangsters toting a shotgun and Tommy gun in addition to their sidearms, and a nervous young lady with one arm in a sling. And here's myself thinking I might wrap up the whole situation in a single night.*

Polly heard his long, deep sigh and looked over from her chair.

"You okay?" she whispered.

"Sure. Dandy. Just dandy."

"Do you suppose that Miss Coteau is going to show up?"

"With a gun? God, I hope not. Too many guns out there already. If anybody starts shooting, the cross fire will be murder. She's worried because the guy they call the Boss has a reputation for flying off the handle and shooting at anything that moves. Let's just pray nobody pulls a trigger and starts a small war."

Polly shuddered.

"By the way," McIntyre said, "I wanted to say thanks. You know, for all the detective work. And all the help you've been to your aunt and uncle. Maybe when all of this is settled you and I could go take a look at your Curtiss Jenny."

"Yes, I'd like that," Polly said. "The Jenny's nothing special, but it is in good shape . . ."

"Shhh!" McIntyre whispered. "Listen!"

The scraping sound coming from the direction of the storage shed sounded like the door being dragged open. McIntyre and Polly stepped down off the porch away from the pool of light from the window and stood side by side peering into the dark. The dim illumination from the yard light cast someone's shadow on the shed wall. A faint yellow speck of light appeared at the door opening.

The figure carrying the flashlight had opened the shed door to look inside. The flashlight didn't give enough light for him to see that the two figures asleep on the two camp cots were nothing but rags and old pillows arranged under the blankets. In the dark, they looked like people.

McIntyre and Polly heard another sound, the clank of a steel can striking a rock or the lid of the can itself banging against the can. The person with the flashlight jerked around in surprise: in less than a moment the shadow on the wall had become a silhouette against bright flames showing through the cracks. The figure made a few tentative steps into the shed, yelled something, yelled again, then turned and ran out the door.

Charlie Nevis. No doubt about it.

"Shall I go into my act now?" Polly whispered.

"Not yet," McIntyre said. "Give it a minute."

As McIntyre had figured, the arsonist had chosen the back corner of the building, the corner that would be furthest from the door and hidden in the most darkness. The fiery glow crawled up the wall, becoming more intense every second. Now they could hear the crackling of the flames and could smell the smoke.

"We'll wait a minute longer," McIntyre whispered. "Let's stay over here in the shadows. We need to pretend we just woke up and realized there's a fire and came rushing out."

"Won't it look funny that we're fully dressed?"

"Damn. I didn't think of that. Hey, look what he's doing!"

Charlie Nevis was scurrying around the end of the shed, yelling as he went and waving his flashlight.

"Hey! Put it out! Stop! They're not coming out, dammit! Throw some dirt, get that fire out! They're still in there! They didn't get out! We've gotta help them!"

Charlie stopped at the corner, yelling at the unseen arsonist in the shadows. McIntyre signaled Polly to stay put and crept ahead, hoping to see who Charlie was yelling at. But before he got to that point, he heard the heavy *pop* of a handgun and saw Charlie duck for the cover of the shed's corner. Charlie pulled his own revolver and fired back.

Charlie stumbled back toward the doorway and looked in again, but the flames had reached the boxes and crates and turned the inside of the shed into a furnace. Charlie turned one way and then the other, obviously in a panic and not knowing what to do. He lurched back to the corner of the building, pointing his gun at somebody back there.

The fire burned through the wall planks and with surprising speed. Flame raced along the floor, licked up the door frame, and caught the front wall. Overhead the rafters were alive with crawling fire. One after the other, the beams burned in two and sections of roof began falling down into the inferno.

Before McIntyre could stop her, Polly went into her act. She ran toward the blazing building, waving her arms and screaming bloody murder.

"Aunt Hattie!" Polly screamed. "Uncle John! Oh, no! Aunt Hattie! Aunt Hattie! Uncle John! Oh, no! Oh, they didn't make it! Oh! Oh no!! Somebody help! Oh! Oh!"

A perplexed-looking Charlie Nevis turned toward her, but it was obvious that he had no clue what to do.

"What is it?" he managed to say.

"Aunt Hattie!" Polly screamed. She clenched her fists to her waist and doubled over in agony like a kid who's been punched in the belly. "And Uncle John! They were afraid the gangsters would set fire to the lodge to burn it down! They were sleeping in the shed where they'd be safe! Oh, no! *No!* They didn't make it out in time! They're dead! I know it, I know it!"

Nevis shielded his face with his forearm and tried to see into the shed even though there was nothing to see except flames and smoke. Burning rafters crashed down. Charlie jumped back from the eruption of sparks and embers.

Polly ran back toward McIntyre and pretended to trip. Down she went onto her belly, rolling like a kid on a lawn until she rolled into the shadow of the trees. Down she stayed. Looking to see where she had gone, Charlie Nevis saw Ranger Tim McIntyre instead, in full uniform and holding his .45 service revolver.

"I'm arresting you, Nevis. Arson and murder. Hand me your gun and be very, very careful. How could you do this? John and Hattie had nothing against you or your sister."

"It wasn't me!" Charlie Nevis cried. "It was them! It was them!"

"Damn you, Nevis!"

McIntyre would later testify that he didn't know who had shouted at Nevis. All he knew was that someone had, and in the same instant he had seen Vinny coming from behind the shed aiming his handgun in their direction. He brought his own .45 revolver up and dropped the arsonist, surprised to see Charlie fall as well. His bullet hadn't gone anywhere near Charlie. That's when he realized the Boss was charging toward them, shooting and cursing as he came. McIntyre went down on one knee and steadied his revolver to take a shot, but before he could squeeze the trigger there was a rifle shot. It came out of the dark woods off to his left. The Boss staggered a few steps forward, fell down, twitched once or twice in the light of the flames, and lay still.

"Who's that?" McIntyre called. He trained his revolver on the woods.

"A ranger," came the reply. Russ Frame. Frame and his .303 Savage.

The roar of an engine reached their ears. The driver of the gangster car was not going to stick around. The sedan tore away down the Grand Harbor approach road and straight toward Major Angel and his posse of citizen riflemen.

The two rangers hurried to where Charlie Nevis was sitting on the ground holding his leg and whimpering. Polly walked up to them, straightening her blouse and patting her hair into place. *She's quite the calm character*, McIntyre thought.

"I'll go get those gas lanterns from the porch," she said. You okay?"

"I'm fine."

From the distant moonlit woods bordering the main road came a burst of rifle shots. Several rifles, as if a half-dozen hunters had all spotted the same deer at the same time.

"I'd say your city pal is in trouble, Charlie," McIntyre said as he knelt down to look at Nevis's wound. Russ Frame retrieved one of the battery lanterns and held it steady while McIntyre used his pocket knife to cut the pants leg away. Nevis's skin was clammy and his eyes were staring. He was going into shock.

"The bullet didn't hit the bone," McIntyre said. "You're lucky, Charlie."

Charlie groaned.

McIntyre wrapped a bandanna over the wound and tore the pants leg into strips for a tourniquet. He was standing up again when Jamie Ogg came hurrying up.

"Did I miss anything?" Jamie asked.

"Well . . . the building's on fire. I shot the one they called Vinny. Somebody shot Charlie. Ranger Frame shot the Boss. Otherwise it's been a pretty quiet night. Oh, except for the major's friends shooting their deer rifles down along the main road. Where's your truck?"

"Parked on the Grand Harbor approach road. There's a trail through the woods right there."

By this time a trio of male guests from Small Delights had come to see what was going on. Catherine Croker and her manager, Thad Muggins, were hurrying from the direction of Grand Harbor.

"Did you move your road block out of the way?" McIntyre asked.

"Yessir. I towed the log off the road."

"Good. You and Russ put Charlie in your truck and take him into town to the doctor. If the doc says he's okay to travel, haul him on down to the county jail and book him for assault with a weapon, attempted arson, and attempted murder."

Another volley of rifle shots echoed in the distance.

In the east, the sky was turning from deep black to light gray. The full moon would be down behind the Rockies in about an hour. Deliberately and without any attempt to hide his disrespect for the woman who had probably caused all of this, McIntyre cast a cold look at Catherine Croker as she approached. He turned his back on her and went to take one of the gas lanterns from Polly. McIntyre's deliberate snub made Catherine veer off like a battleship making a turn at flank speed; she scurried to catch up with the two rangers who were leading her brother away.

"Polly," McIntyre said, "you think you could organize Mr. Muggins and a few bystanders into a fire brigade and start up the fire pump? I suppose we should dampen down the ashes. Maybe spray the surrounding trees in case any embers flew off into the woods."

"Sure!" Polly said. "I'll take charge of that. Afterward we can sit down to a nice peaceful breakfast."

The remainder of the morning at Blue Spruce Lake was relatively quiet. Catherine Croker returned to her lodge to telephone a lawyer for her brother, but she would be coming back to Small Delights to "settle this." A contrite Thad Muggins was helping hose down the remains of the storage shed with the assistance of a lodge guest who had always wanted to be a fireman. Polly supervised breakfast preparations in the Small Delights kitchen while Ranger Tim McIntyre sat at a table in the dining room with a mug of coffee.

He heard footsteps and turned to see Major J. Lee Angel and another man coming across the room toward him. He waved to two empty chairs at his table and got up to fetch the coffee carafe and two more mugs.

"Ah, just the thing!" the major said. "Hot coffee! What a night! Eh, neighbor?"

"A famous party indeed, simply famous!" the neighbor replied. "We're in your debt for the invite, Ranger McIntyre!"

"Are you going to tell me what happened?" McIntyre asked.

" 'Cannon to the left of them,' " said the Major, " 'cannon to the right! Into the valley of death . . .' Charge of the light brigade and all that. Pardon my excitement. Rather too much tea from the old flask whilst standing guard, I imagine. What happened is this. Our little band of neighbors, having had word by shortwave radio of a possible fracas that evening, took up positions along the main road leading south. The long, long road toward Denver? The moonlight was excellent! The light was good enough that when a large buck deer stepped across the road I was able to count the points on his antlers.

"Directly we saw the glow of the fire north of us and in a matter of minutes, as you had predicted, here came that bloody dark sedan. Heeding your admonition against killing anyone, our first sniper simply put a bullet into the boot, what you colonials call the 'trunk' of the sedan. Second man placed a shot very neatly through the engine bonnet—'hood'—which caused one side of it to pop open. The automobile began to accelerate until another sharpshooter put out one of its head-lamps. A fine shot. At which point your Chicago boy decided to make a stand! Auto skidded to a stop. He leapt out, flung open the boot, and came up with what appeared to be a shotgun and a bloody deadly-looking Thompson submachine gun."

"Was anyone hurt? Of your bunch, I mean?" McIntyre asked.

"Bless you, sir, not a scratch! With the shotgun, he took aim at the dark woods where we were, holding it by his hip you know. But when he touched the trigger the only thing we saw was a flash of fire and an explosion. When the smoke cleared he was still standing stock-still in the moonlight. We found the shotgun after he'd left. Totally wrecked. Barrel all burst and torn apart. Must have been something inside the barrel when he fired the thing, that's what we deduced."

"Modeling clay," McIntyre said.

"What's that you say?"

"Nothing," McIntyre said. "What about the Tommy gun?"

"That's another odd thing. Had that gangster in my sights, don't you see? What I mean is, if he began spraying us with Thompson bullets I was going to put him down with a .303 bullet in the leg. Or higher up. But the Thompson misfired, too."

"Misfired?"

"Surprised us, I assure you. Pointed the bloody thing in our direction and apparently pulled the trigger. We heard a popping noise, saw him fumbling around to recock the whatchacallit, loading lever, heard another pop, and that was it. That's when he threw the Thompson back in the boot and slammed it shut.

Fired a few pistol rounds at us—all into the treetops—and raced away down the road. My neighbors managed to perforate the sedan a few more times."

"Glad nobody got hurt," McIntyre said.

"Odd about those weapons, though," the major said.

"We might talk to Ranger Russ Frame about it," McIntyre explained. "He snuck into the Grand Harbor parking lot the other night and had a look at those guns in the trunk of their car. I'm pretty sure he jammed modeling clay down the shotgun muzzle, which would make it blow up when anyone fired it. And he showed me bullets he'd taken out of the Thompson and replaced."

"Aha!" Major Angel said. "Aha! Good lad! Wager they were squib loads! Further wager that your Frame chap was either a scout or a commando in the recent trouble with Germany."

"Squib load?"

"You remove the bullet from a cartridge, see?" the major said. "Wrap a rag around the jaws of your pliers so as not to mar the lead, of course. You dump out the gunpowder except for a few grains. Reseat the bullet, load the cartridge in the magazine, and presto! Shooter chap pulls the cocking lever, chambers the squib, pulls the trigger, and the bullet goes about halfway down the barrel, where it becomes stuck. Even if it doesn't stick and makes it all the way out the end of the barrel, there's not enough gas pressure to recock the weapon."

"Apparently Frame put a half-dozen of these squibs in the Thompson magazine."

"Certainly," the major said. "One of 'em bound to become stuck in the barrel. Now, if you wanted to cause real damage you'd put a red load under the squib."

"Red load?"

"Take gunpowder from two or three of the squibs. Packed into a single shell casing. Called a red load. Your villain pulls the trigger, Pop! Nothing seems to have happened, but the bullet from the squib has plugged his gun barrel. Only he don't know it yet. Cocks the weapon a second time, pushing the red load home. When that one goes off it's likely to blow off the entire breech and barrel and very likely part of the shooter's anatomy."

"Major Angel?" McIntyre said.

"Yes?"

"You're a dangerous man!"

"Thank you."

The first light of morning appeared over the eastern forest horizon and became entangled in the high trees for a few minutes before flowing down the shingled roof and log walls of the Small Delights Lodge. It entered through the dining room windows and came to rest on the wooden floor. McIntyre sat with the two men, a thick white porcelain coffee mug between his palms. He could smell sausages being cooked and could hear frying pans being moved on the stove top. After breakfast, he reflected, it might be a fine day to go fishing.

Ranger Tim McIntyre didn't know who had phoned headquarters, but he was glad when RMNP Supervisor Nicholson and Dottie arrived. The supervisor would sort out the bits and pieces, Dottie would write down the details for the report and the entire Blue Spruce Lake situation would be all tied up in a blue ribbon.

Making good her threat to return, Catherine Croker marched into the dining room. She huffed and muttered to herself as she took a seat at the table. Supervisor Nicholson sat at the head with Dottie on his left.

"Ranger McIntyre," he began. "Your plan didn't go exactly the way you wanted? What do we have now, two homicides? Lying out there under tarps?"

"Unforeseen circumstances," McIntyre replied.

"There will need to be a hearing," the supervisor said. "You and Ranger Frame will explain everything to the judge. Polly will be a witness. So will Charlie Nevis. Let's begin with you telling me what happened."

"Yessir. You sent me out here to investigate a rifle shot . . ."

"No. Skip over all of that. Start with last night. I know the first part. Frankly, I don't think I could stand to hear the whole story again."

"Yessir. There wasn't time to report it to you, but an employee at Grand Lodge overheard the Chicago boys making plans to torch the storage shed at Small Delights. As soon as I heard about it, Polly and I set up surveillance. I instructed Jamie to be ready to block the main road to prevent escape. Ranger Russ Frame showed up and volunteered assistance. In fact, he reconnoitered the situation that night, which was a help."

"So far, so good. Then what?"

"Polly and I stood watch. A little after midnight we saw somebody with a small flashlight prowling around the storage shed. It turned out to be Charlie Nevis. At about the same time, a fire started at the back corner of the shed. We—Polly and I—ran toward the scene. Charlie ran around to the back of the shed with a gun, yelling at someone to put the fire out."

"Can you account for why he did that?"

"Yessir."

"Continue."

"We were about halfway to the shed when we heard a pistol shot. I instructed Polly to drop to the ground. I pulled my service revolver and moved forward. When I got to where I could see the back of the shed, I saw Nevis and the man called Vinny pointing guns at each other. Vinny saw me coming—the fire was lighting up the whole area by then—and shifted his aim and pointed his pistol at me. I stopped and aimed and fired first, and he fell. Right then I heard another shot and Charlie let out a yell and he fell down, too. I didn't know where that shot came from. But I turned and saw the Boss running toward us—he had been over at Grand Harbor during all this—and he was shooting, too. Luckily for me and Charlie, Ranger Frame had come on the scene. He shot the Boss with his deer rifle."

The supervisor listened patiently as McIntyre and Polly described the subsequent events, including extinguishing the fire and the arrest of Charlie Nevis. When they had finished, the supervisor turned to Catherine Croker.

"Speaking off the record," he said, "in my opinion you need to be more selective with your guests. I don't think the thug who drove away will be coming back to pay his bill any time soon. Polly, the national park is going to take over Small Delights now. As we earlier discussed."

"It's not fair!" Catherine screamed. "I deserve priority! I'm the most logical buyer for Small Delights and I should have it!"

Supervisor Nicholson regarded Catherine in his usual calm way and waited patiently until she sat down again. Everyone around the table waited to see what he would say next.

"Mrs. Croker. I understand your situation. You would like to expand your lodge, connect it to this one with a nice road flanked by modern cabins for tourists. It would give you a virtual monopoly on tourist accommodations on Blue Spruce Lake."

She made no reply.

"Just for the moment," he continued, "I'm going to overlook your brother's confession that the both of you connived with a criminal element to force John and Hattie out of here. We will be bringing charges. It might lead to your losing both your license and your property."

Supervisor Nicholson drank off the last of his coffee and Polly took his mug to get him a refill.

"If you recall," he continued, "all owners of private property

213

within the park signed contracts when the park was established. Including you. That contract very clearly states that if a property owner wishes to sell his or her property, the park has a right to purchase it at a fair market price. The park may decide not to buy it, but we do have the first option. Secondly, the contract stipulates that if any activities or accidents on private land, within the park, can be seen as a threat to the natural surroundings or to the inherent aesthetic values of the area, the park has the right to force a sale. And has first priority as purchaser."

He took the fresh mug of coffee from Polly and nodded his thanks.

"In my view—and my supervisors will agree with me—this feud at Blue Spruce Lake has been the direct cause of at least one shooting, one assault and attempted murder of a ranger while on duty, one attempted drowning, and two cases of blatant arson, the storage building and the garbage truck. In addition, we now have two dead men lying out there. In my opinion, we have a case for acquiring the property and shutting down Small Delights for good."

Catherine Croker began to sputter and protest, but Nicholson silenced her with an upraised hand.

"Fortunately, Miss Sheldon has offered a solution that will save us the trouble and expense of going to court. Her aunt and uncle have been wanting to sell Small Delights and only held on to it because they thought Miss Sheldon might wish to take it over and make her living here. Together they have made the decision to sell it to the park. They will take up residence in Denver."

"But!" Catherine said, "but what does the park want with it?"

"Catherine, you said earlier that you deserve to have priority regarding this property. But you were wrong. The priority is with the people of these United States. All people, without exception, and all citizens of the distant future, have a right to natural beauty, a right to witness nature untouched by human greed. That's who has the priority. As park supervisor, I have an obligation to those future generations to preserve and protect this place, to keep it as it is for as long as I am able. So, in answer to your question of what we want with it, the park service wants to remove all of these buildings, plant native trees and grass over the roads, and take down the telephone and electric wires. In short, what we want is to put it back, as nearly as possible, the way it was before civilization arrived."

"But with no place to stay, how can anyone come enjoy it? It doesn't make sense!"

"There will be a parking area just off the main road. They can rent lodgings outside the park. They can walk to the lake. I'm not sure you'll understand this, Catherine, but in building this country of ours, men and women pitted their strength and ingenuity against raw nature. That's how we became who we are. Most of the population will never come here to see this national park, but they need to know that it is here. For most of them, it's enough to know that it is being kept for them as a reminder of who their ancestors were and who they are. Every citizen of the United States is entitled to the assurance that their children and grandchildren will always have a wilderness to visit. The village can furnish plenty of rooms and camp-grounds for whoever wants to come. The park will provide campgrounds, too."

Catherine Croker stood up so quickly that her chair went skidding backward. Without a word, she grabbed up her purse and portfolio of papers and stormed out of the dining room. As the door slammed shut behind her, Polly looked around the table.

"Can I offer anyone more coffee?" she asked sweetly. "How many can stay for lunch?"

After lunch, the supervisor and Dottie got into their car to return to town. McIntyre would stay behind to wait for the coroner's ambulance. He found himself alone with Polly in the dining room.

"Quite a speech," McIntyre said. He got a tray from the sideboard and began helping Polly clear the dishes from the table.

"Really was," Polly agreed.

"I always took Nick for the strong silent type. But put a dime in him and wow! Isn't there a line in *Huckleberry Finn* that says 'my, don't he talk, though'? I guess Catherine Croker won't be scheming to acquire Small Delights now."

"Which reminds me," Polly said, "Uncle John and I were arranging what to do with various stuff. He's found a warehouse store in Denver that will buy the bedding and crockery, and a salvager who will come for the light fixtures and plumbing and that kind of thing. John gave me this to give to you. It's all filled out. All you have to do is take it to the courthouse."

McIntyre unfolded the stiff piece of paper and looked at it.

"He's giving me his truck?"

"Yes. He said you stuck by him like no man ever has, and he'd rather see you have his pickup truck than sell it. There you go. It's not in the best of shape, but I'm sure you can fix it up just fine. You'll want to repaint the doors to cover up the sign."

"Oh, I don't know," McIntyre said. "Just imagine Vi Coteau's face when she sees me drive up in a truck with SMALL DELIGHTS painted on the door."

Polly went silent.

"What's the matter?" McIntyre asked.

"Nothing," Polly said. "I was just imagining it."

GLOSSARY
THE LANGUAGE OF THE LOCALS

"Altitude": up high enough in the mountains to brag about it, as in "we were hiking at altitude," or as in "we were camped at altitude." Usually above the treeline (see "timberline"). "Relative Altitude" is one of two things heavily stressed by real estate salesmen, the other being "view." As in "Sure, your yard is mostly rocks and steep as a barn roof, but it sits above the village and has a great view!"

"Cabin camp": these were originally intended to be a step up from a tent camp. A slight step. A typical cabin camp consisted of five or ten one-room noninsulated 10 × 12 cabins furnished with one or two beds, a wood-burning cookstove, a single light bulb hanging from the rafters, and a small table with two chairs. If advertised as "rustic," the cabins had an outhouse "up the hill" and a water tap in the middle of the parking area. "Semi-modern" meant there was a central bathhouse with hot and cold running water and possibly a water tap inside the actual cabin itself. "Modern" got you a cabin with a bathroom inside, unless that particular cabin had already been rented, in which case you got semi.

"Chinook": a warm wind, often called "the snow eater." Saying "chinook wind" is regarded as redundant and makes you sound like a tourist. It is permissible to say "it's chinooking" even if it makes you sound like a non-English speaker. A chinook becomes most noticeable in winter when warm air sliding down from the Divide turns the snow into sloppy mush. Skiers do not like chinooks.

"Chipmunk": countless scientific man-hours have been spent cataloguing the characteristics of this pointy-nose little rodent. Thanks to all those generations of intrepid biologists and illustrators, we can now say with confidence that a chipmunk is not a ground squirrel, gopher, prairie dog, or marmot. Some tourists, however, have yet to appreciate the difference and gleefully send Junior to give peanuts to the "chipmunks," which actually turn out to be brown bears.

"Creek" pronounced "krik": any dribble of water that appears to be moving. The rule is that a creek must have an unimaginative name. Thus we have Willow Creek, Beaver Creek, Rock Creek, and Pine Creek. If those seem too daringly descriptive, we resort to calling them North Fork, Middle Fork, or Miller's Fork. Fork of what, does not need explaining. Any dribble that becomes too deep, wide, or turbulent to wade across is termed a "river" much to the amusement of out-of-state visitors who live near the real ones.

"Crevice, crevasse": being primarily granite and suffering extremes of heat and freezing, the Rockies are prone to cracking. Any crack may be called a "crevice," mostly for dramatic effect as in "wow, would you look at that crevice." The exception is any crack in those ice fields that locals erroneously refer to as "glaciers" when they (the cracks) become Frenchified into "crevasses." If your foot slips and you become lodged in one,

218

you don't care what they are called. You only want somebody to come get you out.

"Clearing": for reasons no one has adequately explained, forests sometimes have expanses of open grass, usually flat and fertile, where no trees, or only a few trees, grow. Some clearings are created with chain saws and bulldozers but will revert to forest if left alone long enough, for reasons I cannot adequately explain.

"Divide": the Continental Divide, an imaginary line running along the top of the Rocky Mountains but not always at the highest points. It is called the Divide because creeks and streams on the west side (known as the Western Slope) flow toward the Pacific Ocean, while those on the Eastern Slope of the Rockies drain toward the Atlantic.

"Dry fly": an emblem of fruitless hopes consisting of some feathers, thread, and chenille wrapped around a hook, which the fisherperson is convinced resembles an actual insect. The dry version is intended to float on the surface of the water and attract trout. The wet version is intended to sink beneath the water and fool the fish into thinking it is an emerging insect. Samples of both versions may be seen festooning willows, aspen, pine, dead logs, rough logs, and articles of clothing, not to mention certain protruding appendages such as noses, ears, and fingers.

"Elk": local jokers have a story about a tourist who asked "what time of year do the deer turn to elk" hah hah hah. Elk are taller and heavier than deer and have longer antlers and can run faster, which is good to remember if you are ever tempted to send Junior out onto the meadow to pose with one of them. Local lore also believes that "the Indians" (whoever they were) called the elk "wapiti," a word no one could pronounce until a ranger with nothing else to do came up with the rhyme "hippity hoppity it's a wapiti."

"Front Range": I don't know about other states the Rockies run through, but in Colorado the long line of high mountains dividing the state into two halves is itself divided up into "ranges." To the north we have the Mummy Range, so named because the collection of peaks resembles either a reclining mummy or a severely constipated boa constrictor; the Never Summer Range in which there actually is summer every year; then the Front Range (for which there is no correlative Side Range or Back Range); and then the Arapaho Range named for the Indian tribe we stole it from (sometimes referred to as the Indian Peaks, but God help any Indian who would try to claim any of it).

"The gate": as in "who is manning the gate" or "I'm only going up to the gate and back" or "they will give you a map at the gate." The term refers to one of the automobile entrances to the park, where there are no actual gates unless that's what you call orange traffic cones.

"Lichen, Krummholz, and Skree": crusty moss on rocks, stunted and twisted trees at altitude, and loose sliding stones where you want to walk. It's either that, the name of a pop music group, or a story of three squirrels. Hikers have other names for Krummholz and skree but we aren't allowed to print them.

"Lodge": a large private home made of logs chinked with ten-dollar bills and credit-card receipts; a tiny summer shack with grandiose name like Nest of the Eagle Lodge or a silly name such as Wee Neva Inn, Dew Drop Inn, or Lily's Li'l Lodge; a big establishment with a few rental rooms inside and a dozen or more cabins outside, plus a livery stable upwind of a dining room and a volleyball court no one has ever used.

"Moonshine": illegal alcohol. According to folk legend, it was distilled by the light of the moon in order to avoid the authorities. Also known as "shine," "hooch," "popskull," "varnish remover," "who-hit-John," and even "beer."

"Moraine": few terms confuse visitors as much as does the term "moraine." Locals use the term sparingly, because they don't understand it, either. Some say it means a big ridge of rocks that looks as if it was dredged up and stacked by huge machines—it was actually done by a prehistoric glacial flow—while others say it refers to a big treeless clearing. Locals sometimes take visitors to Moraine Park and point at the distant ridge, the flat meadow, and the campground and say "that's the moraine." Residents along Fall River Road live on no fewer than three moraines and none of them knows it.

"Mountain sickness": also known as "altitude sickness." Do you feel clammy, yet feverish? Dizzy and diuretic? Have a hangover-size headache? Nausea, aching joints, death wish? Have you been bitten by a wood tick lately, or have you sipped water from the stream? If not, you probably have mountain sickness. Go home.

"National Forest": a usually vast area set aside and under the protection of the U.S. Department of Agriculture and managed "for the greatest good of the greatest number in the long run." Land within national forests is used for logging, mining, grazing, and recreation.

"National Park": a usually vast area set aside and under the protection of the U.S. Department of Interior and managed so as to preserve and protect it in its natural state for the benefit and enjoyment of future generations. The principal ideal is expressed in the slogan "take nothing except pictures, leave nothing except footprints." (Which, by the way, would get you arrested in the Louvre.)

"Park": a flat open space in the mountains, often named for a pioneer and ranging in size from a few acres (Allenspark, Hermit Park) to hundreds of square miles (South Park, North Park). Locals joke about tourists who arrive in Estes Park Village and ask where to find the roller coaster and Ferris wheel, or the caged animals. No one in human memory has ever laughed at that joke.

"The park": Rocky Mountain National Park, the only important industry of Estes Park and the only reason for the village's existence. Villagers speak lovingly of trails and peaks and lakes in "the park" but roughly seventy percent of them have never ventured off its blacktop roads.

"Pass": (1) a slip of paper allowing you to bring your car into the park. But you already knew that. (2) In local parlance, a "pass" is a route over the mountains. There are more of these than you might assume, most of which are inaccessible. Foreigners to Estes Park might be confused by the fact that El Paso del Norte in New Mexico lies south of the village, while South Pass crosses the Wyoming Rockies to the north.

"Ranger": there are two kinds, and woe to him who confuses them. In the USFS a ranger is an important chieftain in charge of a very large district of the national forest. In the NPS a ranger might or might not be a temporary summer employee, i.e., a schoolteacher wearing a uniform and badge. A national forest symbol shows Smokey the Bear wearing a flat ranger hat, which national forest rangers don't wear but national park rangers do. Park rangers are known locally as "flat hats" and sometimes "tree cops." National forest rangers can jerk your permit for grazing, mining, logging, or commercial recreation and thus are known locally as "sir" or "mister."

"Sam Brown": in addition to the iconic flat hat, park rangers used to wear iconic Sam Brown belts (presumably invented by the iconic Sam Brown), a wide leather belt attached to a narrower leather belt that went over the shoulder. Some say the function of the shoulder strap was to support a heavy pistol and holster. Some say it was left over from WWI, when the shoulder strap was used to drag wounded soldiers out of harm's way.

Some say the function of the shoulder strap was just to make the uniform look cool.

"The S.O.": supervisor's office, or the central administration building from whence flows a relentless stream of orders, regulations, recriminations, requests, and regrets. For some reason, employees seem to like pronouncing "S.O." with a suggestive pause after it as if a letter were missing.

"The S.O.P.": a manual of Standard Operating Procedures. Updated on a weekly basis until no office shelf is sturdy enough to hold it, the S.O.P. dictates How To Do Everything, from what to tell people in the event of nuclear holocaust (pray) to how to install the toilet paper (roll from the top, not the bottom). Temps in search of answers to questions (I just saw a bear climb into a visitor's car, what do I do?) have been known to disappear only to be found years afterward as desiccated corpses hunched over the S.O.P. Equally useful is the Compendium, revised almost annually, which tells everyone how to do everything and what not to do. It has been said that the flat hat rangers live in fear of offending it and won't even visit the restroom without taking the Compendium along.

"Summer hire": with more than a million visitors traipsing through the national park each year, the park depends heavily on summer employees to keep everything (particularly restrooms) clean and functioning. They maintain hiking trails, clean toilets, paint signs, clean toilets, direct traffic, clean toilets, answer questions, clean toilets, pick up trash, and sometimes the rangers help them clean toilets.

"The Canyon": there are two major highways between Estes Park and "the Valley." One of them follows the Thompson River and is always called "the Canyon" as in "I'm going down the Canyon to the Valley to pick up some toilet paper at Sam's Club if you need anything." The other route, Highway 36, doesn't have a name. It also doesn't have much of a canyon.

"Timberline": 10,500 feet above sea level. Or thereabouts. Early settlers discovered that at that altitude the trees would not grow large enough to be cut down for lumber. And "timberline" sounded more euphonic than "lumberline." Some modern fussy little know-it-all decided that it should be called "treeline" instead, which confuses things because stunted, runty little trees can be found higher than 11,000 feet in some locations. Which, like having a word like "timberline," doesn't matter in any imaginable way.

"Up top" or "Up on top": locals who say they drove "up top" or took guests "up on top" are referring to the highest section of Trail Ridge where they can see snowbanks in August at two miles above sea level. They can also enjoy driving a two-lane highway that (a) has almost no guardrails and (b) drops off more than a thousand feet from the edge of the pavement to the bottom of Forest Canyon. Restrooms are available "up top." Sometimes for a reasonable gratuity, a local high school student will agree to pry your fingers from your steering wheel and drive you back down to your lodgings.

"The Valley": one Estes Parkian might say "I'm going down to the Valley" and another will ask "which one?" and the reply will be "Longmont." This may confuse those who don't know that "the Valley" may refer to any town or city between Loveland and Denver. However, one goes "up" to Fort Collins and "over" to Greeley, both of which are approximately two thousand feet lower in elevation than Estes. You also go "over" to Grand Lake, which is on "the other side," and you go "down" to Allenspark, which is higher than Estes Park (unless you're looking at a road map tacked to the wall, in which case it is below Estes). I hope this clarifies the matter.

ABOUT THE AUTHOR

James C. Work's parents operated a rustic cabin camp on the edge of Rocky Mountain National Park. Whenever he was not in school at nearby Estes Park, he would most likely be found fishing in Fall River or bicycling up the road to the ranger station. Rangers knew him and would sometimes put the old balloon-tire bike in the back of a pickup and give him a ride up the road. By the time he finished high school, "Jimmy" knew most of the rangers of RMNP, at least on the eastern side of the park, and most of the streams, lakes, and peaks. While in college, he had summer jobs with the trail crew and fire crew and worked for the U.S. Forest Service where he fought forest fires and also gave campfire programs.

He holds a doctorate in Victorian poetry and is professor emeritus at Colorado State University. He and his wife and a feisty Westie terrier live in Fort Collins, Colorado.

James edited a definitive anthology of Western American literature, *Prose and Poetry of the American West* (University of Nebraska Press). He has published over eighteen other books including mysteries and westerns; his Keystone Ranch series of mythical cowboy novels set in the 1880s is published by Five Star. The current book, *Small Delightful Murders,* is the second volume of a new series featuring Ranger Tim McIntyre of Rocky Mountain National Park. The first in the series is titled *Unmentionable Murders;* the third in the series will be *The Dunraven Hoard Murders.*

The employees of Five Star Publishing hope you have enjoyed this book.

Our Five Star novels explore little-known chapters from America's history, stories told from unique perspectives that will entertain a broad range of readers.

Other Five Star books are available at your local library, bookstore, all major book distributors, and directly from Five Star/Gale.

Connect with Five Star Publishing

Visit us on Facebook:
   https://www.facebook.com/FiveStarCengage

Email:
   FiveStar@cengage.com

For information about titles and placing orders:
   (800) 223-1244
   gale.orders@cengage.com

To share your comments, write to us:
   Five Star Publishing
   Attn: Publisher
   10 Water St., Suite 310
   Waterville, ME 04901